GUNSLINGER: KILLER'S BRAND

GUNSLINGER BOOK 6

A W. Hart
aka
michael A. Black

A.W. HART

WOLFPACK PUBLISHING
— EST 2013 —

WOLFPACK
PUBLISHING
— EST 2013 —

Paperback Edition
Copyright © 2020 A.W. Hart

Special thanks to Michael Black for his contribution to this novel.

Published in the United States by Wolfpack Publishing, Las Vegas

Wolfpack Publishing
6032 Wheat Penny Avenue
Las Vegas, NV 89122

wolfpackpublishing.com

Paperback ISBN: 978-1-64734-683-6
eBook ISBN: 978-1-64734-695-9

Library of Congress Control Number: 2020935073

Cover photography by Marty Overstreet at Circle Bar T Leatherwords. Cover design by Lohman Hills Creative.

GUNSLINGER: KILLER'S BRAND

The great brand
Made lightnings in the splendor of the moon,
And flashing round and round, and whirled in an arch
Shot like a streamer of the northern morn ...

Tennyson
Montede d'Arthur
1842

CHAPTER 1

THE SOUTHERN AREA OF CALIFORNIA, 1883

The man who'd been hanged had a distinctive brand in the middle of his forehead. His boots were perhaps five feet above the dry sandy earth, as he dangled at the end of the noosed rope, which had been tossed over the branch of one of the more sturdy trees in the once verdant valley.

Seated on his horse Connor Mack was almost level with the dead man's head. His eyes were no more than swollen slits in a grayish purple face, the mouth a twisted gash bisected by a lolling tongue that appeared to have been almost bitten through. A hoard of flies buzzed continuously around the body, which was emitting the putrid odor of a violent death. Connor studied the brand. It appeared to be the letter *P* enclosed within a wide circle. He looked toward his twin sister, Abby, to gauge her reaction. She seemed curious, but fascinated as well. That was the way with her, though. Sometimes she could be the sweetest little angel, full of compassion for some wayward animal or even a snake or crawling bug, and other times she could be disconnected from everything, oblivious to a man writhing in the dust, taking his last breaths. She'd fashioned her long, red hair into some sort of braid and stuffed it up under her hat. Lean and athletic, from a certain angle she could almost pass for a young boy, save for her burgeoning feminine figure.

"Looks like he's seen better days," River Hicks said.

Connor glanced at his mentor. "Want me to cut him down?" He cocked his head toward two perched buzzards about fifty feet away. "Guess we interrupted their meal."

Hicks was about to answer when the crack of three gunshots broke the evenness of the afternoon. His head swiveled and he pointed to a slopping mound of earth extending upward from the uneven mesa. The remnants of a cloud of dust were settling along the open bend in the plain. Someone had ridden through there quite recently.

Hicks pulled back on his reins, twisting his horse's head around the suspended legs of the dead man.

"Sounds like it's coming from just around that hill there."

They left the dangling man and rode forward.

Perhaps a hundred yards away there was an overturned wagon with a team of fleeing horses dragging a broken wagon harness. A man crouched behind the wagon's bed as a group of four riders rode back and forth firing shots at him.

"Don't like them odds much," Hicks said.

"We gonna help him?" Connor asked.

Hicks nodded. "Let's see what's what. Abby, you stay here."

"What?" Her pretty face curled into a confrontational expression. "Why?"

"Because we need you to cover us with you rifle." With that, Hicks drove his heels into his gray stallion's flanks and the horse took off like a cannonball, Hicks's long, black, shoulder length hair flying back from under his hat like dark flames. Connor flashed a grin at his sister and followed Hicks, who already had one of his Colt Peacemakers out. Connor's left hand gripped the butt of his own revolver as he steered his horse with his right. He was naturally left-handed, but he had an ambidextrousness about him and was able to shoot proficiently with either hand.

The two riderless horses, fastened together in a harness and dragging the remnants of the wagon tongue, shot past them, the animals' eyes wide in panic. Connor steered around the runaway team and fixed his gaze on the scene unfolding before him.

The man behind the wagon had a pistol out and was trying to return fire back at the marauders. Several more shots echoed back and forth from both sides, and one of the riders jerked back, dropping his gun and clutching his arm.

Hicks extended his own weapon and fired.

The riders noticed the approaching pair and then dispersed, riding hard in the opposite direction, the wounded one bouncing awkwardly in his saddle.

Connor left his gun in its holster as he slowed slightly, staying behind Hicks. The two of them trotted up to the overturned wagon as the man on the ground looked up at them, his gun now being held down by the side of his leg. It was a massive looking revolver with a 7 ½ inch barrel of blue steel. The frame had gold colored plating surrounding a blue steel cylinder. Connor saw that the man wore no hat and was black. He was big, too, with broad shoulders and a chest that tapered down to a trim waist. His shirt was a ragged tan fabric that was replete with holes and tears. The trousers appeared worn, as well, but the bright blue color, accompanied by the single yellow stripe down the side, labeled the man as former army, as did the leather-flap holster affixed to his belt. He stood ramrod straight as he looked up at them and Connor was reminded of a picture he'd seen once in a book of a large jungle cat, sort of like a mountain lion, but completely jet black.

A panther, he thought.

Hicks replaced his gun in its holster as he brought his horse to a stop. The black man seemed to relax a little.

"We thought you could use some help," Hicks said. His face twitched into a smile. "Though it appeared that you were doing more damage to them than they was to you."

The black man's lips drew back over his teeth, which looked exceptionally white in contrast to his dark skin. "I could've done a lot more if this damn wagon hadn't fallen on my Henry." He gestured toward the butt of what appeared to be a Henry rifle jutting from under the side of the wagon.

"Lucky for them," Hicks said. "I'm pretty sure my shot went high, but I was more or less hoping to just scare them off. Let 'em know more guns were coming. Hard to hit a moving target when you're riding full out."

"It is at that," the black man said.

Connor had figured right: that Hicks had sought to intimidate the gunmen on the horses with only one shot and was pleased now to find out his assumption was correct. Ever since plucking Abby and him from their wretched existence at the Mack farm River Hicks had mentored and taught both of them. They had had been through a lot up to this point and had bonded, becoming almost like a family.

One of choice, Connor thought. But as strong as one of blood.

"I appreciate you coming to help," the black man said. He opened the side gate of his revolver, ejected the spent shell casings, placed them in his pocket, and then stuck the gun into its holster and secured the heavy leather flap. "I came up on them from over that way." He cocked his thumb over his shoulder. "I was on my way to town, and they commenced to riding after me and shooting. I tried to turn and head for them rocks for cover, but the damn wheel hit a shallow gulley and flipped the wagon over." He paused to snort a laugh. "Sent me a flying, broke the horses loose. By the time I go back to the wagon, they was on top of me."

"Let's see if we can help you right it," Hicks said, starting to swing his right leg over his horse's flanks.

"I think I can manage," the black man said, stooping downward and gripping the side boards of the wagon that lay flat on the ground. "But I wouldn't be turning you down, none, neither."

With a quick motion he straightened his body upward, lifting the heavy wagon from its resting place. The thick muscles of his thighs seemed to stretch the blue fabric of his trousers. Connor swung his right leg forward and up, bringing it over his horse's mane, as he slipped his left foot out of the stirrup. He landed on the ground almost simultaneously with Hicks, and they both ran over and gripped the wagon, helping the black man with the arduous task. Connor had never seen such strength in a man. He'd practically lifted the whole thing by himself.

"Let's try to ease her down," the black man said, the strain evident in his voice. "Don't want to break nothing."

The wagon teetered on the two left side wheels for several moments as the three of them pulled back on the frame, slowing the descent of the right side to minimize the chance of any further damage.

The wagon jolted as the wheels hit the ground.

The black man ran to the right side, inspected them, and heaved a sigh of relief.

"Looks like the wheels and axles ain't damaged none," he said as he walked around to the front. "Can't say the same for the damn tongue, though." He strode over and bent down to retrieve a brown hat from the ground.

Connor saw the jagged piece of broken wood protruding from the metallic hitch junction.

"Or that," Hicks said, pointing down at the rifle.

"Aw, hell," the black man said, stooping to pick up the Henry. He held it up and Connor saw that the barrel was bent in the middle, evidently from the weight of the wagon's heavy wooden bottom. "Had that rifle a long time." He tossed it into the bed of the wagon.

"Maybe you could find a gunsmith who could straighten it out," Connor said.

"Ain't likely around these parts." The black man straightened up, placed the hat on his head, and extended his big hand toward Hicks. "Name's John Henry Bardwell."

Hicks pulled off his leather glove and shook the man's hand. "River Hicks." He cocked his head toward Connor. "This is Connor Mack."

Connor shook Bardwell's hand, which felt as calloused as his own. The clip-clopping sound of trotting hooves intruded upon them.

Abby approached on horseback her hand grasping the bridle of one of the two errant horses Connor has seen fleeing before, the ones from Bardwell's wagon.

The black man smiled at her.

"Much obliged, Miss," he said tipping his hat. "You got a way with horses. They don't usually take to strangers none."

She smiled down at him. "Since they didn't see fit to introduce me, I'll do it myself. I'm Abby Mack."

Bardwell nodded and rubbed his hands over the massive neck of the closest horse. The animal seemed to relax slightly. The black man then repeated the gesture, caressing the snout of the other animal.

"Any idea why those men attacked you?" Connor asked.

Hicks glanced at him and raised a critical eyebrow.

Connor immediately knew that Hicks disapproved of the question. His number one rule was not to ask questions that might put you in the midst of somebody else's troubles. Hicks always stressed that it was prudent not to get involved in a fight unless you felt you had to, but once you did, to finish it and move on, so as not to let those troubles of somebody else slow you down.

But Connor was almost sixteen, and big and strong for his age. He'd already seen more and done more than a half dozen full grown men. And he'd taken a life or two as well, although it wasn't something of which he was proud. The ghosts of those men did their reoccurring dances in his dreams almost every night.

Hicks's admonishment of not getting involved hovered over him, but Connor figured he'd earned the right to ask a few questions by virtue of his growing maturity.

Bardwell's head turned slightly as he regarded the young man, then pinched the flesh on his forearm with his thumb and index finger.

"I suspect they didn't like the color of my skin," he said. "They was most likely from the McManus spread and ain't fond of my kind. I'm sort of the leader of a group of Negro homesteaders over yonder, and he don't like us being there. Our farms jut up against the boundaries of his ranch."

"McManus?" Hicks said.

Bardwell nodded again. "Big George McManus. His family's been running things 'round here for long time. Got the biggest ranch in these parts, and now he's trying to drive out those of us trying to homestead."

"Looks like there's plenty of open range," Connor said. "Why's he want to do that?"

Bardwell walked his horses over to the front of the wagon and was studying the broken hitch.

"Word is he's working with the B and D Railroad Company," he said. "Trying to bring the railroad line east through this area. McManus don't want to sell off none of his own land, so he's trying to get the railroad to take ours instead." His heavy lips parted in a smile once more. "'Cept we don't want to give it to him."

"And he don't like it?" Connor said. It was more of a statement than an interrogative.

Bardwell gave a quick nod and looked to Hicks. "I'd be obliged if'n' I could borrow that lariat you got hanging on your saddle, Mister Hicks."

Hicks held out his hand, palm upward. "Be my guest. But what you got planned?"

"I'm looking to rig a temporary hitch so I can pull this thing into town. Got to see about getting this wagon tongue fixed." He strode over to Hicks's horse, patted the animal on the shoulder with a practiced ease, as Hicks slipped the coiled rope off the saddle and handed it to him.

"You know horses," Hicks said. "Learn that in the army?"

Bardwell smirked, then slapped his pant leg. "Yeah, I guess these kind of give that away, don't they?"

"That, and your pistol." Hicks said. "Buffalo soldier?"

"Fifteen years."

"Why'd you leave after that long?" Connor asked.

"Well ..." Bardwell took in a deep breath. "Let's just say I had me some reasons."

He withdrew a long-bladed knife from a sheath on his belt and began carving some V-shaped wedges in the wooden wagon tongue, which was still attached to the horses' harness. Next Bardwell looped the rope through the wedges and then around the hitch on the wagon. Pulling the rope taut, he fashioned another series of loops and then knotted it.

"Looks strong enough, leastways till we get into Sweetwater."

"That's the name of the town?" Abby asked.

"It is. There's a river that runs down from the

mountains over yonder." He made a brief pointing motion toward the north. "It's responsible for this valley area here being as fertile as it is. Only problem is, it runs through McManus's land, and he's taken to damming it up now and again. Forcing all the farmers and other smaller ranchers to pay him for the use of it."

"That don't seem fair," Connor said. He knew from his own upbringing on a farm that water, either from rain or tributaries, was an absolute necessity.

Bardwell uttered a harsh sounding laugh. "The last thing Big George is concerned about is being fair."

"And the law lets him get away with it?" Hicks asked.

"There's a coalition that formed to try and stand against him," Bardwell said. "Some of the smaller ranchers and other farmers. Even asked us to join with them. Sent a wire to the governor, and he sent some county commissioner to come take a look at the situation. We're all hoping he turns out to be fair and makes McManus open up that dam."

"So them men that were shooting at you," Connor said, knowing he was risking incurring more of Hicks's ire. "They McManus's men?"

"More than likely," Bardwell said. "But he's got a whole lot of ranch hands. I don't reckon I could swear to it. And, even if I make the accusation, he'll just say it was the work of the Phantom Riders."

"The Phantom Riders?" Now Connor's curiosity was really getting stoked. The thought of outlaws riding in a group reminded him of a Dangerous Dan story he'd read in the old dime novel book he'd found. "Why do you call 'em that?"

"They ride under a black flag. Been terrorizing the countryside, raiding farms and rustling cattle. All the farms and ranches. Even McManus claims to have had some run-ins with them."

"What do you mean, a black flag?" Abby asked.

"Just an old army expression, Miss," Bardwell said. "Back in the war between the States there was some Confederate units that used a black flag to show they'd neither give nor accept quarter. It became a symbol of those that didn't obey no laws. These Phantom Riders are like that. They wear masks, and leave this brand, burned into something, or someone before they ride off."

"Brand?" Hicks said. "What kind of brand?"

Bardwell smoothed out the long reins over the backs of his horses.

"Can't rightly describe it," he said. "I'd have to draw you a picture."

"Does it look like a P in a circle?" Connor asked.

Bardwell's brow creased. "A what?"

"P," Connor repeated. "Like the letter P."

Bardwell raised his eyebrows and gave a slight shrug. "Well, I don't rightly know. I never been much good at reading and writing."

Connor felt a sudden flush of regret. He hadn't wanted to embarrass this man, and didn't know whether he should apologize or not. Luckily, Hicks reentered the conversation.

"We found a man hanging from a tree back thataway," he said. "Right before we come onto you."

"Hanging?" Bardwell asked. "Like a no-good hanging?"

Hicks nodded. "And somebody branded his face."

Bardwell's expression hardened.

"Sounds like them. Can you show me?"

They rode back toward the dangling man. As they drew closer the two large buzzards alighted from the dead man's shoulders and flew upward, circling overhead.

"Damn things," Connor said.

"Don't say that about them," Abby shot back. "They got a purpose. They clean up what gets left behind."

Connor frowned. Sometimes his sister's ways mystified him. Other times, they worried him.

Bardwell halted his wagon and emitted a heavy sigh and accompanying frown as he stared up at the dead man's face. It was obvious that the buzzards had taken a more than just a few chunks of flesh from the head and neck area, but the man's bloated visage was pretty much intact.

"Know him?" Hicks asked.

"I do." Bardwell snapped the reins, moving the wagon forward positioning it under the hanging figure. He set the hand brake and tied the reins around it. Standing, he took out his knife and brushed away the swarming flies with his other hand.

"It's Howard Layton," Bardwell said. "That county commissioner I told you about."

He sawed through the rope and caught the body

as it fell, taking care to lay the dead man supine in the bed of his wagon.

"Don't look like he's been dead too long," Hicks said. "Judging from the stiffness."

"You know about dead men, Mister Hicks?" Bardwell asked.

Hicks regarded the other man for several seconds, then said, "I've created my share of them."

Bardwell knelt and crossed the dead man's arms over his chest.

"I'd be mighty grateful if'n' you'd come with me to town to report this to the sheriff."

Hicks gestured toward the brand on the body.

"That the sign of the Phantom Riders?"

"That's it." Bardwell took off his neckerchief and brushed away the flies again. He then secured it over the dead man's face.

"Then I guess we'll be going with you," Hicks said.

The letter P in a circle, Connor thought. The sign of the Phantom Riders.

******

THE DOMINION
SOUTHERN CALIFORNIA

Big George McManus stood with his arms crossed on the top rail of the corral as his second born son, Burl, began circling the huge steer. The large corral was ringed with onlookers including McManus's other three boys, Aaron, Freddie, and Little George. Big George's lawyer, Maxwell Tiddy, was also there, standing at the patriarch's side, with a look of frustration on his face.

"Big George," Tiddy said. "Can we *please* discuss the plans for after the election?"

"After the election be damned," McManus said. The short, fat, little attorney visibly stiffened, like he'd been slapped. "That's what I pay you to worry about, ain't it?"

Before the lawyer could answer, McManus yelled at Burl: "You sure you don't want a rope him. He's a big one."

Burl scrunched up his face and shook his head.

That's Burl's way, Big George thought. Always confident of his strength, his ability.

It was too bad Aaron, his eldest son, didn't match Burl in physicality. Aaron had gotten more in the way of brains, but his right hand was underdeveloped and smaller than his left, rendering him less than a full man in Big George's estimation. His youngest son, Little George, had gotten the looks of his father, and his quick temper, but not the size and height of his progenitor. And Fredrick ... Well, Fredrick was Freddie. Always had been, always would be. But it wasn't his totally fault that he was more than a little bit slow mentally. When they'd been kids, Little George had stuck him in the head with a pitchfork. That had made a difference. A big difference.

At least that's what Big George told himself, rather than admit that it had been something inherited that made his third boy only slightly smarter than that imported Texas Bull.

Big George heaved a quick sigh. All of his boys were lacking in some area, and none matched up to him. Obviously, they all had a bit too much of their mother in them in, one way or another.

The animal was a monster, one of those long-horns from Texas, with a massive hump of muscle clustered just behind a solid looking neck. The beast's horns had to spread at least six feet or more. They were long horns, a glossy gray color that curled into sharp hooks at the ends. McManus knew that he wanted those horns mounted and placed over his mantle once the beast's breeding duties were done. But for now, he was more interested in watching his second born match his strength against the massive animal. One bull against another.

Bull … That was the nickname that Burl had acquired as a boy due to his large, powerful body that was like a barrel with a set of arms and legs. Even as a boy he'd been exceptionally strong, able to bend nails and horseshoes with his oversized hands. And now that he'd grown to manhood, the nickname fit like a tailored glove.

If only his mind matched his strength, Big George thought.

Burl was, for lack of a better term, not the sharpest of blades either, but he was well above Freddie. Of McManus's four sons, Burl most resembled his father, but without his sire's deftness of reasoning. Still, that, too, might be considered a good thing. Big George was in no hurry to turn over the Dominion, the name he'd given to his empire, to his progeny. At least not yet. There was still a lot to do, more land to conquer, and a lot more power to be accumulated.

Two men stood off to the side of the senior McManus holding the end of a branding iron in a small bonfire. Wade Kandy, Big George's favorite ranch hand, sat on the uppermost rail at the corner juncture holding a Winchester rifle just in case the four-legged bull bested the two-legged one. But Big George didn't think any intervention would be necessary. Neither did his son, whose heavy, rotund face harbored an anticipatory simper.

"You ready for me to rassle him down, Pa?" Burl McManus asked.

He was shirtless and his big, solid body was covered with a nap-like layer of coarse brownish hair. Big George often thought Burl resembled a bear more than a bull. The late afternoon sun reflected off the large bald spot on the crown of his head. He took after his mother's side of the family in that regard. Big George was very proud that he still had a full head of dark brownish hair, albeit with a few streaks of gray of late.

Burl clapped his big hands together and grinned. "Pa?"

Big George whistled to the two ranch hands by the fire and one held up the iron. It looked ready.

"Go ahead," Big George said. "But don't hurt him none. Remember I bought him for breeding."

Burl snorted and stepped forward. The wary steer's eyes widened and he lifted his right front leg and pawed at the soft earth a bit.

Kandy worked the lever to cock the Winchester and adjusted himself on the rail.

"Should be all right," Big George said. "Burl can handle him."

Kandy kept the rifle leveled at the beast anyway.

Burl advanced a few steps and stopped. The steer was perhaps fifteen feet away from him. The animal's head shifted as one bulbous brown eye scrutinized the man before him. Then the head lowered and the steer charged. Moving with a grace that belied his size, Burl skipped to the right and pirouetted, grabbing one of the long horns in each hand. He slammed his body against the steer's left shoulder and twisted at the same time. The animal continued for several feet more in a small semicircle and Burl's face twisted with exertion. Then the beast slowed, took three more hesitant steps and flipped over onto its right side, Burl Mc-Manus twisting the head up toward his own face like a recalcitrant lover's. When the steer's snout was only inches from his own, Burl pursed his lips and mimicked a kissing sound.

"Well, get your asses in there and brand him, dammit," Big George yelled.

The two ranch hands straightened up and one of them lifted the branding iron from the fire with his gloved hand. The end glowed bright red with the McManus brand: *McM*, enclosed in a circle.

The first one slipped between the wooden rails of the corral as the other thrust the branding iron between the spaces. The first one grabbed it and ran toward the flopping beast.

"Put on his flank," Big George said. "Where everybody can see it."

The ranch hand circled behind the kicking rear legs, which flailed in metronomic fashion in the air. He raised the end of the iron, and then held it against the steer's flank for several seconds creating a hissing sound. The animal emitted a squeal and struggled more desperately, but Burl's grip had the horns firmly secured. He shifted his legs to adjust his dominant position.

The ranch hand removed the brand, checked the site, and then turned to Big George.

"It's done, sir," he said.

"Good. Now get the hell outta there so my son can release the damn thing."

The ranch hand scurried back through the fence.

Burl McManus grinned, shifted his weight once more, and then got to a stooped position, still holding the long horns in his grasp. He then released the steer's head and stood erect. The animal's legs kicked back and forth momentarily, and then it rolled to its feet, standing on shaky legs.

Kandy shouldered the rifle, but Burl held up his hand as he shook his head.

"Ain't no need," he said. "Critter knows who his boss is. He's just feeling the pain of that brand."

As if in testimony to the statement, the steer stood on shaking legs, its rear end shivering, as a stream of urine forming a ridge on the ground. A burst of fecal matter followed.

Burl backed toward the gate, pulled up the securing latch, and slipped through.

Another ranch hand handed him a tan chambray shirt, which Burl slipped on. His immense body was glistening with a patina of sweat and dirt. The shirt stuck to his skin like a glove. He held up his arm, sniffed, and then smirked.

"Might have to take a bath sooner than Saturday night," he said.

Big George laughed. He was exceptionally proud of his big, strapping boy, who was on the path to becoming the next sheriff of the county after next Tuesday's election. And this would be preceded by Aaron being appointed the new County Commissioner, all nice and legal. The McManus brand would be on a lot more than cattle in the near future, paving the way for the new railroad coming in.

"Big George," Maxwell Tiddy said. "Can we at least go in the house? The dust is getting all over me and the smell is terrible."

McManus turned and laughed. If he didn't need this short little pot-bellied bookworm to tend to the legalities, he'd throw the son of a bitch into the corral and watch that burned-ass bull chase him around. But McManus knew that in truth, he did need him. It was a sad fact of recent days that things were done by a different means; not like when he'd first settled here and carved out his ranch, the largest in the territory, if not the state. Then things were done with fists and guns. Law was established by the butt of a rifle, and disputes were settled man-to-man, in the middle of the main street, like they should be: with a fist and a gun.

Now civilization had crept up and bit him on the ass. No longer could he ride into town and knock his way through the damn city council and their puppet sheriff. Things had to be ruled upon in a court of law, and instead of bullets, ballots controlled who got what positions.

McManus drew in a deep breath and exhaled sharply.

He longed to return to those days of yore. And deep down, someday he knew that he would.

"George, please," Tiddy said, holding his hand toward the substantial frontier mansion behind them. "Shall we?"

But McManus heard something and held up his hand. His ears strained to make out the sound. The sound of hooves ... Rapid hooves ... Horses moving fast.

He turned and saw four men riding in, one of them slumped over on his saddle.

As they drew closer he saw it was Pete, Rodney, Jasper, and Lloyd.

Everyone stood silent as Big George began walking toward the approaching riders. They halted their horses and the slumped over one, Lloyd, lolled backward in his saddle. McManus saw that the front of his dirty tan shirt was red with blood. His lips curled downward.

"What the hell happened?" McManus motioned for two of his ranch hands to help Lloyd down from his horse.

"We was out doing what you told us, boss," Pete

said. "And then that nigger, Bardwell, rode up and took a shot at us."

"One man against four?" McManus glared at him. Pete reminded McManus of a shifty coyote, but he was always good at doing those dirty little jobs that had to be done.

"Well, some other riders come to help him." Pete's tongue shot out to wet his lips.

"Riders? Who?"

The cowhand shifted his narrow shoulders. "Dunno. Two men with guns. They was shooting, too. We was outnumbered."

"You were, eh?" McManus said. This son of a bitch couldn't count any better than he could follow directions. "Where's the nigger at now?"

Pete shrugged. "Can't say. When Lloyd got hit, we figured it was better to vamoose."

McManus considered this. "How was it that Bardwell just appeared?"

The shifty coyote shrugged. "Looked like he was headed to town before the fight, I guess."

"How much did he see?"

Pete shrugged again.

McManus turned to one of his ranch hands and said, "Get my horse."

"George," Tiddy said, stepping forward. "Let's not do anything rash. At least not until we have all the facts."

"Shut up," McManus said. He strode next to Pete, who was still mounted on his horse. "You get it all done?"

"Yes, sir. Just like you told us."

McManus turned and walked over to Lloyd who was on the ground now and barely conscious.

"Get the buckboard and take him into town to the doc's," he said.

One of the ranch hands immediately trotted off toward the large barn.

Tiddy came up and stood next to McManus.

"Once again," the lawyer said. "I'm advising you it would be best to find out exactly what happened."

"I already got me a pretty damn good idea what happened."

"I mean," the lawyer continued. "We should have things figured out before we report this to the sheriff,"

McManus turned his head slightly to address him. "The sheriff?"

"Yes. We'll want to make a report that one of our men was shot. It's a preemptive move."

"Preemptive. Like in chess."

Tiddy smiled. "Precisely."

One of the cowhands walked Big George's regal black stallion over, the silver trimmed saddle and bridle already in place. McManus took the reins from the man, hooked his left foot in the fancy stirrup, and swung up onto the animal.

"Hold on, George," Tiddy said. "I'm coming along with you."

"All right," McManus said. "Hurry up and get your damn horse."

Tiddy hustled over to a gray mare tied at the hitching rail in front of the huge stone and timber pillars that gave the mansion what McManus called frontier regality.

Timber and stone ... The solid building blocks of a man's empire.

He saw his four sons were readying their mounts as well.

To all things, there is a season, he thought with a smile, unable to recall the exact wording of the rest of the Bible verse. And this one looks like it's going to become a season of the gun.

✳✳✳✳✳✳

ARIZONA TERRITORY

William Franklin O'Rourke watched as the tall, lean man in a buckskin shirt and filthy pair of black pants walked up to them carrying a trussed up body over his right shoulder as easily as if he were carrying a bed roll. His left hand clasped a long, leather scabbard that was about five feet long along with a half-full bottle of whiskey. Beside them, the heavyset man with the fancy hat, Melvin Bennett, had his thumbs tucked into the small pockets of his vest. A big cigar smoldered from the corner of his mouth. They were in the middle of a huge pasture, at least two hundred yard square, the foliage sparse over the sandy earth.

The man in buckskin stopped and let the trussed body roll off his shoulder and fall to the ground with a sodden thump. O'Rourke saw that it was a man, a boy really. An Indian not more than eleven or twelve; his dark eyes darted back and forth over the three white men.

"That son of a bitch's been pilfering from me for over a month," Bennett said. He removed the cigar from his mouth and addressed the man in buckskin. "Well, what are you waiting for, Quint. Cut his damn throat."

Quint set the long leather scabbard down on a tree stump and carefully placed the bottle next to it. He then stared at Bennett for several seconds before glancing down at the boy. He took in a deep breath and removed a long, thin knife from a sheath on his belt and stooped down next to the Indian. The boy's head recoiled as he saw the blade.

Quint smirked and flipped the youth over onto his face. The Indian made a grunting sound, but said nothing.

He's got grit for someone about to die, O'Rourke thought. He continued to watch with fascination. He'd always dreamed of killing one those savages to claim the title of an Indian killer.

"You ready to die?" Bennett yelled. "You little thieving son of a bitch."

Quint slipped the blade under the rope that bound the Indian's wrists. With a quick upward gesture he cut the bonds, then did the same for the one securing the boy's ankles. The Indian shook his limbs. The man in buckskin stood up and stared down at him. Their eyes locked. Quint pointed to the tree line that was perhaps two hundred yards away.

"What the hell you doing, Quint?" Bennett said. "I paid to you track down that critter."

"And that's what I did," Quint said. His voice was low and gravely. "I tracked him for three damn days. So there he is."

"Well, don't let him go," Bennett said.

The Indian's eyes flashed and he jumped to his feet, running as fast as he could toward the tree line.

"You hired me to catch him." Quint grinned. "I caught him."

The Indian boy ran as fast as he could through the expansive open field. He tripped and fell, then got up, glanced back at them, and continued his run. About ten feet away the tall, rangy man in buckskin took a drink from the bottle of whiskey on the tree stump and set it down once more. O'Rourke looked again at the Indian. He'd gone perhaps close to a hundred and fifty feet now. Fifty yards. And he had at least twice that to get to the distant line of trees at the other end of the field.

"He's gonna get away, dammit," Bennett said. "Shoot him."

"Ain't no sport in shooting a fish in a barrel," Quint said. "It's gonna cost you more."

Bennett stamped his feet. "Dammit, dammit, dammit. I ain't paying you for a job left undone."

The man in buckskin was watching the Indian's progress. He ran his tongue over teeth, made a clicking sound with his mouth, picked up the long leather scabbard, and slipped out an enormous rifle. It was a massive thing, bigger and longer than anything O'Rourke had ever seen in this godforsaken frontier. And along the top it had an extended brass tube of sorts. No doubt it was some sort of mechanism akin to one of those telescopic sights he'd heard about.

"Take him now, Quint," Bennett said. "He reaches them trees and gets out of range, there'll be hell to pay."

Quint spat on the ground close to the fat man's boot.

"You saying you think I can't 'fore he gets to them trees?" he said.

Bennett frowned at the spittle drying in the sandy earth, the lines of his face deepening.

"What I'm saying is, you'd damn well better not let him get away." He transferred his gaze to the running boy again. "Hell, he's almost there."

Quint looked, nodded, and said, "I expect he is. How 'bout we make us a little wager? Double or nothing if'n' I can't?"

Bennett's lips pursed as he glanced from Quint, to the Indian, and then back again.

"I'm paying you to do a job, dammit," he said. "Not to play games. That damn Injun's been bleeding me dry with his stealing and sneaking around. Now do it."

Quint was still holding the big rifle in front of his chest, the skin around his eyes and mouth crinkling from a mirthful grin.

"Double or nothing?" he repeated.

O'Rourke saw that the Indian was nearing the tree line.

Bennett's flaccid cheeks shook, his face almost beet red now.

"All right, all right. Double or nothing," he yelled. "But you'd damn well better get him."

Quint turned and braced the rifle stock against his shoulder, settling his cheek against the finely polished wood and placing his right eye perhaps an inch or so behind the long scope. His left hand held the wooden portion under the barrel as his big right thumb flicked up and cocked back the long hammer.

The Indian continued his run. He was only a tiny target now, no bigger by comparison than a half a match stick.

O'Rourke was amazed at how still Quint was.

He's like a statue, O'Rourke thought.

Suddenly the sound of the exploding cartridge concussed O'Rourke's eardrums and he lost all hearing momentarily. He saw Bennett recoil, and then recover, his jaw gaping in shock and then re-settling into a wide, childlike simper as the distant, running figure jerked like he'd been stuck by a cannonball and tumbled forward, face down.

Quint lowered the rifle, bent to retrieve the bottle, and took another swing.

He said something to Bennett that O'Rourke couldn't discern. His ears were still ringing from the intrusion of the gunshot.

Bennett seemed less affected and was talking now. O'Rourke could see it was rapid speech, accompanied by an attempt to pat Quint on the shoulder.

The buckskin man shook off the fat man's adulation. He turned and picked up his rifle scabbard and slipped the long gun inside.

"I'll be takin' my money now," he said.

O'Rourke realized that his hearing had returned, albeit a bit more distorted and fuzzy than normal.

"Certainly, certainly," the Bennett said, taking a long, finely tooled leather wallet out of his coat pocket and opening it up. He licked his right thumb and began counting out the bills. "Oh, by the way, this is Mr. O'Rourke. He contacted me earlier and wants to speak to you."

Quint's eyes didn't stray from the counting, but O'Rourke didn't mind. In fact, he preferred a man who kept his eye on the important things, like the job at hand, although this buckskinned sharp-shooter had cut things rather close with that wager.

Double or nothing...

But regardless of the brazenness, that had been one hell of a shot. The man's reputation was well-deserved.

Quint folded the money and stuck it into a pouch on his belt. He was wearing a sidearm on his right side and a large, sheathed knife on his left. The man's hair was shoulder length and he had grizzled stubble covering his face. O'Rourke had been ordered by the Chicago office of the Pinkerton National Detective Agency to track the man down and procure his services. Tracking people was O'Rourke's specialty. Hiring killers was something with which he also had experience, although his last foray hadn't turned out as well as expected.

Quint was walking toward him now, Bennett by the buckskinned man's side. The fat man dispatched two of his ranch hands to "Go fetch the dead Injun."

"You had ought to leave him right where he fell," Quint said. "Be a warning to any more of 'em come thieving. Especially with that one causing all that trouble down south a ways."

"Geronimo?" Bennett laughed. "Well, we've got laws coming to the Territory now. Indian agents, too. They find out that one of their charges sneaked off the reservation and got shot, they might start asking questions. Which is why I paid for your discretion as well as your marksmanship."

Quint didn't seem to be paying Bennett much attention. Instead, he was studying O'Rourke, sizing him up.

Noticing this immediately made O'Rourke try to pull in his stomach a bit and stand a little straighter. Not that he was very successful at either. His body was short and stout and he needed spectacles for close-up work, such as reading or shooting. While he was not a pantywaist, by any stretch of the imagination, nor was he a hardened westerner. He'd come West from Boston and had been a Pinkerton Agent for the better part of four years. Wherever the agency sent him, he went. Whatever they told him to do, he did. And now he was once again going to hire a man to do some dirty work ... To do some killing.

"You want something, dude?" Quint asked, his voice low and gravelly. The man's face held a questioning expression, his eyes unblinking and deadly looking.

O'Rourke forced himself to smile. The "dude" comment irritated him. While he was wearing his customary navy blue suit, which was standard dress for the company, he'd recently substituted a wide-brimmed western style hat for his beloved black derby. It was an effort on his part to be less conspicuous, and now this ignoramus had called him a "dude," and he meant it in the pejorative sense of the word, as if a man having retained some culture and learning was a bad thing. But dealing with these uncouth reprobates was part of his job. He mentally recited the Pinkerton Code: *Maintain professionalism. Maintain objectivity. Maintain anonymity. Maintain loyalty to the client.* And last, but most important, *Maintain absolute loyalty to the Company.* He knew he had to choose his words carefully.

O'Rourke felt the strain in his cheeks maintaining the smile. "Say, that was quite a shot."

Quint's eyes narrowed and he looked O'Rourke up and down.

Clearing his throat, O'Rourke said, "What type of rifle is that?"

Quint didn't reply for several seconds, then said, "Sharps."

O'Rourke's mouth felt dry. His tongue flicked out over his lips.

"Looks like a pretty big caliber. Forty-five?"

Quint's nostrils flared, the squint deepening. "Fifty caliber."

"Big enough to stop a buffalo, I'd imagine," O'Rourke said.

Quint made a hocking sound with his mouth and then spat in the dirt once more. "What the hell you want?"

O'Rourke cautiously regarded the spittle as it sank into the soft earth. He gingerly stepped away from it. "I represent a client who wishes to procure your services."

"Procure?" Quint's brow furrowed. "What's that mean?"

"He wishes to hire you."

"Hire me? For what?"

O'Rourke felt his smile waning a bit. He gestured toward the field where the dead Indian lay. "A similar assignment as this one. But it involves a bit of traveling. Some tracking, too."

Quint's hardened expression evened out and his right cheek twitched into something akin to a smile. "I'm listening."

"We're prepared to triple the amount of payment you received today."

"Now you're talking my language, dude." He picked up the whiskey bottle and took another swig, then offered it to O'Rourke.

The Pinkerton man recoiled slightly, but tried not to show his revulsion as he accepted the bottle. He brought his left hand up to wipe off the top, but saw Quint scrutinizing him.

The son of a bitch is watching to see what I do, O'Rourke thought.

He took another deep breath and brought the bottle directly to his mouth with no wipe off.

Maintain absolute loyalty to the company, he thought as he took a drink of the bitter fluid. The things I do ...

CHAPTER 2

SWEETWATER, CALIFORNIA

The town was a more substantial looking place than
Connor had imagined it would be. The main street
had a cluster of various sized buildings including
a bank, telegraph office, saloon, hotel, at least two
mercantile shops, and a host of others. A curving
set of railroad tracks led up to a corner structure
on the northern end and abruptly ended with a
large wooden barricade next to a depot which bore
the sign, *SWEETWATER JUNCTION: B and D
RAILROAD COMPANY.* Across the street was a
huge wooden building with big, fancy windows
and a set of double doors labeled *SWEETWATER
GRAIN EMPORIUM.* As they rode farther Connor noticed the burned out shells of two buildings,
their blackened beams and timbers listing pitifully
on the corner of an adjacent street.

"What happened over there?" Connor asked.

"Phantom Riders came in one night," Bardwell said. "Burned them out. Or so I heard."

Connor pointed to a pile of discarded pieces of lumber sitting in front of one of the charred structures.

"Looks like somebody was thinking of rebuilding or fixing them up."

Bardwell shook his head. "Ain't gonna happen. One was a highfaluting saloon. Called itself The Emporium. The owner raised holy hell with the sheriff after some of the local cowpunchers busted the place up one night. Next thing you know, the Phantom Riders threw a torch through the window. Shot and killed the owner."

"What was the other place?" Connor asked.

"The other used to be an office building for handling legal stuff. Caught on fire the same night. Was a couple of lawyers helping folks with recording deeds and that sort. All the lawyers but one left town or quit, and the one that stayed works for McManus now."

As they went by a saloon called *The Peachtree Palace,* the bat wing doors flew open and a burly man in a white shirt with a fancy vest tossed a tall, lean guy off the boardwalk and into the street. The lean man flopped down and lay there unmoving for several seconds.

"Is he all right?" Abby asked.

Before anyone could offer an opinion the man sprang up from the dusty street and turned back toward the saloon. Connor noticed the man was unbuttoning the front of his pants.

"Sis, don't look," he yelled out, but it was too late.

The man in front of the bar was urinating on the boardwalk in front of the saloon. The stream continued and the bartender burst through with a large cudgel.

The man turned and fled, tucking himself back into his pants as he wobbled away on shaky legs and an uneven gait.

Connor glanced toward Abby, hoping she'd been spared the sight of the unpleasantness, but from the smile on her face he knew she hadn't.

She shot him a knowing look and said, "Oh, don't be such a priss. It ain't like I never seen one before."

Connor knew she had, but he still felt the flush of embarrassment.

"Ain't it a bit early for drunks?" he said.

Bardwell snorted a laugh. "Not for him."

"Man musta worked up one hell of a thirst," Hicks said.

"And he had to let it out," Abby said.

"Seems kinda uncouth," Connor said. "Especially with women folk around."

Bardwell let out a laugh. "Well, he ain't got much to do lately." He jerked his thumb back indicating the direction from which they'd come. "Remember that burnt out building? He was one of them lawyers that quit."

Connor shook his head in disgust as they rode by the man.

"Stable and livery's over there," Bardwell said. "In case you want to be housing your horses for the night."

Connor studied the place. It was constructed out of heavy beams. "Appears to be pretty well maintained."

"The owner's a pretty good smith," Bardwell said. "When he wants to be. Like everyone else in this town."

"He gonna fix your wagon?" Connor asked.

Bardwell shrugged. "I'm sure hoping so."

They passed the blacksmith's shop and stable, then a barber shop, an undertaker's, an emporium, and postal and telegraph office. A big, solid brick and mortar building with *Sweetwater Bank an▸ Trust* on the front window sat next to another, equally solid looking structure that said *County Seat* in gold and black lettering. There were so many buildings with different names that Connor had a hard time taking it all in. Many of them had signs nailed to the front with the picture of a man's face, under which was written in bold block letter: *BURL "BULL" McMANUS FOR SHERIFF.* At the far end of the street a two story church with a tall steeple adorned with a bell and large wooden cross seemed to preside over the area. Quite a few houses lay beyond the church. Connor checked Abby and noticed she seemed as fascinated as he was by the number and variety.

She'll be looking to get some of her licorice candy, no doubt, he thought.

"Sheriff's office is over there," Bardwell said, pointing to the left as they rode under a banner that had been strung across the street from two poles.

Connor turned his head to see what the lettering on it said and was surprised.

Welcome Governor George Perkins.

The governor, he thought. This place must be pretty important.

Bardwell brought his wagon to a halt in front of a wood and stone building with a sign above the door labeled *SHERIFF* and *JAIL*. He wrapped the reins around the brake and hopped down onto the street. Connor took another look at the body in the back of the wagon. There was no canvas top to it, but the handkerchief Bardwell had used to cover the dead man's face was still in place.

Hicks motioned toward a hitching rail and he, Connor and Abby all dismounted.

The dirt felt hard packed under Connor's boots and he noticed the area was very dry. He wondered how successful John Henry would be as a farmer in an area where there didn't seem to be a lot of rain and that McManus fellow hogged all the water.

"Abby," Hicks said. "See to the horses. Don't let them drink too much from that trough."

She nodded.

That girl always does what River tells her to do, he thought. If I would've said that, she'd be sassin' me back.

Still, he was glad that Hicks had invited him along to see the sheriff with Bardwell. That meant a lot to Connor, being accepted as a man, even though he was only sixteen.

But man enough, he thought.

They stepped up onto the wooden boardwalk and Bardwell pushed open the door, knocking as he did. Inside a broad shouldered man glanced up from behind a desk. He had weather-worn face with a thin mustache and a streak of gray in the front of his hair. A large silver star was pinned to the left side of his leather vest. As the man stood, Connor noticed the .45 Colt Peacemaker in a leather holster on the sheriff's right side. The loops in the gun belt held a neat row of cartridges. A rack on the wall held a shotgun and two Winchesters. A stove sat to one side and on the wall behind the desk another door was standing open. Connor could see the metal bars of a cell in that room.

"Afternoon, sheriff," Bardwell said.

The sheriff nodded. "John Henry." His dark eyes shot from Bardwell to Hicks to Connor.

Bardwell removed his hat and took a deep breath.

"This is Mister River Hicks and Connor Mack," he said. "This is Sheriff Dan Thorpe."

The sheriff nodded again. "So what brings you all here?"

"They helped me out on the prairie when I was attacked by some riders," Bardwell said.

"Riders? The Phantom Riders?"

Bardwell shook his head. "Can't rightly say, sir. They wasn't wearing no masks. Appeared to be some from the McManus spread, but I couldn't be sure."

"What happened?" Thorpe asked.

Bardwell gave him a brief summary of the encounter and how Hicks and Connor had helped him. "I think I winged one them."

Thorpe raised his eyebrows. "I'll have to check with Doc on that. See if he's had any new patients.

Anyway, what's this about a dead man?"

"He's in the wagon," Bardwell said. "It's Howard Layton, sir. And he's got the Phantom Rider brand on his forehead."

Thorpe blew out a long breath while shaking his head. "You say he was hung?"

"That's right," Hicks said. "We came upon him just before we heard the gunshots."

"So it's possible the riders that attacked you might have done it?" Thorpe said, looking to Bardwell.

The black man shrugged. "When I came by in my wagon, they was over by the tree where he was. They saw me and commenced to coming after me. I tried to out run them, but I hit a deep rut and overturned my wagon and my horses broke away."

Thorpe considered all of this for several seconds, then reached to a coat rack and grabbed his hat. "I better take a look."

They walked outside and Thorpe stopped suddenly. Connor saw that Abby was standing by the wagon holding the handkerchief that had been covering the dead man's face. She was staring intently at the disfigured visage.

"Aw, sis, what you doing?" Connor blurted out.

The girl turned and stared back at him, saying nothing.

Hicks pushed past them and strode over to her, gently pulling the handkerchief out of her hands. He turned, his face as stoic as usual.

"This is Abby," he said. "Connor's sister."

The sheriff tipped his hat, but his expression

remained rather guarded. He moved to the wagon and stared down at the dead man for several seconds, then shook his head again.

"This is a damn shame," he said. "A *amn* shame."

"You knew him well?" Hicks asked.

Thorpe sighed. "He was one of our county commissioners, in charge of settling land disputes and planning for the development of the area." His eyes moved toward Bardwell. "Was in the midst of deciding on an important issue involving the water rights in these parts."

"I already told them about it," Bardwell said.

"He seemed like a fair man," Thorpe said. "We been having a lot of trouble with these Phantom Riders, and this does look like their handwork."

"Can't you do nothing to catch 'em?" Connor asked.

Hicks shot him a quick frown and Connor realized that was the wrong thing to say.

Thorpe lowered his gaze as he spoke. "It ain't been for lack of trying. They strike, usually at night or out on the prairie somewhere, and by the time word gets back to me here in town, and I get up a posse, they're long gone. It's like they just disappear."

"Like Phantom Riders," Connor said, thinking once more of that Dangerous Dan story he'd read once.

"Oh, they're flesh and blood, all right." Thorpe heaved a heavy sigh. "I had hoped to find their hideout while I still had a job."

"Election coming up?" Hicks asked.

"In a few days. You saw the signs, huh?"

"Hard not to. Your opponent the same McManus John Henry was telling us about?"

"His son," Thorpe said.

"I hates to think what things gonna be like if'n' he gets in," Bardwell said. "I know me and my people all be coming in to vote for you."

Thorpe reached up and placed a hand on Bardwell's shoulder. "I appreciate that, John Henry."

"Why's the governor coming here?" Hicks asked.

"He's supposed to be appointing one of the McManus boys to a county commissioner position. Circuit judge is on the way, too."

Hicks emitted a low whistle.

"This McManus fellow must swing a lot of weight."

"That he does." Thorpe turned. "John Henry, can you bring your wagon down to the undertaker's office? I'll walk with you."

Bardwell nodded and held his hand toward Hicks, who was still holding the handkerchief. Hicks gave it to him and the black man once again covered the face of the corpse. Across the street a few onlookers were staring at the scene.

The thunder of hooves resounded from the other end of town and Connor saw a group of riders coming in hard and fast surrounding a buckboard. He counted six of them, led by a good-sized man riding a magnificent black stallion with the fanciest bridle and saddle harness Connor had ever seen. It was fine, black polished leather trimmed with silver. The other riders were flanking him in what appeared to be an almost-parade of military procession. He heard Bardwell grunt.

"Who's that?" Connor asked.

"McManus," Bardwell said.

He stepped up onto his wagon and untied the reins from the brake. Thorpe began walking down the boardwalk toward the undertakers. Hicks, Connor, and Abby remained by their horses as the procession trundled by at a rapid pace, stirring up a cloud of dust. Connor turned his face away and Abby coughed.

"Ain't too neighborly," Hicks said. "Are they?"

"Wonder where they're going in such a damn hurry?" Connor said. He emitted a cough now, too.

"The doctor's, most likely," Hicks said. "They got what appears to be an injured man in the back of that buckboard."

Connor's eyes followed the wagon. He could see someone lying on the flat bed, but could discern little else.

"That one driving the buckboard looks a might familiar," Hicks said.

"You think they're the ones that was shooting at John Henry?" Connor asked.

Hicks gave a fractional nod. "If I had to harbor a guess, I'd say you could bet on it."

The procession halted next to Bardwell's wagon and the one Connor assumed was McManus thrust an arm out at Thorpe, who was still on the boardwalk.

"What's going on here, Sheriff?" he demanded. His voice was deep and commanding and Connor wondered if the man had a military background.

Thorpe stepped over to Bardwell's wagon and put his hands on top of the wooden sides.

"There's been a murder," Thorpe said.

McManus glared down at him, then looked to the wagon, and then back to the lawman.

"A murder?" McManus said. "Who?"

Thorpe stared back at him for a few beats before replying.

"Howard Layton."

"Layton?" McManus's nostrils flared. "What happened?"

"That's what I intend to find out," Thorpe said. "Now, if you'll excuse me—"

"Not so fast," McManus said. "I want to swear out a complaint."

"Against who?" Thorpe asked.

McManus gestured toward Bardwell. "Him. He shot my man, Lloyd here. We're taking him to the doc's now."

"I already reported it the sheriff," Bardwell said. "Your men attacked me and I only fired back in self-defense."

"Shut up, you black son of a bitch," McManus said. His head swiveled back toward Thorpe. "I want him arrested."

"I can't do that, Mr. McManus," Thorpe said. "No grounds."

Connor was close enough to see McManus's face redden.

"You lilly-livered, nigger-loving son of a bitch. I'll give you grounds."

His hand dropped toward his holster but stopped as the echo of a round tore through the air. Connor whirled and saw Hicks standing there with his pistol in his hand, the barrel pointed at an upward angle, a trail of smoke emanating from the muzzle.

"I wouldn't do that, if I were you, mister," Hicks said. "Otherwise I won't be aiming so high with my next shot."

McManus transferred his stare from Thorpe to Hicks. The large guy on the horse next to McManus appeared ready to draw.

"That goes for tiny over there as well," Hicks said. "Or for any of the rest of your ne'er-do-wells."

A younger man with jet black hair and a striking resemblance to McManus pulled his horse around to face Hicks. "You think you can get all of us, gunfighter?"

Hicks pulled out his second gun with his left hand and his mouth curled into a sly smile. "More than likely, sonny."

"And my gun makes three." Connor removed his Colt Peacemaker from its holster and held it high, aiming for the man on the horse.

"Connor, back off," Hicks said.

Connor lowered his gun but kept it by his leg.

"Who the hell are you?" McManus said, his voice a low growl.

"I'm one of the witnesses that can back up what Mr. Bardwell just said." Hicks cocked back the hammer on his Peacemakers. "Your men, four of them, were circling him and shooting after his wagon overturned. He just shot back."

"That ain't what they told me," McManus said.

"Then they're lying," Hicks said.

Thorpe had his gun out now as well and spoke in a loud voice.

"McManus, if you're so worried about your wounded man there, maybe you should be getting him over to the doc's instead of threatening us here."

McManus held his gaze on Hicks a moment longer before glancing back to the sheriff. He sat on his horse for several seconds in silence. Connor couldn't help but admire what a fine animal the steed was, its black coat shiny and taut over the chiseled musculature. The sleek beauty of the horse's midnight blackness, however, was marred by the ridge of a raised, white outline of a brand on its left flank

McM enclosed in a circle.

Connor understood the need to document ownership of such a horse, but couldn't help by feel that the brand spoiled the creature's beauty. This seemed to be more of a boastful proclamation.

McManus turned toward the buckboard. "Get him outta here. Take him to the doc."

The buckboard driver snapped the reins and the craft lurched forward, the horsemen separating to let it pass.

"Come next Tuesday," McManus said to Bardwell. "After the election, we'll be coming for you, *boy.*"

"And I'll be waiting," Bardwell said. "*Boy.*"

A tremor shook McManus's face as his lips curled

into a snarl, but he said nothing. The two men sat only about twelve feet apart, their eyes locked, neither wanting to be the first to look away. Finally, McManus turned his head and motioned with his hand. The procession trotted down the street after the buckboard. Hicks lowered and uncocked both of his weapons before slipping the left one into its holster. He then half-cocked the pistol he'd fired and opened the side loading gate. After ejecting the round, he replaced it with a fresh cartridge. Connor holstered his weapon as well.

Thorpe blew out a long breath and replaced his gun in its holster. He turned to Hicks.

"I appreciate the support," Thorpe said. "But next time let me handle things."

"You sure looked like you were handling things, all right," Connor said. "River saved your bacon, by my way of recollection."

The lawman was about to say something, but Hicks spoke first.

"You're absolutely right, Sheriff. I'm not an apologizing man, but if I was, that's what I'd be doing."

Thorpe's mouth tightened.

"Let's get this body to the undertaker." He turned and began walking.

Bardwell flicked the reins and his wagon jolted forward. He stared toward Hicks and Connor and winked.

Connor grinned.

"John Henry knows you saved that worthless sheriff's neck."

"I ain't so sure you should be calling him worthless," Hicks said. "It's not always that easy being a lawman. Pay's low, and the pats on the back are few and far between. Man in a position like that, he's got to maintain his self-respect as well as the respect of the townsfolk. If he appears weak, he's a goner."

Connor compressed his lips. He knew River was right. A man loses the respect of others, he quickly loses it for himself.

"So you're saying that you wasn't really apologizing, but you were just saying so to let the sheriff save face," Connor said.

"Never apologize. Remember that." Hicks shot him a wink. "But you're learnin', boy."

"Did you see that awful brand mark on that pretty Stallion?" Abby said.

"Yep. M C M in a circle," Connor said. "Must stand for McManus."

"And a whole lot more," Hicks said. "Judging from the looks of things around here. Come on, let's get our horses bedded down in the stable and then get us a room at the hotel."

"We're staying here?" Connor asked.

"For the time being," Hicks said. "At least till this powder keg simmers down a little bit."

"Why?" Connor asked. "Wouldn't it be better to head on out?"

Hicks nodded. "Better, but also more dangerous. There's the three of us out on the range against the possibility of who knows how many of McManus's range riders trailing us looking for trouble. Don't like them odds any."

Connor clucked his tongue. "Didn't figure on that."

"Besides," Hicks said. "It's been way too long since I slept on a genuine feather bed, not to mention Abby most likely wanting to buy a bag full of that licorice candy she's so fond of."

Abby smiled.

They began walking their horses down the street toward the blacksmith/livery stable.

Connor glanced back over his shoulder and saw one of the McManus crew staring after them.

******

McManus slammed some money down on the bar of the Peachtree Palace and motioned for the bartender to set up glasses for him and his men. He surveyed the place. They'd made some improvements since the last time he was here. The poker room and gambling tables were the same, but some bright gold wallpaper now covered the walls; and the chandelier that Kandy and the boys had busted a month or so ago had been reinstalled. That was good. The best bar in Sweetwater needed a bit of elegance.

Of course, he thought. It's also the *only* bar in Sweetwater.

That amused him as he remembered how the Phantom Riders had driven out the other, officious Emporium at the far end of town. The new owner had it coming, though, because he hadn't shown the proper amount of respect to the McManus brand,

and the son of a bitch had gotten what he deserved: a burnt out shell of a building and a bullet in his gut for good measure.

He remembered another Bible verse from his long ago childhood days: As ye sow, so shall ye reap.

Good advice to keep in mind. It had also been a sound business decision.

The adjacent law office was putting too many funny ideas into the heads of the townsfolk and ranchers. And especially those damn homesteaders. Now all the worthless lawyers were gone, except Tiddy, and he was necessary evil at the moment.

McManus glanced at the set of stairs leading to the second floor, where the rooms were, and saw they'd added a bit of carpeting to them. He wondered if they'd added any new girls as well. The current selection was getting a bit tiresome.

"What'll it be, Big George?" the bartender asked, his mouth twisting into a nervous grin.

"What do I usually have?" McManus said. "Your best whiskey. And none of that rot gut stuff you got sitting over there." He jabbed a finger at the assortment of bottles sitting in front of the long mirror that ran the length of the wall behind the bar. "Drinks for everybody."

A cheer emanated from those accompanying him.

His reflection stared back at him, and McManus removed his hat. What he saw more than pleased him. He'd changed so little over the years.

Sure, I'm a bit heavier with a few strands of gray, he thought. But I still look pretty damn good.

Maybe it was time to order him up a new wife. A younger model to replace his dearly departed, Sadie, who'd died five years ago. Or was it six? She'd been good for popping out the babies and raising them through the early years, schooling them and such, until he took over and made men out of them. The task had washed the life out of her and her disappointments became more and more obvious. McManus wasn't surprised when Freddie came rushing into the house that morning blabbering that ma had hung herself in the barn.

But, such was life.

The Dominion would go on. So would the McManus brand.

The barkeep moved down the bar and used a key to open a special cabinet then removed a dark bottle. Then he came back and filled Big George's glass first, smiling nervously all the while. The smile remained in place as he began serving the others. The ranch hand McManus had stationed outside came up and whispered into Big George's ear.

"After dropping the body off at the undertaker's," the man said. "The sheriff went back to his office and the nigger went down to the blacksmith's shop. Looks like his wagon's broke, just like they said."

McManus considered this. "Go check on Lloyd."

The cowhand eyed the whiskey on the bar and licked his lips.

"You didn't hear me?" McManus said.

The ranch hand blinked, nodded and then scurried out the doors.

Little George and Burl, shouldered their way on

either side of their father.

"Pa," Little George said. "Why'd you let that sidewinder get the better of us back there?"

"Not to mention taking guff from that soon to be ex-sheriff," Burl added.

McManus was sipping his drink. It tasted good. He licked his lips then set the glass down on the counter. He half turned toward Little George and brought his hand up quickly, grabbing his son's neck.

"How many times I got to drill it into you?" Big George's voice was a low growl, his face only an inch away from Little George's. "Nobody *ever* gets the better of me. Nobody."

"But, Pa—" Little George croaked.

Big George tightened his grip, cutting off any further words from his son.

"You ain't listening too good, are ya?"

Little George made a gurgling noise.

"Aw, Pa," Burl said. "We was ready to take them on. We coulda got 'em."

Big George released his hold on his son's neck and swiveled toward Burl. He had doubts his hand was big enough to span that bull's neck, so he shot him a withering stare.

"Neither one of you got the common sense of damn mule." He blew out an exasperated breath. "Sure, we coulda shot it out with them, and most likely we'd a got 'em. But did you see the way that tall, lean fella handed them guns? He'd a taken some of us with him, that's for sure. Plus he had that young one with him, and that no-account sheriff as well."

Burl said nothing. Little George hunched forward and massaged the front of his neck.

"But that damn sheriff siding with that Bardwell got me riled up," Burl said.

"And when you're elected to replace him after Tuesday," Big George said, "we'll deal with the both of them. You two need to learn to be smart about things. A good general always picks his battles."

"But what about the nigger shooting Lloyd?" Burl asked.

Big George picked up his drink and watched the amber liquid swirl inside as he rocked the glass.

Big George turned and stared at the reflection of the three of them in the mirrored wall.

One big, dumb and strong and the other a shorter, impulsive version of his father. But they were his blood, his progeny.

That couldn't be chosen, nor could it be changed, at least for the short term.

There's always time for me to start a new family, he thought.

"Pa?" Burl said.

"Think," Big George said. "We got the governor and that circuit judge coming to town."

"So?" Burl said.

"So ..." Big George's nostrils flared. "We got to be mindful of how we're doing things."

"Huh?" Burl's face wrinkled. "What you mean?"

Before he replied Big George sighed and savored some more of his drink.

This stuff wasn't bad, he thought.

"I got me a way to deal with Bardwell," he said. "All nice and legal like." He tossed down the remainder of the whiskey and motioned for the bartender to refill the glass. Then he leaned back and yelled, "Kandy."

Wade Kandy shifted away from the bar and walked down to stand by Big George.

"Sir?" he said.

Big George was always impressed by Kandy's looks, manners, and capableness. There was an elegance about him, from his well-coiffed pompadour to the silver belt buckle to his fancy, intricately inlayed black boots with the ostentatious Texas Spurs.

It was too bad he wasn't blood. McManus knew Kandy would be far better suited to run the Dominion than any of the four boys.

But blood was blood, he thought.

Big George turned and placed a hand on his foreman's shoulder and leaned close.

"Take one of the boys and ride back to the ranch," McManus said, the plan already forming in his mind. "There's something I want you to fetch."

✶✶✶✶✶✶

ARIZONA TERRITORY

O'Rourke drummed his fingers on the high desk top. The waiting for confirmation from the Chicago Office was always the most difficult part of the job. He mentally repeated the creed of the Pinkerton

National Detective Agency: *Maintain profession-alism at all times; maintain objectivity; maintain anonymity; maintain loyalty to the client; and last-ly, maintain absolute loyalty to the Company.*

The client's anonymity was a given. O'Rourke had never even met the man. The arrangement had been handled totally through the Chicago Office. All that was known to O'Rourke was that he lived somewhere in Oregon and was rich and deter-mined.

Obsessed is probably a more accurate descrip-tion, he thought. And *very* rich.

"When we gonna be catching that train, dude?" Quint asked.

The lean bounty hunter was standing so close that O'Rourke was very cognizant of the man's pungent body odor. It was deplorable. That buck-skin outfit smelled like it had never been washed.

But then again, could one wash the stench out of the dried, dead skin of an animal?

Regardless, the outfit would have to be discard-ed soon.

"I'm waiting on a telegram," O'Rourke said. "Then we're going to invest in some wardrobe ad-justments."

Quint raised one eyebrow and looked askance. "Huh?"

O'Rourke took in a deep breath out of frustra-tion and regretted it immediately.

The stench, he thought. Oh, Lord.

After quickly exhaling, he forced a smile.

Quint stared at him for a few seconds, saying

nothing, then snorted in apparent disgust. He reached into his pocket and removed a leather pouch and a corncob pipe.

"If'n' you and me gonna get along, dude, you're gonna have to start talking so I kin understand ya."

O'Rourke watched the man's long fingers pack the dark tobacco into the bowl of the pipe. He didn't mind the smell of pipe tobacco that much, and at least it would offset the odiferous buckskin. He reached into his pocket and withdrew a match, handing it to Quint.

The bounty hunter acknowledged the move with a slight nod, plucked the match away, and ran his thick, blackish thumbnail over the primer igniting the red phosphorus and sulfur head.

"We're going to have to buy you some new clothes first." O'Rourke said.

"Clothes? What fer?"

O'Rourke took in another deep breath, through his mouth this time, before he replied. How could he explain the tenants of the Company to this ignoramus?

"Part of what my employer does is maintaining anonymity."

"Ano what?"

"Anonymity," O'Rourke said. "It means not being noticed.

"Not being noticed ... Why does that matter so much?"

O'Rourke considered his next words carefully. "Your reputation precedes you. And we'd prefer this be handled in a discreet fashion."

"Discreet?"

Oh, Lord, O'Rourke thought. Do I have to explain the damn dictionary?

"So it's not so obvious who did what."

Quint puffed on the pipe, blowing clouds of smoke through both of his nostrils. "What difference does that make? I thought you said them three was wanted."

O'Rourke coughed. The smoke had a bitter redolence after all. Almost as foul as a cigar or cigarette after all. This third-party hiring was shaping up to be bit more difficult than he'd figured. "Well, one of them is."

Quint smirked around the pipe stem. O'Rourke noticed the man's teeth were as discolored as the dirt under his fingernails. "And the other two ain't."

It was more of a statement than a question so O'Rourke merely raised an eyebrow.

"All righty, dude," Quint said, puffing on the stem. "But none of them new clothes is coming out of my end."

Before O'Rourke could answer the sharp, beeping sound of an incoming telegram intruded.

Finally, O'Rourke thought. Turning to the telegraph operator, he said, "Please tell me that's for me from Chicago."

The clerk ignored him, tapping out a quick acknowledging response.

The sounds of more Morse code followed and the clerk was busily scribbling down the letters on a pad. After a solid two minutes of transcribing, the beeping noise ceased and the clerk heaved a heavy sigh. He wiped his upper lip with his finger and turned to O'Rourke.

"You want me to transcribe it all nice and pretty for you?"

"Just give it here," O'Rourke said, holding out his open palm.

The clerk held his hand out as well.

O'Rourke rolled his eyes, reached into his vest pocket, and withdrew two Indianhead pennies.

"Here." He tossed the coins onto the counter top and grabbed the notepad. The clerk's handwriting was atrocious, but O'Rourke could make it out.

FOR OROURKE STOP PROCEED AS PREVIOUSLY DIRECTED STOP SUBJECTS BELIEVED TO BE HEADING WEST FROM LAST KNOWN LOCATION STOP AGENCY ASSETS INVESTIGATING NEW REPORTED SIGHTING STOP MORE TO FOLLOW STOP CONTACT HEAD OFFICE IN TWELVE HOURS STOP

"That the one we been waiting on?" Quint asked.

O'Rourke nodded, tore the paper from the pad, then stuffed the page into his coat pocket.

It would have to go into his report.

"It is," he said in way of reiteration.

Quint sucked on the pipe but it had obviously gone out. He mashed his thumb into the bowl and replaced it into his pouch.

"So, where we headin'?"

"West," O'Rourke said. "But first—"

"I know. Them new clothes."

O'Rourke gave a fractional nod.

"Let's get to it, then." Quint snorted. "But like I

told ya, none of them new clothes is coming out of my end."

He picked up the scabbard containing the long rifle and headed for the door.

O'Rourke remembered the magnificent shot Quint had made earlier with the fleeing Indian and felt a sudden, but familiar thrill.

A long range kill, he thought.

This was going to be something to watch.

CHAPTER 3

SWEETWATER, CALIFORNIA

Connor heard the periodic, clanking sound of metal being pounded on metal as he, Abby, and Hicks approached the shop. The blacksmith was a big, sour looking man with a drooping gray mustache and distended belly that stretched the front of his dirty apron. His bare arms were replete with solid muscles that stood out under his hairy skin. His left hand used a pair of tongs to transfer a glowing piece of curved metal from the fire to the anvil where he smacked it with his hammer. Connor saw that the metal was a horse shoe. The blacksmith gave it another smack, and then one more before pausing to look at the three of them.

"Want something?"

"You run the livery stable?" Hicks asked.

The blacksmith grunted in the affirmative.

"We want to board our horses."

"How long?"

"Tonight for sure," Hicks said. "Maybe longer. Depends on if we like the town."

The blacksmith eyed the three of them and his gaze lingered over Abby. He licked his lips and then smirked.

"Don't expect you will," he said. "Ain't much to offer 'lessin' you're farming or working a ranch. And you all don't look the type for neither." He rattled off the price and Hicks took off his glove and reached into his pocket.

"We'll pay for tonight in advance," he said. "And if we stay longer, we can settle up then."

"Sounds good enough to me." The blacksmith put the horseshoe back into the fire and set the tongs down. He held out his big, calloused palm. "Name's Baker. Otis Baker."

"River Hicks." He dropped the coins in the blacksmith's hand.

Baker slipped the money into his apron pocket and pointed toward the adjacent building.

"Stable's over there," he said. "Food and water's off to the side. You can leave your saddles on the rail, if'n' you like. Make sure they're in there proper and the stall door's closed."

They led their animals through the adjacent shop and toward the interior of the stables.

After unsaddling them, Hicks removed his saddle bags and opened them. Connor saw him remove a pair of wrapped towels from each one. Hicks laid the folded material on the ground and gingerly unwrapped them. They contained two small, glass tubes filed with clear liquid. He checked the seal on both, and then rewrapped the tubes and put them back in the separate saddlebags.

"Those what I think they are?" Connor asked.

Hicks shot him a squinted look. "A little something I got from Zubal before we left Woodman."

"You mean Hope Springs," Abby said. "They changed the name back, remember?"

Connor remembered, all right. They'd had a close encounter back in Arizona with a corrupt mayor who'd named the town after himself. They'd been there to deliver some liquid components to the railroad: one container of glycerin, and one of nitric acid. When mixed together, they formed nitroglycerin. Zubal, their friend and associate, had been in charge of mixing up the explosive, and it had come in handy. Connor was surprised that River had kept some, but he also remembered that as long as the two chemicals were kept apart, they wouldn't blow up. But once they were mixed ...

"You expecting trouble?" Connor asked.

"Just staying ready for it," Hicks said. He told Abby to wipe the horses down and brush them. He turned to Connor. "Let's go check in at the hotel." He grabbed his saddle by the horn and slung it over his shoulder. "Grab Abby's saddle as well as yours."

Connor grinned. "You ain't gonna take Mr. Baker up on his offer to leave them here on the railing?"

"Not without knowing this place a little better." Hicks glanced at Abby. "Meet us at the hotel once you finish?"

She nodded.

"Can you find your way down there by yourself?" Connor asked.

"Of course." Her pretty face contorted into a quick frown. "I'm not helpless, you know."

"We didn't figure you was," Hicks said, his lips curling into a grin. "Especially with that Trantor pistol you got in your boot. You can handle the likes of that blacksmith and any others like him who look at you crossways."

Abby's frown flipped into a smile.

Connor was amazed at how obedient Abby was around River. She always accepted whatever he said, albeit with an occasional smart aleck remark, but that was the extent of it. Whenever Connor said something to her, it was certain to start her on one of her rants, arguing all the way. He guessed that was just the female in her coming out. Maybe one day she'd respect him as much as she did River.

As they came out of the stable area Connor heard loud voices arguing. He shot a glance toward Hicks, who had obviously heard them as well. They were emanating from the blacksmith's shop. Hicks increased his pace and Connor struggled to keep up. Not only was he a bit shorter than Hicks, but he was encumbered with the two saddles. He managed to round the corner of the building and saw John Henry Bardwell holding the bridle of one of his two horses, the wagon behind them.

"I told you to get outta here, nigger," Baker said in a loud voice.

"All I'm asking for is to get my wagon tongue fixed, Mister Baker," Bardwell said. "Ain't no call to talk to me like that."

The blacksmith was as tall as Bardwell and much heavier and Connor wondered which one would come out on top if they commenced to tangling. He'd been amazed out on the range at Bardwell's strength when he'd picked up the wagon, but Baker's arms were huge.

My money would be on John Henry, he thought. But that might be only because I like him.

"What you gonna pay for it with?" Baker said. "A promise?" He picked up his hammer and held it in front of him in a menacing gesture. "I don't run a business here on promises and credit."

"I'm good for it, Mister Baker. And I got to get this here hitch repaired."

"And I said *git.*" The thick muscles in Baker's forearm rippled as he rotated the hammer. The horse Bardwell had been holding tried to take a few backward steps, obviously a bit spooked by the argument.

Connor dropped both saddles and cleared his throat. The two men turned toward him.

"We got our horses situated," Connor said. "My sister's finishing up with the rub downs."

Baker's face was still set with an ugly expression.

"What's going on here, John Henry?" Hicks asked.

The black man reached up and patted his horse's snout, calming the animal.

"Mister Baker, here," Bardwell said. "Don't seem to want to have none of my business."

"Your business?" Baker made huffing sound.

"Offering to pay me off with some of your damn corn? That you ain't even harvested yet? Like I said, I don't run no charity outfit."

"You low on funds John Henry?" Connor asked.

Bardwell raised his eyebrows and took in a deep breath. "You might say that. What money I have got to be used for supplies right now. I'll be needing to sell some of my crop next month at the grain exchange 'fore I get some more."

"Ha!" Baker snorted and pointed with the hand not holding the hammer. "That's just what I mean. I do the work, and I'll never be seeing that money for doing it."

"Here," Connor said. "If that's all that's holding things up, I'll pay for it. How much?"

Baker seemed taken aback by the offer. His mustache wiggled as his mouth worked back and forth. After a few more seconds, he spat out a price.

"Fine," Connor said, reaching into his pocket. "Half now, and the rest when the job's done. Fair enough?"

Baker stared at him, then wiped at his mustache, smearing the gray hairs with black soot. "You gonna pay all of it yourself?"

"If I have to," Connor said.

Bardwell looked stunned. "Connor, you don't have to do—"

"It ain't a question of having," Connor said quickly. "It's a matter of helping out a friend."

Baker snorted in disgust. "It's your money, if'n' you want to throw it away. Put your damn wagon over there, Bardwell. I'll get to it when I can."

"It's a simple job," Bardwell said. "I could do my-self if—"

"When I can get to it," Baker said, his voice rising, his eyes fixed on the other man.

"And that means today," Connor said, handing the blacksmith some coins. "If you want to get paid the rest."

The burly blacksmith glared at him, inhaling so his huge chest expanded up over his sagging belly, and slipped the money into his pocket.

"I mean," Connor said with a grin. "We may not be staying around here too long."

Baker frowned. "All right. Soon as I finish this shoe."

Connor winked and nodded. Bardwell said nothing more and turned his horses toward the area that Baker had designated.

"That'll be extra if'n' you're leaving your horses," Baker said.

"No, sir," Bardwell said. "I'll be taking them with me." He nodded to Hicks. "And I'll be returning your lariat as soon as I untie that hitch."

"Fine," Hicks said. "We're staying at the hotel."

Bardwell looked at Hicks and then to Connor. A broad smile was on the black man's face. "If you give me an address where I can get a hold of you, I'll send you that money when I can."

"Not much chance of that," Hicks said. "We move around a lot." He started walking. Connor picked up both saddles again and ran to catch up to him.

"Are you mad at me?" he asked.

Hicks cast him a sideways look. "Just wondering why that money we worked so hard to earn is burning a hole in your pocket, is all."

Connor tried to shrug, but the burden of the saddles made this difficult.

"I don't know," he said. "It just seemed like the right thing to do, is all. Besides, we made all that money delivering that nitro—"

"And you can't wait to spend it?"

Hicks continued with his long strides toward the hotel.

Connor felt frustrated. Like he'd somehow let River down. "I don't know. I told you, it seemed like the right thing to do. A good deed, and all."

Hicks smirked. "You ever heard that old saying that the road to hell is macadamized with men's good deeds."

"Macadamized?" Connor said. "What's that mean?"

Hicks grinned. "It means crushed, and that's the way you can end up if you ain't being careful about getting in the middle of someone else's fight all the time."

******

Abby had come to the front of the stables and had seen the argument and the intervention by her brother. She saw them leave and then the black man, Bardwell, began untying the knots that had held his wagon hitch together. The blacksmith had gone back to his pounding and Abby wondered why he seemed to dislike Bardwell so much.

Growing up where they did, she and Connor hadn't been around many black folks, although her father, Jonas, had ranted and raved at how depraved they were. But she disregarded everything that evil man had ever said, him and his other two lecherous sons. Abby had never been so glad as to get out of there and leave all of them behind. And then they'd met Zubal Jefferson during their trip to Arizona with the nitroglycerin. He was such a nice man. It was hard to believe that he'd been a slave once. She remembered the awful stories he told her about it while they were riding together in the wagon. They hadn't been that dissimilar to the existence she and Connor had been subjected to before River came along and whisked them away.

River … her knight in shining armor.

Bardwell stood up and began walking his horses in a wide circle in front of the stables. The beasts were still in their harness. When he saw her he paused and tipped his hat.

"Miss Abby, what you still doing here?"

"River told me to rub down the horses," she said.

"You be needing some help?"

She shook her head. "No, I'm done. He said to meet him back at the hotel."

Bardwell's brow wrinkled slightly, like he was concerned about something.

"Well, I'm going back that way myself," he said. "I'll walk with you, if'n' you'd like."

That sounded fine to Abby. She was somewhat fascinated by this big, dark skinned man. In a way, he reminded her of River, although she knew he couldn't be as fast with a gun. He was powerful, though. And he was also kind of handsome, in his own way.

She stepped over and rubbed her hand over the snout of one of Bardwell's horses. The animal snorted in contentment.

"Like I said before, Miss, you got a way with horses."

Abby smiled. She gripped the bridle line and helped Bardwell steer the animals away from the stables and out into the street. The blacksmith glared at them as they passed his shop and brought his hammer down on the glowing red metal with a loud bang.

"I'll be back to give you a hand, Mister Baker," Bardwell called out. "Soon as I walk this young lady to the hotel."

Baker frowned and continued his pounding.

"Why is that man so disagreeable?" Abby asked as they walked.

Bardwell was silent for a bit, then said, "Some folks are just like that, all full of bitterness and hate. Best to avoid 'em if'n' you can. Anyways, you should never let them bring you down."

"You sound like River," Abby said. "He's always telling my brother and me about things like that."

"I'm beholding to him," Bardwell said. "To your brother, too. You all are good folks."

As they passed the mercantile shop Abby slowed down and studied the storefront.

"I'll bet they have licorice candy in there," she said.

"I believe they do."

She stopped. "I'm going to get me some."

Bardwell smiled and stopped as well. "I'll tell you what. I'll go in there with you, and if'n' Mister Wilson, he's the owner and a pretty fair man, will extend me a line of credit, I'll be able to pay your brother back that money he advanced me."

"Connor gave you money?"

"To get my wagon fixed. But I felt mighty bad letting him do it."

Abby shrugged. "He's got nothing else to spend it on. And he likes helping people."

"He's good folk, like I said. Reminds me of some of the good men I served with in the army."

There it was, the army reference again. Abby was burning with curiosity about why he'd left it.

They brought the horses to a nearby hitching rail and Bardwell secured the reins. As they stepped up onto the boardwalk they saw two riders rapidly approaching at the other end of town. As they drew closer Abby could see that they'd been part of the McManus group who'd menaced them before. She frowned, wishing they could leave this town and all its troubles behind them. But then what would become of John Henry? Still, it was like River was always telling her and Connor: *Don't go borrowing somebody else's troubles, because you'll always have plenty of your own.* But saying it was one thing, living it another. Just like when River had ridden onto the Mack farm that day and rescued them from that bleak existence. Hadn't he been borrowing their troubles back then?

The street was starting to fill up with people walking to and from. A man and woman on the boardwalk were passing by the store. The woman's eyebrows rose as Abby and Bardwell stepped to the mercantile shop and he opened the door for her. The woman's lips puckered into an O shape. Abby was secretly delighted that his chivalry had affected the old hag thusly.

Giggling with delight, Abby entered the store. It had rows of barrels filled with grains and beans. Bushel baskets of potatoes sat opposite them, and row after row of canned goods lined the wall to her right. On the left were stacks of burlap sacks labeled flour, sugar, and other things that Abby couldn't discern. Straight ahead she saw a man standing behind a counter where several big glass jars contained long, black sticks of licorice and other candies. Her mouth began to water at the thought of the sweetness to come as she moved to the counter.

The man behind it smiled and said, "There's a young lady that knows what she's looking for."

Abby didn't answer him. *A young lady* ... She didn't like it when people referred to her as that. It felt wrong somehow. Too prissy. But then again, she didn't want to be considered a young man, did she?

She saw some red and white peppermints alongside the licorice, and they looked delicious, too. Her fingers sought the coins in her pocket and she wondered what would be a prudent amount to spend.

"You let me know when you're ready, young

lady," the store clerk said. He turned and addressed Bardwell.

"I figured you'd be coming in today, John Henry. I got your usual supplies packaged up for you."

"Well, Mister Wilson," Bardwell said. "I run into a little trouble on the way into town. My wagon's down at the smith's being repaired."

"Trouble?"

"Yes, sir. Some men chased me. Fired some shots. I rolled my wagon. Broke the hitch."

"Riders?" Wilson's face showed alarm. "The Phantom Riders?"

"These were some of McManus's men," Bardwell said. "I think."

Wilson heaved a sigh and shook his head. "McManus. His crew is good at causing trouble. They just got that chandelier repaired in the saloon from the last time. How bad's the damage to your wagon?"

"Bad enough that it's gonna take most all of the money I brought with me." Bardwell paused and Abby glanced up at his face. She saw his lips compress, and then he spoke again. "I was hoping you'd extend me a line of credit until I can get some of them crops into you."

Wilson's mouth tightened into a thin line. "Well now, I do feel that you and the other homesteaders deserve some consideration, the way McManus has been blocking that river water. And until that's settled I know it's not going to be getting any better."

Bardwell closed his eyes, shook his head. "No, sir, it ain't. And to make it worse, the county commissioner was murdered today. We found him out on the prairie."

"That Layton fella?" Wilson's mouth was agape. "Lord. What happened?"

"Looked to be the work of the Phantom Riders," Bardwell said.

Wilson shook his head. "No way of knowing for sure now, but rumor had it that he was coming down on your side in that dispute."

Bardwell took in another deep breath. "Mister Wilson, sir, about that credit …"

Wilson held up his hand. "I'd like to help you out, John Henry. I really would. But with Layton being dead, there's no way of knowing how this thing will play out."

"I understand, sir. But if'n' there's any way you can reconsider, I give you my word I'll get that payment back to you as soon as I can."

Wilson held up his hand. "I don't doubt that. Perhaps you have something you could give me as collateral?"

Bardwell blew out a slow breath. "Well, I ain't got much. He reached into his pants pocket, withdrew a shiny gold colored medallion, and handed it to Wilson. "That there's a medal they give me from the army. Should be worth something."

Wilson accepted the medal and turned it over in his palm. "It'd be a damn shame to melt this down." He placed it in his pocket and pointed to the gun on Bardwell's side. "But how about that fancy pistol and holster?"

Bardwell said nothing for several seconds, then

nodded and stripped off his pistol belt.

Wilson pulled the weapon out of the holster. Its gold colored frame shone as brightly as the medal. "This an official U.S. Army gun?"

"Forty-five caliber U.S. Cavalry Model Eighteen Seventy-Three."

Wilson raised an eyebrow. "Why does that sound familiar to me?"

"It was standard issue for U.S. Cavalry. The same kind Custer and his men had at the Little Bighorn."

Wilson placed the gun and holster under the counter and said he would write up a receipt and agreement. He grabbed a small notebook and a pen and inkwell. The bell on the door jingled and a cowhand came in.

"I'll be with you in a minute," Wilson said.

"No hurry," the cowhand said, and began looking at the array of saddlebags and ropes on a table near the door.

Abby remembered seeing the damaged Henry rifle in the wagon and knew that giving up his sidearm would leave Bardwell defenseless.

"John Henry," she said. "You're giving up your gun?"

Bardwell didn't look happy, but he shrugged. "Got little choice right now."

"But we can loan you the money."

He shook his head. "You all have already done enough. I ain't expecting no more, and I don't want no charity."

This is one proud man, she thought.

She didn't like the idea of giving in, but, then

again, as River always said, *Don't get in the middle of things that aren't your concern.*

"When you're finished with that," she said to Wilson, "I've decided on which candies I want."

"And they'll be going on my line of credit," Bardwell said.

Abby turned toward him in surprise.

He smiled. "It's the least I can do."

She smiled back and figured she'd accept the offer. That was another thing River was always telling her and Connor: *Never look a gift horse in the mouth.*

As they left the store and stepped out onto the boardwalk Bardwell was carrying several wrapped bundles of supplies and Abby had her bag of candies. She saw three men standing by Bardwell's horses. One of them cast a lustful glance at Abby. He had a crazy look in his eyes. She immediately felt like reaching for the Trantor pistol in her boot.

"I'd appreciate it if'n' you'd not be bothering my horses," Bardwell said.

"*Your* horses?" the crazy looking one said. He had four round scars lining the left side of his face, from cheek to temple, and his eyes seemed to bounce around in his head as he looked from Bardwell to Abby. Then his mouth curled into a feral looking smile. "We was just checking them for the McManus brand. They look like some that was stole from us."

From us, Abby thought. He must be one of the McManus boys.

"Well, they ain't," Bardwell said, stepping down

to the street. He towered over the crazy looking man and the two others.

"My father says you're a thief, nigger," the crazy one said. "What you got to say to that?"

The two men with him laughed.

"Your father's wrong," Bardwell said. "Freddie."

At the mention of his name the crazy one's smile turned into a sneer.

"My name's Fredrick. I don't like anybody calling me Freddie."

Bardwell said nothing.

Freddie canted his head and focused on Abby. "So what's your name, sweet stuff?"

Abby didn't reply.

Freddie reached out and grabbed her bag of candy, ripping it from her hand.

"Hey," she said. "Give that back."

He held the bag just out of her reach as his other hand came up and fondled her breast.

"What you hiding inside that no-good shirt?"

Bardwell tossed down his packages and stepped forward. The crazy one danced back into the street, tearing open Abby's bag and plucking the licorice and peppermints into his mouth. His lips curled back over crooked, yellow teeth.

Bardwell reached out to grab the bag out of Freddie's hand. He spat the candies into Bardwell's face.

Abby was already bending down to retrieve her Trantor pistol from her boot when someone grabbed her from behind. She felt the bow of a rope slipping over her upper torso, pinning her arms to her sides. She tried to kick the shin of her attacker, but he shoved her and she went down hard onto the boardwalk, pain racing up her left side. The Trantor went fumbling from her grasp. One of the other men picked it up.

"Fredrick." He held the gun up. "Look at this."

Bardwell lashed out and punched the man in the stomach. He bent over and fell into the nearby horse trough, the water splashing up over the sides. The other man jumped at Bardwell, but he swiveled and caught his adversary with a powerful uppercut. The man's head jerked back and Bardwell grabbed him with both hands and thrust him away. The fourth man who'd roped Abby swung a roundhouse punch at the black man, but Bardwell ducked and then grabbed the man's arm, twisting to literally lift and throw him from the boardwalk. He smashed into Freddie, who was just drawing his gun. The collision knocked the weapon from Freddie's grasp. Stumbling backward, Freddie tossed the ripped bag of candy into the street and came up with a long-bladed knife. The sinister, feral smile returned.

"I'm gonna cut you up real good, nigger," he said. "And then I'm gonna do the same to your little white whore."

He rushed at Bardwell jabbing with the knife. The two men circled in the dusty street. A crowd was beginning to form and Abby heard a cacophony of yells, most of which were undecipherable. She screamed Connor's name, and then River's.

Bardwell and Freddie came together like two unlikely lovers, each struggling for dominance, grunting and breathing heavily. Their bodies moved into the center street as one, and then they twisted and fell. More sounds of exertion and hissing radiated from them, followed by a sudden shriek that transformed into a keening wail. The writhing motion ceased and both men were momentarily still, then Bardwell rose up, breathing hard. His dark face was covered with sweat and dirt as he stared down at his supine opponent.

Freddie's hands fluttered about over his stomach and Abby saw that the blade had been buried in his gut, almost to the hilt. The keening sound gradually changed to a series of softer audible gasps, the crazed expression now one of surprised wonderment. She managed to regain her footing and tossed off the encircling rope. Her left side burned with pain, but she managed to bend down and retrieve her pistol from the boardwalk.

Sheriff Thorpe and a young man wearing a deputy's star broke through the crowd and he stopped a few feet away from the jerking body in the dirt. Glancing at Bardwell, he said, "Oh, Lord."

Just as Bardwell started to speak River and Connor appeared. They joined the sheriff. Then several other men bustled forward, one of them Abby recognized as the patriarchal McManus. He shoved onlookers out of the way and knelt by his son's side, his face vivid with rage.

"Who did this?" he demanded.

"Mr. McManus, calm down," the sheriff said. "The best thing for you to do is get your son to the doc's."

McManus stood as more of his men joined him. One of them was the big fellow Abby had seen earlier. McManus had referred to him as Burl, and the picture of his face was on the election poster. He glared at Bardwell and reached for his gun.

Hicks was there with his Colt already out. He raised it and pointed the barrel at the big man.

"Don't even think about it," Hicks said.

The smaller, McManus boy jumped forward, starting to pull his gun as well. Before he could clear leather, however, Connor jumped forward and brought the barrel of his Colt Peacemaker down on the younger McManus's head. He crumpled.

The father stood, gesturing toward Freddie.

"Get him to the doctor," he yelled. "Now. Move."

Burl McManus stooped down and carefully picked up his brother. Tears streamed down his huge face. Big George McManus told more of his men to attend to his other son, then McManus turned to the sheriff and thrust his hand in Bardwell's direction.

"Are you going to arrest him?"

Thorpe shook his head. "I was on the way over here and saw the whole thing. Freddie was the attacker. John Henry was only defending himself."

McManus shook with rage. "What?"

"You heard the sheriff," Hicks said. "We saw it, too. So did all these here folks."

"Your son came after my sister," Connor said. "Pulled a knife. There was nothing else to do but stop him."

A murmur of ascent began to circulate from the

crowd, but McManus stopped it with a baleful look.

"You're all a bunch of nigger-loving cowards," he said. "And you'll all pay for your lies." His head surveyed the crowd, which had fallen silent. McManus once again pointed toward Bardwell. "I demand he be taken into custody."

"For what?" Connor yelled. "You heard what everybody said. Your boy was trying to knife him."

McManus stared down at him. "I don't know what kind of white trash pile you and that little bitch crawled out of, sonny, but this ain't over by a long shot."

"It's over, all right, McManus," Thorpe said. "And I'm taking those three in for disturbing the peace." He pointed at the three men who'd been with Freddie.

"We didn't do nothing," one of them said.

Hicks pointed his revolver at the man's head and said in a low, cold voice, "Best keep your mouth shut before I put another hole in that fat head of yours."

The man's lips clamped together and he said nothing.

McManus turned toward the sheriff. "A fine piece of pie this is. My boy gets stabbed and you're arresting his friends."

"They have it coming," Thorpe said. "I saw what happened, and as long as I'm sheriff, that kind of conduct won't be tolerated in Sweetwater."

An echo of supporting comments from the crowd, which had become substantial, began to permeate the air.

Good, Abby thought. The sheriff's standing up

to that evil bastard and the townsfolk are on our side.

McManus stared at the sheriff and a crafty looking smile crested his mouth. "Is that so? You interested in justice, and all that, eh?"

"Like I said, as long as I'm wearing this star …" Thorpe returned the other man's stare, then moved forward with his deputy to strip the three suspects of their weapons.

"Well, McManus said. I got some *justice* news for you. I just finished taking a statement from my ranch hand that was shot by this nigger."

Bardwell straightened up and glared at the other man. "Better be watching what you keep call me, Mister."

Big George McManus uttered a laugh. "You ain't nothing to me, boy, and you don't scare me, none. Even if you and the rest of your yellow bellied kind ride under a black flag."

Bardwell's face wrinkled in apparent confusion. "What the hell you talking about?"

McManus pointed at him. "You denying you're one of them?"

"One of who?" Bardwell said.

McManus flashed a sly smile and said. "The Phantom Riders."

A sudden hush fell over the crowd, and before Bardwell could answer, McManus turned back toward the sheriff. "My ranch hand, Pete Koors will swear to it, sheriff. So will the rest of my boys. Arrest him, dammit."

"That's a pretty wild charge, McManus," Thorpe

said. "What are you basing it on?"

"Pete told me that him and some of my other men were out on the range when they seen Bardwell here stringing up Howard Layton. Seen him using a branding iron, too. When they chased him, he shot one of my other hands, Lloyd Miller."

"That ain't the way it happened at all," Bardwell said.

"Says you," McManus shot back. He spat in the dirt next to the black man's foot.

"Just a minute," Thorpe said. "Even if they did say that, it's their word against his."

"And ours, too," Connor said, motioning toward Hicks and himself.

McManus glared at him for several seconds, then turned back to the sheriff. "It's as clear as the nose on your face. It's them damn nigger homesteaders. They wear masks to cover their black faces. And everybody knows this one's the leader of them."

Thorpe's hand reached up and adjusted his Stetson on his forehead. "I'm afraid I'm not following you, Mr. McManus, but like I said, all this sounds pretty flimsy. I ain't arresting nobody at the present except for these three troublemakers."

"So why don't you go see how your boy's doing?" Hicks said.

"I figured you'd say something of the sort," McManus said. "But we got more. We got evidence."

Someone in the crowd yelled out: "What kind of evidence, Big George."

Abby tried to see who'd said it, but there were too many people now. She knew McManus was

an evil man and figured he'd seeded the onlookers
with some of his own people.

"Evidence?" a loud, mellifluous voice said, from
behind the group. "I have that right here."

The crowd parted and a short, fat looking man in
a black suit standing to the rear of the crowd came
sauntering forward carrying a long, burlap sack.

Abby recalled that she'd seen the man ride in on
a gray mare along with McManus.

"Who're you?" Abby heard Connor ask.

"That's Maxwell Tiddy," Thorpe said. "He's Mc-
Manus's lawyer."

"Fancy name for a crook," Hicks said.

Tiddy shot him a malevolent look and continued
forward. "*This* was found concealed in Bardwell's
wagon." He held up the burlap sack. Abby saw that
it contained something cylindrical and about three
feet in length. Slowly Tiddy withdrew the material
from the hidden item like a circus magician reveal-
ing his surprise. It was a branding iron and he held
it up for all to see. On the end of the rod was a circle
containing the brand. It was the letter *P*.

The Phantom Rider's brand.

A collective gasp burst from the crowd that had
gathered and the buzz of conversation increased.

"I ain't never seen that before in my life," Bardwell said.

"I wouldn't expect you'd admit to it," Tiddy said,
turning to Thorpe. "But it's circumstantial proof
that he was involved in the branding and murder
of Howard Layton, just like the McManus men
said. They caught him in the act and were trying

to make a citizen's arrest when this gunslinger and his … catamite attacked them."

"That's crazy," Bardwell said. "What reason would I have to kill Mister Layton?"

"Because," Tiddy said, leaning forward and speaking in a loud voice. "Howard Layton had been out at the Dominion earlier today. He confided to my client and myself that he had made his decision about the water rights dispute, and was deciding in our favor."

A hush fell over the crowd.

"He also told us, Mr. Bardwell," Tiddy said. "That he felt it was his civic duty to ride out to your place to inform you of such."

"And that's when you killed him," McManus said.

"That's a lie," Bardwell said.

Thorpe hitched his hat up on his forehead, an expression of concern and bewilderment on his face. The deputy stood next to him, his mouth agape.

"Well, what are you waiting for, Sheriff?" Tiddy said. "Take him into custody. The charge is murder."

"He's the leader of the Phantom Riders," McManus said. "And justice, all nice and legal, shall be served."

CHAPTER 4

ARIZONA TERRITORY

O'Rourke found the smell of the saloon distasteful—a copious mixture of cigar smoke and alcohol, but felt he had little choice but to endure it. After receiving the confirming telegram from the home office to hire the barbarous Quint and proceed westward toward California, the only train O'Rourke could book passage on was one heading eastward toward Santa Fe, New Mexico. It irritated him that in order to proceed west, as directed, they had to first go in the opposite direction. But the only other avenue of travel would be to book passage on a northbound stagecoach to the Trans-Atlantic Railroad Line up in Colorado or the Utah Territory, and that would be even more time consuming, not to mention infinitely more uncomfortable. Additionally, he also had to worry about keeping his charge on a short leash. Quint seemed to attract trouble like a magnet attracted iron filings. O'Rourke watched as the lean bounty hunter stood nose-to-nose with a big brigand who was almost a head taller and most likely seventy pounds heavier. The sleeves of his red and black shirt were rolled up exposing forearms almost the size of horse hocks.

This could develop into a bit of a problem, he thought. If Quint ended up incapacitated, or quite possibly dead, how was he going to explain it to the head office?

O'Rourke felt under the lapel of his navy blue suit jacket for the 1878 nickel-plated Colt Frontier .44 caliber revolver he wore in a leather shoulder-holster. The weapon had a short barrel, but it was effective for short distances. Or so he'd been told. He found the prospect of drawing it a bit intimidating. They were in the midst of a sea of rowdy drunkards, many of whom no doubt knew the big, bearded man with whom Quint was now portentously engaged. And virtually all of them appeared to be armed as well. Drawing his own pistol and trying to back them off seemed to be an arduous task, not to mention that although he'd drawn his weapon upon two previous occasions, he'd never actually shot anyone.

Suddenly it was difficult to swallow. He felt a troublesome knot had formed in his throat and coughed to clear it.

Nobody took notice. Neither Quint nor the other man moved.

Finally, the big man said in growling tone, "I

don't cotton to nobody messing with my gal."

"That so?" Quint shot back. "Who sayin' she's *your* gal?"

O'Rourke assessed the creature the two men were squabbling over. Her lips peeled back exposing a mouth of horribly crooked dentition, and her ample bosoms threatened to spill over the tight black fabric of her low-cut dress.

"Whadda ya say, Honey Pot?" the big man said. His voice was low and very deep "Tell this greenhorn four-flusher who you belong to."

Honey Pot just emitted a cackling laugh. "Aw, Moose, sweetie, he didn't mean nothing. Just wanted to buy me a drink and pass a little time. I got plenty nuff for both of you."

The big man, Moose, seemed to take this as an admission of propriety.

"Hear that, four-flusher?" he said. "She's mine."

"You better clean the goose shit out of yer ears," Quint said. "She said nothing of the sort."

"Maybe then you and me best get to tanglin' then." Moose drew out a knife and slammed it point first into the top of the bar.

"Dammit, Moose," the bartender said. "That's the third time in two weeks you damaged my counter top."

"Shut yer mouth," Moose said. "Your call, four-flusher. Knife or gun?"

Quint eyed the big Bowie knife standing perpendicular to the bar and grinned. He removed the green suit jacket that O'Rourke had just purchased for him, popped the cufflinks from the fine, ruffled white shirt, and rolled the sleeves up to the elbow. His limbs were long and sinewy, but looked emaciated compared to the big man's.

"Been a long time since I was in a good knife fight," Quint said. "You gonna give me one, lard-belly?"

Moose's lips curled back into a sinister leer.

"I'm gonna cut yer belly open and feed you your guts," he said.

Quint winked at him and danced back a few steps, reaching into the long, leather rifle scabbard that was leaning against the bar next to his stool. His hand came up with the same long bladed knife that he'd used to cut the ropes securing the Indian boy.

O'Rourke closed his hand over the butt of his gun and stepped to the side.

"All right, that's enough," he said. "We have a job to do, and a train to catch in less than an hour."

"Stay outta this, dude," Moose said. "This is between me and him."

"Yeah, do that," Quint said. He licked his lips and waggled the knife in his hand, motioning the big man toward him. "You want to talk, or fight?"

Moose's face curled into an expression of pure rage and his big fist grabbed the Bowie knife from the top of the bar. He crouched down, the large bladed weapon in his right hand, his left palm open and extended in front of him.

O'Rourke thought about the chances of stopping the man mountain with one shot. It would be problematic if the round hit him in the barrel chest or one of his extremities. And O'Rourke always kept the hammer of his revolver over an empty cylinder chamber for safety purposes. The damn things were known to go off if dropped. He'd often fantasized about killing a man. He'd almost gotten a chance a while back with a drunken Indian. Now he wasn't sure whether he wanted to try it or not.

Where was the damn law and order in this one-horse town?

The question was answered for him when the bartender slammed a sawed-off double-barreled shotgun onto the bar and said, "All right, dammit, everybody back off and let them two fight. First one to draw blood wins."

"The hell with that," Moose said. "I'm doin' some cutting."

Quint's face twisted into a smile. "You all heard him."

The bar patrons seemed to move back in unison, providing the two combatants with a substantial area approximately fifteen feet square. The chants for Moose to "stick him" radiated from the pervasive dissonance.

The big man snarled and lurched forward, a grizzly closing in on a mountain lion. He thrust the Bowie knife forward toward Quint's chest, but the smaller man pirouetted out of the way with the grace of a ballet dancer. Moose twisted his massive arm into a backhanded slashing motion, but once again, Quint danced out of range. This seemed to enrage the bigger man and his grin transformed into a snarl. He lumbered forward now, arms extended, and this time Quint brought his own blade up and outward so quickly the movement could barely be seen.

Moose recoiled and glanced at his right arm. A crimson dribble sprang from the inner aspect of his forearm.

Quint raised his eyebrows, the smile still on his face.

"Quit now, big man," he said. "Before I get real serious."

The thick cords in Moose's neck rose like lines being pulled taut on a docking ship. He swung the Bowie knife in a wide, looping movement, but Quint stepped in and under the arc of the swing and brought his knife upward into the big man's expansive gut, once twice, three times before darting to the side.

Moose took three halting steps forward, the Bowie knife slipping from his fingers and crashing onto the wooden floor. His left hand curled around his stomach as he sunk to his knees.

A hush fell over the room. The chants stopped. People watched as the big man went down on one knee, reached his right hand over toward the edge of the bar for support, then emitted two long, wet sounding gasps before tumbling forward, his large, curly-haired head knocking over one of the brass spittoons. As his immense body rolled over onto its back, his breathing continued for a half dozen short gasps, the last of which ended abruptly causing a translucent red bubble to form over his gaping mouth.

Still no one talked in the bar.

"Moose's dead," someone muttered.

"Can't believe it," another said.

Quint stood off to the side, his eyes darting over the stunned faces, his lips drawn back in a cheerful simper. After a few more seconds of silence a wail commenced from Honey Pot and she threw herself on top of the mountainous carcass, crying inconsolably. This seemed to interest Quint a bit and then his lips closed over his teeth, but the smile remained. He bent down and grabbed the edge of Honey Pot's dress and used it to wipe off his blade. Then he stepped over to the bar, grabbed the leather scabbard, and motioned to O'Rourke to start heading toward the door. O'Rourke withdrew his Colt and held it by his hip, the barrel pointing outward.

"Clear the way," he said, using what hoped would sound like an authoritative tone. He pulled back the left side of his lapel to display the large silver shield of the Pinkerton National Detective Agency that was affixed to his belt. He hoped that no one would pay too much attention to the lettering and only react to the sight of a badge. A few people in the crowd stood fast, but Quint merely shoved them out of the way.

"Give 'em passage," the barkeep said. "It was a fair fight."

The few resistors in the crowd stepped back, and the barkeep's voice boomed again.

"But you owe me money for damages, mister."

Quint paused and squinted over his shoulder at the barkeep.

"How much?" he asked.

The barkeep's tongue traced over his lips. "Well, three dollars'll cover it."

Quint raised his eyebrows and tilted his head in what appeared to be mock concentration, and then he flashed the grin again.

"Check my big friend's pockets and if he ain't got enough to cover it, just call it even, considering I provided you with the entertainment. Come on, O'Rourke."

They made it to the door and pushed through the swinging doors and into the street.

O'Rourke kept glancing behind them as they walked toward the train depot. He could feel the sweat running down his face and neck.

No one appeared to by following them.

"You can put your gun back in its fancy holster," Quint said. "They ain't gonna be coming after us."

"How do you know?"

Quint shrugged. "I just do. You track people long enough, you learn how to read 'em."

O'Rourke slipped the Colt back into the shoulder holster. Another quick glance over his shoulder confirmed Quint's prognostication. No one was following them.

"You ever use that thing much?" Quint asked.

"Upon occasion."

Quint smirked, and O'Rourke got the impression the bounty hunter didn't believe him, but he wasn't about to share his life story with this reprobate. They were almost at the depot now. He silently recited the company tenants once more: *Maintain professionalism. Maintain objectivity. Maintain anonymity. Maintain loyalty to the client.* And last, but most important, *Maintain absolute loyalty to the Company.*

This was proving to be a most challenging assignment.

✵✵✵✵✵

SWEETWATER, CALIFORNIA

Connor, Hicks, and Abby sat across from Sheriff Thorpe in the small office area. The door leading to the cell area beyond them was closed, but the caterwauling of the three McManus men in custody for disturbing the peace could be heard. Outside the late afternoon was fading into early evening.

"They're gonna be yelling at John Henry all night," Connor said. "It ain't fair."

Thorpe turned to his deputy. "Lucas, go on in there and tell them ne'er-do-wells that they ain't gonna get any supper if they keep that up."

The deputy rose to his feet, his expression showing less than stern resolve.

"That the only help you got?" Hicks asked after Lucas had closed the door behind him.

Thorpe nodded. "He's young, unsure of himself. I been trying to work with him." He blew out a long breath. "But come next Tuesday, after the election, we'll probably both be out of a job."

"Tuesday?" Connor said. He counted the days on

his fingers. "That's only five days away."

"Four and a half," Abby said. "This one's almost done now."

"When's that circuit judge supposed to get here?" Hicks asked.

"Day after tomorrow, I expect," Thorpe said. "In the morning. The governor'll be here that afternoon."

"What's this judge like?" Hicks asked.

"Judge Robertson," Thorpe said. "He's a fair man."

The cell block area was silent now, but as Lucas came back through the door the yelling stated up again.

Thorpe shot him a baleful look. The deputy shrugged.

"I told 'em, sheriff."

"Want me to go back and give 'em a piece of what I got on my mind?" Connor asked.

"That wouldn't do no good, boy," Thorpe said. "Besides, I suspect that McManus will be sending someone down to pay their fines soon, and I'll have to release 'em."

"Boy?" Connor said. "I ain't no boy. I'm prit near a full grown man."

Hicks shook his head and Connor fell silent. The lawman's condescension was irritating, but it was clear that River wanted Connor to button it up.

Easier said than done, Connor thought. He pursed his lips.

"I don't know why you locked up John Henry in the first place," Abby said.

"Didn't have much choice, Miss," Thorpe said.

"You're not saying you believe that cock and bull story about finding that branding iron in Bardwell's wagon, are you?" Hicks asked.

Thorpe shrugged. "Again, what choice did I have? That was the Phantom Riders brand, all right. And with Tiddy making that claim in front of everyone … Well, you saw that crowd."

"Can't you at least let him out of jail?" Abby asked.

Thorpe shook his head. "That'd be the worst thing I could do. The Phantom Riders have been terrorizing a lot of folks around here. I let John Henry go before a trial, there'd be a lynching for sure."

"The sentiment turned against us pretty quick out there on the street," Hicks said.

"It doesn't seem fair," Abby said.

"Life seldom is," Hicks said.

"But John Henry didn't kill that Layton fella," Connor said. "He couldn't have. Those McManus boys are lying."

"That's very possible," Thorpe said. "But it's going to have to be proven in a court of law. And keeping him here, where I can keep an eye on him, is the only safe thing to do."

"Makes sense," Abby said. "He doesn't even have a gun."

"Tell me about these Phantom Riders," Hicks said. "Any idea who they are?"

Thorpe shook his head. "There are plenty of suspects. They've got to be locals, that's for sure, but they wear masks, and must have a special group of horses that they keep hidden away. I've tried to track them, look for their hideout, but nothing."

"How many of them are there?" Hicks asked.

Thorpe shrugged. "It varies. Sometimes four, sometimes six. Even as many as eight."

"Who they been hitting?" Hicks asked.

"Mostly of the local ranchers. They robbed the stage when it was coming in. Shot up the bank once. Killed two innocent women and an eight year old child that time."

"They ever hit the homesteaders?"

"A few times. Left burning crosses in front of their homes."

"They ever shoot any of them?"

Thorpe brought his hand up and stroked his mustache in contemplation. "Well now, a couple of them have disappeared, but there's no way of knowing if that was the Phantom Riders doing, or if they just up and left after going bust."

"Did McManus's place ever get hit?" Hicks asked.

Thorpe shrugged again. "So he says. Came in here a couple of times complaining about them rustling his cattle. But the Dominion, that's what he calls his ranch, is so damn big that it's impossible to tell what happened there."

"I wouldn't believe that evil man even if he was swearing on a stack of holy Bibles," Abby said.

"How are we gonna help John Henry?" Connor asked. He felt deflated.

Thorpe frowned. "The best thing you can do, if you want to help him, is to get him a lawyer."

"A lawyer?" Connor said. "Where we gonna find one in *this* town?"

Thorpe's face assumed the contemplative cast once more. "I been thinking that over myself. Tiddy's already said he'll be acting as the prosecutor. He may not look like much, but he's slicker than shit on a shovel in a courtroom."

Hicks was studying the sheriff. "You look like you've got an idea."

"I do," Thorpe said. "There's a man in town here who holds a law degree, although he's got no official practice. Maybe you could talk him into representing John Henry."

"Sounds like that's the best plan," Hicks said. "Where can we find him?"

Thorpe stood and picked up his hat.

"I'll show you." He turned to the deputy. "Lucas, bar this door after me, and don't let nobody in till I get back. Got it?"

The deputy rose to his feet and nodded.

"Come on," Thorpe said. "But I want to warn you, you might not like what you're gonna see too much."

Hicks and Connor exchanged looks.

"What's that mean?" Hicks asked.

The sheriff didn't answer. He motioned for them to follow them as he pulled open the door and went out.

I don't like the sound of that, Connor thought. But then again, how could things get much worse?

✳✳✳✳✳

THE DOMINION

Big George McManus sat in front of his massive stone fireplace and contemplated the way this hand had played itself out. Planting the branding iron had been a stroke of brilliance, like dealing himself an ace off the bottom of the deck, or getting a pawn crowned as queen in the penultimate moves of a chess match. Now the court would do what his men had failed to do—get rid of Bardwell, and what was even better was that it'd all be nice a legal. And it would correspond to Aaron's appointment, the governor's arrival, and Burl's election to sheriff. He was pleased with his perspicacity. He'd be putting the McManus brand on the entire territory.

But then there was the matter of Freddie. He'd had that grayish look of pending death when McManus had gotten down to the Doc Ingraham's office. The doctor's words still hung in McManus's memory:

I managed to stop the bleeding, stitch up the wound, all right, but the concern I had is with his bowels.

When McManus had asked him what the hell that meant, the doctor explained it to him.

"The knife went into his abdomen on a downward angle."

"So what's that mean?" McManus asked.

"It means that if it pierced his bowel, and there's no way of me knowing that unless I open him up more, that he could come down with peritonitis."

"What's that?"

"It's when the waste material from the intestines mixes with his bloodstream. Spreads infection throughout the body." The doctor's face was grim. "It's damn near always fatal."

"And there ain't nothing you can give him for that?"

Doc Ingraham shook his head. "I'm afraid it ain't a good way to go."

With that, McManus ordered his men to get a buckboard and transport Freddie back to the Dominion. Better that he die at home, in familiar surroundings, his father and brothers near. McManus felt bad about Freddie, but if it was one of his sons that had to precede him in death, he was glad it was this one.

In fact, he thought. This might even be a blessing.

Freddie had never been right in the head after that accident, and his conduct always bordered on the wild side of things. He was undependable as far as assigned chores, and even when he did do something, it was usually all messed up. Any way you looked at it, the boy was a pack of trouble.

Messing things up, hurting some girl, Big George thought, and me having to smooth things over and get him out of it.

The faces of Freddie's many transgressions with women flashed thought Big George's mind's eye, like a parade of jezebels. Some of them had been downright pretty, too, before he commenced to cutting on them.

Trying to find a permanent place for him down the road in the McManus Empire would have been problematic at best, and most likely damn near impossible.

So in a way, he thought, Bardwell's done me a favor.

The realization of the irony brought a smile to his face.

McManus had always had an affinity for the games of skill and patience, and his latest series of deft moves reminded him of a chess game using real live pieces.

The sound of a scream broke his reverie and Little George came running into the room.

His temple was starting to show a nasty bruise where that gunslinger's pup had cracked him. But that would heal all right, and it wouldn't spoil the lad's looks. After all was said and done, that's what his son would be most worried about.

"Pa, Freddie's getting bad. Like he's going out of his head."

He's always out of his head, McManus thought. But he said, "Go tell Juanita to fetch some towels and boil some water. Doc said we got to keep him comfortable while he fights off this fever."

Little George nodded and started out of the room.

Not that hot towels and bed-rest was gonna make that much difference ...

Big George McManus took in a deep breath, made peace with his son's pending death, and thought about how he could use the upcoming role as the grieving father to his best advantage. He needed to have somebody in town, somebody to monitor things and report back here to him. Somebody dependable …

"Hey," he called out after his son.

Little George stopped and turned.

"Yeah, Pa?"

"Go find Kandy and tell him I want to talk to him. Pronto."

✳✳✳✳✳✳

SWEETWATER

Connor followed close behind Hicks and the sheriff as they walked down the boardwalk. Abby was at his heels, talking up a storm. It was either feast of famine with her. She'd be babbling on and on, or not saying anything for hours on end. At this point all she could talk about was how evil this place was and how they needed to do something to help John Henry.

"I think that's what we're trying to do, sis," he said finally, hoping it would shut her mouth.

But it didn't. She resumed her incessant raving about how nice John Henry was and then abruptly ended with, "And he bought me licorice and peppermints."

"I wish you still had some to occupy your mouth for a while," Connor said.

Abby frowned and punched his shoulder.

He was secretly impressed that he'd barely felt

the blow. His upper body was developing every day he was feeling more and more powerful. At sixteen, he was almost a man, and couldn't wait to get all the way there.

Someday, he thought, I'll be as strong and as fast and as good with a gun as River.

Hicks and the sheriff stopped in front of a white, wood frame building situated on the corner of the main street and a lesser one that branched off toward a cluster of houses. The sign in front said *Demar's Restaurant.* Inside the place had a dining room area with eight tables, each adorned with red and white checkerboard table cloths. Most of the tables were occupied with men drinking coffee and smoking. A haze hung in the air and the room fell silent as the sheriff's presence was noticed. He waved to the group and the conversations gradually returned.

"That lawyer fella works in here?" Hick said.

Thorpe nodded.

"What is he?" Hicks asked. "The cook?"

"No. The dishwasher."

Connor was amazed when he heard this, and apparently Hicks was as well. The lean gunslinger turned his head toward Connor and they locked eyes. Reading the look on Hicks's face told Connor that this was probably not going to be a good experience.

They followed Thorpe through the door.

A pretty, dark haired woman welcomed them as they entered and asked if they all wanted to be seated together.

"Actually, Rose, we're here to see Rance."

The woman's brow furrowed and her eyes darted from Thorpe to Hicks and then back to Thorpe again.

"Is he in trouble?" Her voice was hardly above a whisper.

"No, nothing of the sort," Thorpe said.

The woman led them through a door that opened up to the kitchen. A man stood over a big metal stove stoking a fire with one hand and holding the handle of a big iron skillet with the other. He was short and round bellied.

Must be enjoying too much of his own cooking, Connor thought as they continued past the man and into a second room that was situated at the back of the building. A tall, thin man with an unkempt crop of blond hair stood hunched over a large metal tub that was filled with stacks of plates, cups, and pots. His hands were immersed in the murky water.

"Rance," the woman said. "Sheriff wants to see you."

The man's head jerked around and his eyes widened as he saw the sheriff. He straightened up and grabbed a dingy looking towel to dry off his hands. Connor saw the skin on the man's fingers was all puckered from being in the water. The woman studied each of them briefly before stepping back through the door and disappearing into the kitchen area. Despite the myriad of odors in the place, and the pungent fragrance of the strong soap, Connor could smell liquor on the man. Then he recognized him. It was the drunk who'd been kicked out of the saloon as they'd all ridden into town earlier. The guy who'd urinated on the boardwalk.

Connor noticed that Hicks seemed to recognize the man as well. They exchanged dubious looks.

"Sheriff," the man, Rance, said. "I'm real sorry about that incident earlier. I didn't mean any harm."

"Incident?" Thorpe said.

Rance shot a quick glance at Abby and then back to Thorpe. "Ah, in front of the saloon. I assure you it won't happen again. Especially if there's a young lady present."

Thorpe's brow furrowed and he shook his head. "Whatever it is you're referring to, it ain't what we're here to talk to you about." He half-turned toward Hicks and said, "This is James Rance," Thorpe said. "Came here from back East."

Connor studied him. The tall, rangy man did have something of an intelligent look to him, but, Lord, he reeked. The residual alcohol on the man's breath mixed with a powerful body odor. He was a drinker, this one, and hadn't had a bath in who knew how long. Connor had seen this type before in many of the town's they'd passed through. The kind that would need a shot in the morning just to get moving and then wipe his finger around the inside of the glass for a parting lick before shuffling over to tackle all the dirty dishes from the night before.

"You know something about the law, I take it?" Hicks asked.

Rance's jaw twitched. "Well, I have my law

degree." He paused and the corners of his mouth curled into a smile. "Just not so many clients at the moment."

Thorpe cleared his throat. "I don't know if you heard or not, but Howard Layton was murdered."

"Layton?" Rance appeared quizzical. "I know that name sounds familiar, but I can't quite place him."

Thorpe's frown deepened. "The county commissioner that was here to mediate the water rights dispute between McManus and the homesteaders."

Rance nodded in recognition. "Now I remember. You say he was murdered?"

"That's right. He was hung. Branded, too. Looks to be the work of the Phantom Riders."

"Tragic. I heard tell he was a good man."

Thorpe waited for several seconds, then said, "John Henry Bardwell's been arrested and charged with the crime."

"John Henry?" Rance's face took on a look of disbelief. "That is shocking."

"Shocking?" Connor said. "It's a downright lie."

Hicks held up a hand to shush him.

"What's this got to do with me?" Rance asked.

"Like I said, Bardwell's been charged with the murder," Thorpe said. "We got that circuit court judge due in the day after tomorrow, and Maxwell Tiddy's appointed himself prosecutor."

"Tiddy." Rance's face tightened.

"So," Thorpe continued, "Bardwell needs somebody to defend him in court. Somebody who knows his way around a courtroom. Besides Tiddy, you're the only one qualified to do that around here."

"Me?" Rance's eyes widened. "I … I'm hardly …" He let his words trail off.

"I'd say that appears to be about right" Connor said. "This fella don't look like he knows one end of a law book from the other."

Rance recoiled like the words had physically slapped him. He glared at Connor but said nothing.

"Mister," Hicks said, "I don't reckon our paths have ever crossed, but the sheriff here says you got some legal schooling, and that's a hell of a lot more than any of the rest of us have. And John Henry Bardwell seems like a good man. He's between the rock and the hard place on this, and needs some-body to try and give him a hand up."

The dishwasher's head lowered, his eyes staring at the floor.

"I'm not sure I can."

Connor snorted in disgust. "John Henry's gonna be on trial for his life, and this fella's the only one you say can help him?"

Hicks held up his hand again. He was staring intently at the dishwasher's eyes.

Rance remained bent over for several beats, then seemed to straighten up. Reaching for the string that secured his apron, he pulled the knot loose, slipped the apron over his head, and tossed it aside.

"Rose," he called out in a loud voice. "I'll be back to finish these later." With that he dipped his hand into the tub of dishwater and then ran his fingers through his hair. It did little to organize the disar-ray.

"All right, sheriff," he said. "If it's convenient with you, I'd like to confer with my client."

Hicks and Connor exchanged another pair of dubious looks.

Looks like things can and did get worse, Connor thought. I should've known.

✷✷✷✷✷✷

SOMEWHERE IN THE ARIZONA TERRITORY

The jostle of the departing train did a lot to settle O'Rourke's nerves. He'd spent the better part of an hour sweating nervously back at the depot, worried that some of the dead man's friends from the bar would muster enough courage to come after them with shooting on their minds. They hadn't, but the anxiety still remained. His mouth dry, his palms wet, his stomach roiling, he hated the feeling. He also hated knowing that deep down he was envious at the precision and skill that Quint had shown in the knife fight. This hooligan in buckskin, now clad in a civilized suit of clothes, was a ruthless killer, but one of consummate skill. First he'd made that unbelievable shot killing the fleeing Indian—a moving target at an incredible distance, and then bested a man who was almost twice his size in physical combat.

Well, O'Rourke thought, perhaps he wasn't quite that big.

But Moose, or whatever his name was, did have a considerable advantage in both size and strength.

Quint, on the other hand, had a whole lot of quickness. And skill.

A train conductor moved through the car lighting a series of oil lamps which gave off a combined, but flickering, brightness. O'Rourke turned toward the window but saw only his own reflection due to the ubiquitous darkness outside. Night had descended, and with it the recollection of the second death he'd witnessed that day. He looked at Quint, who was sharpening the blade of his knife on a leather strop. The fine white shirt that O'Rourke had purchased for him at the mercantile shop back there was now already dappled with splotches of crimson. Moose's blood, no doubt. Knives were messy things. And it didn't seem to bother Quint at all.

"Where did you learn to use a knife like that?" O'Rourke asked.

The other man continued to slap the blade against the thick strand of leather.

O'Rourke cleared his throat and was set to speak again when Quint replied.

"Used to hunt buffalo," he said. "We'd shoot a bunch of 'em, then skin 'em. Used my knife more than I did my gun."

"I've heard there were quite a few of them back in the day."

Quint shrugged. "Not no more. They're just about all gone now. Injun's too. They used to depend on the herds for food, clothing. The railroad had one of them photographers take a picture of me and another fella standing next to a pile of buffalo skulls that was prit near as big as a small hill."

O'Rourke recalled having seen such a picture in a book.

"So when the buffalo were gone, that's when you became a bounty hunter?"

Quint stopped with the strop and ran his thumb horizontally over the edge of the blade, testing its sharpness. Seemingly satisfied, he sheathed the knife and jammed it into the pocket of the leather rifle scabbard. O'Rourke could see the butt of a pistol in there as well as the shoulder stock of the huge Sharps.

"Thereabouts," Quint said. "Trackin' and killing's about the only two things I'm good at doing."

O'Rourke silently affirmed that statement and felt the pang of jealousy rise again.

"I take it you've killed your fair share of men as well as buffalo," he said.

Quint placed his rifle scabbard down on top of O'Rourke's carpetbag, leaned back into the seat, and lowered the fancy hat O'Rourke had purchased for him.

"Wake me when we get there," Quint said.

"How many men have you killed?" O'Rourke asked.

Quint's extended his index finger and poked the brim of the hat, lifting it slightly to uncover his eyes.

"You talkin' white men?"

The question took O'Rourke slightly by surprise. The thought such a distinction hadn't occurred to him. He nodded.

"Oh, twenty-five, or so," Quint said, lowering the hat once more. "Well, twenty-six counting that man-mountain back there. The lower portion of his face curled into a smile. "But if'n' you throw in Indians, Mexicans, and niggers, I done lost count."

Indians, Mexicans, and nig—. He let the distasteful word drop, but his curiosity gnawed at him. He wanted to know more.

"Is there a difference?" he asked. "In the way you do it?"

Quint's lips twitched slightly, like he was shooing away a pesky fly.

"Well, that downright depends," he said.

"Depends? On what?"

"On what the killing's for. If'n' it's man with a price on his head, you want to make it a nice, clean shot through the chest or gut. With the gut it takes 'em longer to die, so the chest is best to keep the face so's the law can recognize 'em. That's got a lot easier since so many of them wanted posters nowadays have them pictures on 'em."

The invention of photography has been a boon to the Company as well, O'Rourke thought.

But he couldn't help but be impressed. This backwoods assassin had a thimble full of sophistication to him. And he had obviously warmed up to a subject with which he had extensive knowledge.

"Killing up close or at a distance" Quint said. "Don't rightly know which one I like best." His face took on a look of perverse ecstasy. "Makin' that long shot always has some challenge to it, but when you're up close, you can look 'em right in the eye."

He turned, his face resembling a sinister jack-o-lantern. "Just like that big fella back there."

"What about that pistol?" O'Rourke asked. "You ever use that?"

"When I have to."

O'Rourke decided to try a bit of humor.

"Are you as good with the pistol as you are with the rifle?"

"As good as I need to be." Quint squinted at him. "I'm sittin' here, ain't I?"

"Yes, you most certainly are."

O'Rourke recalled the gunslinger, Hicks, and his prowess with a gun. Whichever way this one played out, long shot or up close and personal, it was indeed going to be a spectacle to watch.

CHAPTER 5

THE DOMINION

Big George McManus watched through the main window on the front of his house as some of his men lit the torches he'd order strategically placed around the corral. Earlier in the day Burl had wrestled the bull in that same space, and things were seemingly all falling into place. Now, his master plan was askew, requiring some quick finagling, and his third born son lay dying in the room down the hall.

Not just dying, McManus thought. Screaming all the damn way.

The fever the doctor had warned them about had begun to arrive. Ingraham had given Big George some laudanum to ease Freddie's pain, but had cautioned him: "It's known to be habit-forming."

Habit-forming! As if his son had that much time left. Regardless, Big George had already decided not to give Freddie any of it. Any McManus would go out like a man, not in some drug induced haze.

But those damn screams … They were enough to drive a man crazy.

McManus slammed the meaty portion of his fist against the window frame.

"That damn moaning going to go on all night?" he muttered.

Aaron McManus, his first born, sat in a chair a few feet away. They were alone in the room.

"He's in a bad way, Pa," he said.

"Bad way? Hell, he's dying."

Aaron rose and walked over, placing his hand on his father's shoulder.

"Best we can do is make him as comfortable as we can," Aaron said. "Maybe there's a chance—"

"A chance?" Big George noticed it was Aaron's deformed hand that he'd place on his shoulder and shrugged it off. He was the smartest of his boys, but also the weakest. Even Freddie had more grit.

"What about that laudanum the doc gave you?" Aaron asked.

Big George shook his head. "Forget about that."

Aaron stared at him, looking almost like he was about to say something, but remained silent.

The sound of horses' hooves signaled the approach of riders.

That would be Kandy, McManus thought.

He strode toward the door and pulled it open with a violent jerk, saying over his shoulder, "Go find Burl and Little George. We got some reckoning to do.

"Pa, ain't there been enough violence?"

McManus stopped and stepped back to his eldest son, standing almost chest to chest with him. He was bigger than Aaron, and more physically powerful as well. It was apparent that this one took after his mother a little too much. He'd gotten more than his share of the brains, but none of the gumption. And that damn hand …

Their eyes met and Big George brought his open palm upward and slapped Aaron's face. The blow wasn't meant to be that hard, but McManus had inadvertently put more force behind it that he intended. Aaron reeled to the side, but kept his footing.

Good, McManus thought. At least he didn't fold up like some sissy.

Aaron's dark eyes were piercing, as a blush of red formed on his right cheek.

"Don't ever question me again," Big George said. "Now go find 'em."

He turned and stormed through the still open door arriving in the expansive courtyard that was now partially illuminated by the glow of the torches several yards away. Kandy rode up followed by the three ranch hands that he'd gotten out of jail. The horses snorted as they were reined to a stop.

Kandy dismounted, secured his horse to the hitching rail, and pulled three gun-belts off of his saddle. He slung the belts with guns over his shoulder and approached McManus. About ten other ranch hands had gathered around, three of them holding burning torches. McManus acknowledged

Kandy with a quick nod and turned his gaze on the three other riders. They sat on their still horses, heads bowed.

"Fines all paid in full, boss," Kandy said, patting the assortment of gun-belts. "And I've got some other news you ain't gonna believe."

"Later," McManus glared at the three ranch hands. "Get your asses over here. Now."

The three hurriedly dismounted and the other ranch hands took charge of their mounts. They shuffled toward Big George, who continued to watch their every step with a glower of utter contempt. When the three men stood in a line in front of him, he placed his hands on his hips and spat in the dirt.

Behind him Burl, Little George, and Aaron clamored through the door of the main house and joined their father.

He continued to glare at the three men. The silence was predominant, save for an occasional snort from one of the horses.

Suddenly a loud wail drifted from the direction of the house.

It was Freddie.

One of the three men recoiled slightly.

McManus reached out and seized the front of his shirt.

"You hear that?" he asked, his voice low and guttural.

The ranch hand's head bobbled up and down.

McManus pulled the man closer. "Now, you tell me what the hell happened there today."

The man tried to speak, but all that came out was croaking sound.

McManus pulled him closer, so that they were almost nose-to-nose.

"Tell me how my boy ended up laying in there with a hole cut his gut."

"It wasn't our fault, Mr. McManus," one of the ranch hands said. "We was waiting outside the store, just like you told us to, and then Freddie, well, you know how he is with pretty girls ... He went over to her and—"

"Shut your damn mouth." McManus said.

He thrust the man he'd been holding away and the man stumbled backwards. By this time the line of other ranch hands had surrounded the trio.

McManus glanced toward the corral. The torches had been affixed to each of the four corners, casting a flickering luminance over the square enclosure.

"Put 'em in there," McManus said. He turned to his three sons. "Burl, you want 'em one at a time?"

Burl unbuckled his gun-belt and handed it to Little George. He grinned as he rolled up the sleeves of his shirt. The flickering light from the burning torches skipped over his nearly bald head.

"I'll take all three of 'em at once," he said as he strode forward.

A discord of grunts and anticipatory murmurs circulated through the ranch hands as they pushed and shoved the three hapless men toward the rails of the corral and then surrounded the three railed sides that were adjacent and facing the barn.

"Get in there and act like men," McManus said. "Show me how you should've protected my son."

The three men were roughly shoved through the fencing and they staggered to regain their balance. Burl McManus wedged his oversized bulk between two of the horizontal rails and entered the corral, a wide grin on his huge face. He clapped his big hands together and then balled them into fists the size of grapefruits.

"Let's see what you got," he said.

"Go get 'em, Bull," one of the perimeter ranch hands yelled.

Another seconded the suggestion with, "Whip 'em good."

The three ranch hands exchanged furtive glances, and one broke away from the other two in a full-out run across the corral. Burl sidestepped to his right to cut the fleeing man off and grabbed his right arm. He then shifted his weight and wrenched the arm downward. The ranch hand flopped down, his face a mask of agony. He lay squirming in the dirt holding his appendage.

Burl turned to the other two with a grin.

"Looks like that coward's gonna be tied up for a bit. How about you two? Want to make a sport of it."

The huge man held up his hands and waggled his fingers in a come-hither gesture.

The two men rushed him, their arms flailing.

Burl planted his feet solidly in the dirt and held his bent arms out in front of him, accepting the blows on his shoulders and forearms. They seemed to have little effect, like they were punching a tree trunk.

Big George McManus watched as the large hands of his second born shot out and seized the two ne'er-do-wells. He slammed the two men together with such force that it caused them to squeal in pain. One seemed more affected than the other, and Burl let that one slump to the ground. Drawing back his immense right fist, he punched the man he was holding. The man's nose made a crunching sound and a torrent of blood spouted from it like a pierced water bag. Burl drew his fist back again and struck, this time with an uppercut motion into the ranch hand's abdomen. He repeated this blow several times, each one sounding more sodden than the last as it landed. Finally, he let the hapless ranch hand drop just as the other one was getting to his knees.

Several feet away the first man had managed to struggle to his feet, holding a limp right arm to his side and walking with a distinct limp. He turned and tried to head for the barn, but Burl was upon him after three loping strides and snared his neck. He whirled in a circle bringing the man's head in contact with the closest rail post. It made the sound of a melon being smacked against a rock. The man dropped like severed clothesline.

Burl turned and strode over to the third man, who was just regaining his shaky footing. Burl shoved him down and the man rolled over on his back. The beaten man by the barn was struggling to stand now, and Burl ran over to him, grabbing the man and pulled him close. His large arms encircled the man's chest in a bear hug and the expulsion of the air from his lungs made a hissing sound. He howled pitifully until the noise ceased.

Burl repositioned his grip around the man's neck and said, "Watch this, Pa."

He made a sudden jerking motion and a sudden cracking sound cut the air. The man's body went limp.

McManus watched as Burl, his shirt now clinging to his body with sweat, let the lifeless body fall to the dirt. He started for the other two when Little George yelled to him.

"Let me do one of 'em."

Burl's sweaty face turned toward them and split into a grin.

"Well, come on, little brother."

Little George ducked through the rails and entered the corral. He walked to the supine man, who was now beginning to stir, and kicked him in the side.

"Hey," Little George said. "Get your ass up. I'm giving you a chance."

The ranch hand slowly rolled to his knees and peered up at the younger McManus.

The light from the torches flickered on Little George's features. He wore a fancy gun-belt trimmed with silver, and carried a second gun in his left hand, holding it at chest level.

"I'm giving you a chance to do what you should've done when it came to saving my brother."

Little George tossed the gun in front of the man

and stepped back a few feet. The revolver lay in the dirt in front of the kneeling man.

"Please," the man said. "I ain't done nothing to deserve this. None of us have."

"Pick it up," Little George said. "You yellow belly."

The man wiped the dribbling blood from the corner of his mouth and shook his head.

Little George's features twisted into a snarl.

"I said pick it up!"

The kneeling man took in a deep breath, glanced around, and then reached for the gun.

Little George's right hand flashed down to his holster and came up with his Colt Peacemaker. Cocking back the hammer in one smooth motion as he extended his arm, he fired one shot, which struck the kneeling man in the chest. He recoiled, then tried to bring his own gun upward.

Little George fired again, this bullet seeming to strike the man in the shoulder.

He once again recoiled, but his pistol continued to rise.

"Kandy," Big George McManus shouted.

Kandy drew his pistol and shot the kneeling man in the forehead. He flopped down in a heap.

Little George whirled, his face now twisted in anger.

"What'd you do that for?" he yelled. "I coulda handled him."

Kandy just shrugged, and re-holstered his weapon.

"Pa," Little George said. "Why'd you have him do that?"

Big George gazed at his youngest son and snorted.

"You never, ever give a man a loaded gun and invite him to take a shot at you," Big George said. "You think I want to lose another of my boys?"

Little George's snarl turned into a frowning pout.

"Shucks, Pa," Burl said, stepping over and plucking the gun from the fallen man's fingers. "What makes you think it was loaded in the first place?"

Little George whirled back to glare at his older brother.

"Gimme that." He snatched for the gun, shoved it into its holster, and climbed through the rails to head back to the main house.

"They all dead?" Big George asked.

Burl snorted. "If'n' they ain't, they oughta be."

McManus grunted an approval.

The surrounding crowd of his ranch hands stood in utter silence now, the hoots and catcalls for Burl to "whip 'em" had long since faded away as the brutality escalated.

Every mother's son of 'em knows that it coulda been them in there getting beat down if they crossed me, Big George thought.

"Take them out and burn their bodies," he said to Burl. "And do it far enough away from the house so that I don't have to smell them any."

Burl's face twitched into a smile and he motioned for some of the onlookers to get the bodies. He grabbed one of the torches and walked to the gate of the corral.

Ashes to ashes, Big George thought, remembering another part of a Biblical line. He filled the rest of it in himself: And so goes anyone who crossed paths with me.

His eyes searched for Aaron, but he was nowhere to be seen.

Weak son of a bitch, Big George thought. Where the hell's he at?

Then, from inside the house, he heard the sound of Freddie's screams once again.

******

SWEETWATER

Connor woke early and peeked out the window of the hotel room. The sun hadn't come up yet, but the sky was that mixture of pink and gray, so he knew it wouldn't be long. The hotel room Hicks had procured was large and spacious, with two beds. Connor had elected to give one to Hicks and the other to Abby. Hicks had made such a conniption about finally getting a chance to sleep on a feather bed that Connor didn't want to spoil his fancy. So he'd spread his bedroll on the floor and used one of the saddles for a pillow. The floor was hard and flat and less comfortable than sleeping on the ground, but it had felt good to be able to take off his boots and not have to worry about some critter crawling inside one of them. But he still didn't feel rested. The old ghosts, the faces of the men he'd killed, had come back for one of their periodic visits. The deeds had been done, and Connor knew in each case he'd been left with little or no choice, but the ghosts persisted.

Would he ever be free of them?

He listened to the sonorous breathing of both Abby and Hicks.

They were sound asleep.

He wondered how they'd slipped into slumber so easily and so quickly. He'd lain awake for a long time thinking about poor John Henry and that liquor-laced excuse for a lawyer they'd managed to hire to represent him. Hicks had seemed to have the same reservations as he about this James Rance's competence. He may have studied law at some artsy-fartsy school somewhere back East, but this was the West, and Connor had a feeling this one was gonna be decided with a gun or a noose with thirteen loops. And Connor wasn't about to let that happen.

Still, River had told him that this wasn't their fight. Hicks had agreed to help John Henry by hiring the lawyer, but it was clear that was to be the extent of it. They were just staying in town here until Hicks deemed it safe for them to travel again.

As he would no doubt say, *Don't go borrowing another man's troubles when you got your own breathing down your neck.*

Good words to live by, Connor thought. But sometimes easier said than done.

He liked and respected this man, John Henry Bardwell, and the thought of abandoning him to the likes of McManus weighed heavily on Connor.

Their brief meeting last night when they'd introduced Rance as his attorney had proved less than reassuring. Bardwell thanked Rance for his help, but didn't seem impressed by the man's qualifications. Connor left after Barwell had requested that his horses be housed at the livery overnight. When Connor returned to the jail the would-be lawyer had gone back to his dishwashing job and Abby had left for the hotel. Hicks was in conversation with the sheriff, and didn't say anything about the situation as he and Connor headed for their room.

It had the makings of a real bad situation, like a sore that was bound to fester.

He threw off his blanket and sat up.

The slow, sonorous breathing by Abby and Hicks continued.

Connor fastened his pants and belt and then grabbed his boots, slipping them on as quietly as he could, making sure he'd gotten each foot into its proper setting. He needed to urinate badly and didn't want to use the chamber pot with Abby in the room. Standing with his back to her out on the range was one thing, but in the same room where she might wake up at any moment, held too much potential for embarrassment.

Looks like I'm heading for the outhouse, he thought, and figured to grab the pitcher on the bureau and fill it with water when he went downstairs so they could all wash up. There was a rain barrel and a pump in the rear yard. He rose to his feet as quietly as he could, his knees cracking as he did so, and stepped gingerly to the dresser. The pitcher still had some water in it from last night, and it made a sloshing sound as he hefted it.

He was almost to the door when Hicks said, "Don't forget to take your gun."

Connor turned and smirked. River's voice was as clear as a bell. He hadn't been asleep after all.

"Yes, sir," Connor said, going back and reaching for his gun-belt.

After removing his Colt Peacemaker from its holster and jamming it into his belt line, he adjusted the barrel so that it didn't point down at his privates. Even though he normally kept the hammer over an empty chamber for safety reasons, Hicks had always stressed that you treated every gun like it was loaded and dangerous.

"Respect your gun," he often said, "and it'll respect you."

Connor always took everything River said to heart. After all, if it weren't for him, he and Abby would still be suffering at the hands of their father, Jonas Mack and his two evil sons. That day that River Hicks had ridden onto the Mack farm burned in his memory as vividly as if it had been yesterday. The constant beatings Jonas and his two favorite sons had administered to Connor, their lustful glances at Abby ... Both he and his sister knew in their hearts that Jonas wasn't their real father. He was just an evil surrogate, and they'd shed him like a snake's skin. As Connor made his way down the hallway toward the staircase, he continued to remember that fateful day. He'd given a beating to both his "brothers" before he and Abby had accepted River's invitation to ride off with him. It had been the beginning of their real lives—A new beginning, at any rate.

And what adventures had awaited them. It was like a real-life version of the old dime novel he'd found and kept: Dangerous Dan, the consummate gunfighter. Little had Connor known when he'd found the scared and dirty copy wedged between a barrel and a wall in the general store back when he was a pup, that one day a real, live Dangerous Dan would arrive and whisk him and Abby away.

And now he was on the cusp of becoming a man, and not just any man. He'd taken pains to model himself after River, who was always teaching him about things—guns, shooting, and being a real, live Dangerous Dan. And he was always listening.

Listening, and learning.

He heard someone stirring at the base of the staircase and he shifted the pitcher to his right hand and pulled the gun out of his beltline with his left. It was mostly dark below on the first floor. There was no one behind the long counter where the clerk had signed them in.

He heard another creaking sound.

Should he cock back the hammer?

He decided not to. That was another thing River had stressed.

"Once you pull that hammer back, that trigger becomes real sensitive. Just touching it can make it go off, and you never want to waste one of your shots with a careless miss."

Connor flattened against the wall and moved

downward as quietly as he could. The stairs creaked and moaned with every step. His eyes were becoming accustomed to the darkness a bit more, and he saw a flicker of something down below.

Was it the last vestiges of the moonlight glinting off the barrel of a gun?

Connor made the split second decision to descend more rapidly. If there was somebody lying in wait in the shadows of the lobby, in all probability they were well aware of his descent on the stairway. Creeping down would only give them more time to aim.

He jumped the rest of the way down the staircase, landing with a pounding thud on the first floor landing. His eyes swept back and forth.

Someone moved off to his left.

Connor raised his gun and now cocked his revolver. The distinctive four clicks of the hammer being pulled back echoed ominously.

"Step outta them shadows," he said. "Or die."

"Don't shoot," came the reply. "I'm not armed."

The voice sounded familiar, but also somewhat slurred. Second later he knew why on both counts as James Rance inched forward in a halting stagger. His foot bumped against something and an empty glass bottle rolled toward Connor.

"After I finished up my duties last night," he said. "I came by here to see if you all were still up."

Connor uncocked the hammer and lowered it to the half-cock position. He'd need to realign the empty chamber of the cylinder again, but this was hardly the time or place. Another of the lessons

River had stressed was to use prudence and caution while you were still in what might be considered hostile circumstances.

"What for?" Connor asked. He kept the gun by his leg rather than placing it back into his beltline.

"I wanted to discuss the case."

"Huh?"

"The prospect of going to trial," Rance said. "I didn't want to say too much last night in front of those McManus men."

Connor remembered the ill-conceived meeting with Bardwell last night at the jail. That formidable cowboy from the McManus ranch had come to pay the fines of the three ne'er-do-wells who'd been arrested. Connor was angered that the trio was getting off so easy, with twenty-five dollar fines for disturbing the peace when they'd punched Bardwell and menaced Abby. They'd also made some threatening comments to Bardwell about seeing him hang and him not having a place to go back to even if he wasn't. Connor wanted to tell them to shut their mouths, but Hicks held up his hand and dismissed all further conversation with a fractional shake of his head. He later explained that having the three men in close proximity to Bardwell's cell held more dangers than if they were released.

"Besides," Hicks had said with a smile. "It pretty much looked like John Henry got the better of all three of them. And that Big George McManus fella don't appear to be the forgiving sort."

Connor instantly knew River was right, as usual.

I still got a lot to learn, he thought. But I'm betting I still know more than this sorry excuse for an attorney standing in front of me.

He nudged the empty bottle on the floor with the toe of his boot.

"Yeah, it looks like you come here to talk about the case, all right."

The sun was starting to filter in through the windows now, adding some illumination to the hotel lobby. Connor saw that Rance's face was flushed.

"Well, I sat down in the corner over there and must have dozed off."

The man's excuses, his sloppy demeanor, even his boozy smell reminded Connor of Jonas Mack and his partiality for the corn liquor. Although Connor had seen River partake in a drink or two from time to time, he'd never appeared inebriated, and Connor had vowed to emulate that behavior. He stepped over the bottle on the floor and headed for the rear door of the hotel.

"Go back and crawl inside your bottle, mister," he said. "I got to go to the outhouse."

"That's hardly a hospitable greeting for a man who came to you in good faith," a voice said from above.

Connor looked upward and saw Hicks leaning against the banister on the second floor landing, his forearms resting on the arch of wood, his big Colt Peacemaker in his right hand.

"Mister Rance," Hicks said, straightening up. "Why don't you plan on joining us for breakfast in an hour or so down at that fine establishment where you work? What's the name of it again?"

"Demar's," Rance said. He stooped and recovered the bottle from the floor. "I'll be there."

He turned to go and Hicks called out to him.

"Make sure that empty's the only bottle you bring."

Rance stopped, glanced back up over his shoulder, and nodded.

CHAPTER 6

SWEETWATER

An hour and a half later Hicks, Connor, and Abby sat at a table in Demar's across from James Rance, who still smelled like a brewery and appeared to be in dire need of his morning medicament from a liquor bottle. He toyed with his plate of eggs, bacon and biscuits, while Connor, Abby, and Hicks were almost finished with theirs. There were a few other patrons in the place and two of them, a rotund man with a gray beard, and another equally beefy, but younger fellow yelled over to their table.

"Hey, Rance, ain't it a little too early for you to be thinking about solid food?" the gray bearded one said.

"Maybe he wants to dirty up them dishes some so he has something to wash," the other added. He punctuated his sentence with a cackle.

Hicks silenced both of them with a single glance

and they went back to sopping up their egg yolks with the remnants of their biscuits.

The effect on the lawyer was obvious.

"Mr. Hicks," he said. "Perhaps we were a bit premature in our decision for me to represent Mr. Bardwell." He swallowed and Connor noticed the man needed a shave.

A bath, too, he thought, as Rance's pungent body odor wafted over the table.

"I thought we already discussed that last night," Hicks said. "Bardwell needs someone to defend him. Somebody that knows the law."

He picked up his coffee cup and drained it, then held it up for Rose, the proprietor and waitress to give him a refill. She disappeared into the back room which Connor knew from their visit here last night, contained a big stove. Rose came through the door with a coffee pot and refilled Hicks's cup. She raised her eyebrows at Connor, who held his cup up toward the pot. After refilling his, Rose glanced toward Abby, who shook her head. The woman then glared at Rance and said, "Come see me in back before you leave out of here."

She disappeared through the swinging door.

Rance was visibly shaking. His tongue flicked out over dry lips and he started to get up.

"If you'll excuse me, I've got to check on something."

Hicks's hand shot out and grabbed the other man's right wrist. Rance winced in pain as Hicks exerted pressure.

"Sit down," Hicks said in a low voice.

"But she wanted to see me," Rance said.

"That can wait." Hicks exerted more pressure and the lawyer emitted a groan.

After Rance had dropped back into his chair, Hicks leaned closer and spoke in a low voice.

"Is there a barber shop in this town?"

Rance nodded.

"And a bath house?" Hicks asked.

Again, Rance nodded again, then said, "My arm. Please. You're hurting me."

Hicks's dark eyes scanned the lawyer then he released his grip. "How about you? You got a clean, Sunday-go-to-meeting suit of clothes?"

Rance rubbed his right wrist and shook his head.

"I used to," he said. "I ... I sold them."

"Sold 'em?"

"To the undertaker. It was a fine suit. And shirt, too. He uses them to dress up those who are laid out for their wakes."

"For their wakes?"

"Yes," Rance said. "Once the service is over with, he removes it before the casket's buried. That way he can use it over and over again."

"Well, you're gonna go down there and tell him you need it back," Hicks said.

"I can't do that."

"Yes, you can. Tell him you're going to use it this one time, just like for one of his wakes, and then you can bring it back to him."

"I'm not sure he'll be agreeable to that."

"I don't care if he's agreeable, or not," Hicks said. "Tell him he can either give it back to you, or get ready to wear it himself in a casket, if I have to come down there to talk to him."

Rance appeared nervous, but gave quick grunt of agreement.

Hicks reached into his pocket and removed some coins. "But first, you go to the barber shop and get a shave and haircut. Then go down to the bathhouse."

Rance stiffened and looked across the table at Abby, his face reddening. He compressed his lips and gave another curt nod.

"And lay off the booze until after the trial's over," Hicks said.

Rance shook his head slightly. "I can't do that entirely. I'll get the shakes."

"You already got 'em, from the looks of things," Hicks said. "Let's make sure they don't get any worse."

"But that's why I need a drink," Rance said. "To steady my nerves. You know how it is."

"Yeah, I know how it is." Hicks leaned closer to him. "Mister, I'm telling you right now, I got a low tolerance for a drinking man that can't handle his liquor."

The gray bearded patron who'd spoken before had apparently been listening and he chuckled. Hicks transferred his gaze to him.

"I got a low tolerance for your kind, too."

The smirk vanished from the man's face and he immediately went back to finishing his breakfast.

Hicks turned back to Rance. "You're his lawyer, dammit."

Rance's eyes drifted downward toward the floor and he shook his head. "And he deserves better."

"He does at that," Hicks said. "But you're all he's got."

Rance picked up the coins and started to place them in his pocket.

Connor reached over and grabbed his arm.

"Want me to stay with him, River?" Connor asked. He was thinking he'd like nothing better that to ride ram-rod over this tenderfoot with a penchant for whiskey.

"Maybe that's a good idea," Hicks said. "Take him outta here now and get him cleaned up. Then the two of you meet me down at the jail in about an hour. Me and Abby will go down and tend to our horses at the livery stable."

Connor held out his open palm and Rance dropped the coins into it.

One of the two obese patrons emitted a gravely laugh.

Once again, Hicks glared at the man, raising one eyebrow as if in warning.

The laugh abruptly stopped.

Hicks shook his head. "Remember that we promised Bardwell we'd see that his horses got fed and that we'd go check on his place."

"I can do that," Abby said. She'd been sitting there in silence for virtually all of the conversation.

Hicks again shook his head.

"I don't want you riding out there alone."

"Why? Because I'm a girl?"

"Because I don't want any of us riding the range

alone. Not with them Phantom Riders everybody's always talking about circulating."

With the mention of the Phantom Riders conversation stopped in the restaurant and the eyes of all the other patrons settled on them.

Hicks made a show of looking around, returning their stares and when things returned to normal, he called out to the lady proprietor.

She came sauntering over.

"You want something else, Mister?"

Hicks smiled at her. It reminded Connor of a cat eyeing a canary in a cage.

"Fix me up two plates of eggs, bacon, and biscuits," Hicks said. "And put 'em in a basket."

She pulled out the small tablet in her apron and began writing with a pencil.

"We'll take our check now," Hicks said. "Leave the basket order off it."

She stared down at him for several seconds. "You ain't paying for it?"

"Just bill it to the sheriff," Hicks said. "It's for him and the prisoner."

A frown creased her pretty face.

After leaving the restaurant Connor watched Abby and Hicks walk down toward the jail with the basket. As he and Rance went down the street toward the barber shop, Connor thought about the possibility of getting his own hair clipped a bit. It had grown outt some since the last cutting, and he'd always preferred to keep it on the short side, even though River wore his hair long and tied in a ponytail. But his primary task was to watch Rance and make sure he got spruced up a bit. Still, that task was starting to seem more and more problematic as Connor considered all that it entailed. Even after the cutting and scrubbing was done, he could hardly afford to sit on the man until it was time for the trial to begin.

We'll just have to do the best we can, he thought.

When they stepped inside he saw there was one other patron inside getting his hair cut. Connor studied the reflection of the man in the mirror and recognized him as one of McManus's henchmen. It was the handsome, square-jawed cowpoke with the ornate spurs on his fancy boots. Connor recalled someone calling the man by the name Kandy. The McManus cowpoke stared back and his hands shifted under the white and black striped drop-cloth that was covering his body. The handsome face smirked, and all thoughts that Connor had of getting his own hair trimmed vanished from his mind. He immediately wondered if Kandy had unholstered his gun under the drop-cloth.

He smiled back, doing his level best not to show concern, and undid the leather thong from the hammer of his Colt. He removed the weapon, set the hammer at half-cock, and opened the side gate.

The barber, a rotund fellow with a mostly bald head and heavy mustache and sideburns jerked slightly.

"Hey, sonny," he said. "I don't want no trouble in here."

"Me neither, *sonny*," Connor said as he rotated the cylinder to the empty chamber, removed a cartridge from one of the holders on his gun-belt, and slid the bullet into the open chamber. He then closed the gate and carefully lowered the hammer back into place before re-holstering the Colt.

Kandy's grin widened.

"That looks like a mighty big gun for a boy who's still wet behind the ears," he said.

Connor wished he could think of a felicitous reply. He tried to imagine how River would handle a challenging insult like that, but could think of nothing appropriate. But then again, Hicks could stop a man cold with just a glance, like he'd done earlier in the restaurant. When somebody looked at him, they saw trouble walking.

With me, he thought, they see a kid still wet behind the ears.

But he knew the space behind his ears was dry.

Still, Hicks's other oral lessons about life and survival rang in his ears: *Don't go looking for trouble, or it'll find you. But don't go running from it, neither.*

"Mister," Connor said. "If you ever get the gumption to feel behind my ears to check 'em, just let me know."

He returned Kandy's simper with one of his own and ostentatiously left his gun unsecured by the leather thong.

The handsome cowpoke winked at him and leaned back, closing his eyes. The barber began slopping some lather onto the man's jaw.

Connor saw no further movement under the drop-cloth so he allowed himself to relax, but only slightly.

Someday, he thought, me and this fella Kandy are going to tangle.

✳✳✳✳✳✳

Abby and Hicks went inside the jail and saw Thorpe bending over a basin on the stove. He was shirtless, but had his gun-belt buckled around his waist. He regarded them quickly as they entered, and then nodded and splashed some water on his face. Abby took notice of the sheriff's semi-naked body. He looked to be in pretty fair shape, with lots of hair on his chest and just a small roll of fat around his waist. She'd seen both River and her brother in various states of undress, but the sight of this stranger stirred some new interest within her. He wasn't a bad looking man.

Hicks held up the basket. "We brought you some breakfast. Some for John Henry, too."

Thorpe shot them a grin and picked up a straight razor.

"Appreciate that," he said. "Just let me get presentable." He cocked his head toward the cell block area. "Lucas is escorting him to the outhouse. Should be back shortly."

Hicks set the basket on the sheriff's big desk and walked over to the wall where a plethora of wanted posters were affixed. He began studying them. Abby wondered if his picture was up there.

"We're getting that Rance fella cleaned up some," Hicks said.

Thorpe snorted a laugh as he leaned toward a

small mirror that was hung on the juncture of the stove pipe. He brought the edge of the straight razor to his cheek and scrapped off some beard growth.

"That might be an all-day job," he said, between strokes.

"Sure enough," Hicks said. "What's his story, anyway? He sounds like he's got some schooling, but ..."

He let the rest of his sentence hanging.

Thorpe scrapped under his chin with careful precision.

"Came out here from back East," he said. "On the way in the Phantom Riders held the stage up. They got Rance and the other passengers out and stripped and robbed them. Shamed him real bad. Rode him into the middle of town on a rail in his long johns and dropped him in a pile of horse manure before riding off." He paused to do a couple more swipes with the razor before swishing it in the basin water. "Poor fella never really got over the embarrassment of it. Hung out his shingle to practice law, but nobody came by to even give him the time of day. Then the Riders came back and burned down saloon next to his office, and that caught on fire, too. He ended up selling off whatever else he had and after that money run out, Rose at the restaurant felt sorry for him and gave him a job washing dishes."

"And he crawled inside a bottle and wouldn't come out?" Hicks said.

The sheriff squared off his sideburns and rinsed his face with the water from the basin. "That's about the size of it." He folded the straight razor closed and removed the mirror. After placing both items in a desk drawer, his retrieved his shirt which had been hung on the back of his chair and slipped it on.

Just then the sound of a door slamming in the cell block area became audible.

"Appears they're back," Thorpe said, tucking his shirttails in his pants and then opening the lid of the basket. "This smells good. Thanks."

"You're welcome," Hicks said. "Rose has got the bill waiting for you down there."

Thorpe grunted a laugh and the door separating the office area from the cells opened. Lucas, the deputy, stepped through. "All set, sheriff."

Thorpe removed one of the plates from the basket and told Lucas to give the other one to Bardwell. "And make sure you get that plate and spoon back."

Lucas frowned.

Abby moved over to the basket. "I can go give it to him.

Thorpe lifted an eyebrow as he looked at Hicks.

"We'll both do that," Hicks said. "I want to talk to him. You mind, sheriff?"

Thorpe, whose mouth was already full of biscuit and egg, shook his head and waved them on.

They went through the door and Abby saw Bardwell sitting on the bunk, his head in his hands.

"Morning, John Henry," Hicks said.

The black man looked up and then smiled, but it was the smile of the forlorn. He stood.

"Mister Hicks. Miss Abigail. I appreciate you coming by."

"We brought you some breakfast." Abby pointed to the basket.

"Just make sure you give us back the spoon," Hicks said with a grin.

Bardwell's smile lightened a bit and stooped down as Hicks slid the plate through the slot in the bars.

"Connor'll be by in about an hour or so with your lawyer," he said.

Bardwell was already busy scooping the eggs into his mouth. He bit into a biscuit and then ate two of the strands of bacon. "Mister Rance?" His body jerked in faux mirth.

After chewing furiously, he started using the biscuit to sop up some more of the ruptured yolk, then paused and peered at Hicks and Abby through the bars.

"Mighty sorry for my manners," he said. "I ain't ate nothing since yesterday morning."

"They didn't feed you last night?" Abby said.

"Didn't bother me none. I didn't feel much like eating, no way."

Bardwell shoved the rest of the biscuit into his mouth.

"We housed your horses in the stable last night," Hicks said. "Want us to leave them there for now? Until this is settled."

Bardwell's head jerked at the words, then he went on with his eating. After several seconds he paused again and shot a glance up at Hicks.

"You mean until they hang me?"

Abby felt like someone had slapped her. She

glanced at Hicks, who was staring down at the floor.

"I know things ain't looking so good right about now," he said. "But don't go counting yourself out before the battle starts. They got a circuit judge coming in and the sheriff says he'll do his best to get you a fair trial."

"A fair trial." Bardwell's words sounded flat.

"That's what he told us."

Bardwell shoved the last bit of the food into his mouth and chewed thoroughly. After he swallowed, he pointed to a bucket off to the side of the door with a ladle hooked onto the side.

"Mind getting me some water, Miss Abigail?"

Abby turned and picked up the bucket, hoisting it up to the bars where Bardwell could reach through.

After quenching his thirst, he nodded a "thanks" to her and handed the plate and spoon back to Hicks.

"I ain't no fool, Mister Hicks. I know how things work."

Hicks said nothing.

Bardwell continued. "I told you before, I was a buffalo soldier. Connor asked me why I left the army."

Hicks stared at him, still not saying anything.

"Well, sir," Bardwell continued. "I was with the Fifth Cavalry. We'd been tracking some Comanche braves that jumped off the reservation, killed some cattle belonging to one of the ranchers. Orders came down that we was to track 'em down, bring 'em back to Fort Ellis for trial." He stopped, took in a deep breath. "By whatever means necessary." He paused again. "Well, we tracked 'em back through the hills, found their new camp. The lieutenant in charge split us up. Had my squad circle around in back of them. That was a common tactic we used. If we rode straight in, most of them bucks would skedaddle out the back way."

"So I've heard," Hicks said.

The smile appeared on Bardwell's face again. "Them Indians was something. Always crafty, never weak. Never had much, but they was something."

"Heard that, too" Hicks said.

The smile vanished from Bardwell's face as he spoke again.

"It was early in the morning, around first light and after the lieutenant sent us around the back of the camp, the rest of the company rode straight in. Somebody fired a shot, don't know if it was them or us. The Indians started running. The next thing we knew, the lieutenant had his saber out and commenced to cutting. Other soldiers were shooting … Nobody came up on our position, so we rode on in." He stopped again, his eyes holding a sadness, his face a picture of world weariness. "That's when we saw what was happening. No braves in sight. Only old men, squaws, and children. They was being cut down like cattle, some of them still alive, a whole passel of them dying. I rode in, yelling for them to stop, but they wasn't listening. I got up next to the lieutenant and grabbed his arm, then I knocked him off his horse."

Bardwell's head drooped.

Abby saw a tear splash onto the wooden floorboards.

"At least it stopped the killing. Turns out the braves wasn't even there," he said. "And the only reason they'd killed them cattle is that the crooked Indian agent that was supposed to deliver them a herd of cattle on account of there not being no more buffalo, had sold the cattle to a bunch of Mexicanos down by the border, leaving them Indians to starve."

"That's awful," Abby said.

Bardwell wiped at his eyes. "Well, when we got back to the fort and reported, it turned out that B Company had already rounded up the braves that had been rustling. They'd already brung 'em back and the trial was over with." He took in another deep breath. "There was five of 'em. The major ordered them left on the gallows, all of them were just hanging there. They court martialed me the next day. Striking a superior officer. Booted me out of the army. After fifteen years."

Nobody spoke for the better part of a minute.

"I'll never forget how them Indians' faces was, all swelled up and bloated in the hot sun," Bardwell said. "Just like Mister Layton's face yesterday." He blew out a long breath. "And that's how mine's is gonna look 'fore too much longer, I reckon."

After assuring Bardwell that they'd be back with his lawyer, Hicks and Abby stepped into the sheriff's office. Two men in blue suits and derby hats were standing in front of Thorpe's desk. One of them had on small, gold, wire rimmed spectacles and was clean shaven. The other was older, harder, and had a bushy mustache. They both turned and regarded Hicks and Abby as they entered.

Thorpe was talking fast to the two of them. Abby listened, trying to pick up the gist of the conversation. There was something about the two of them that set Abby on edge, almost as if she'd seen them before, even though she was certain she hadn't.

What does that mean? she wondered.

"… and I certainly do appreciate the agency's help," Thorpe was saying. "I've heard of the fine things you've done working with the railroad. When I was a boy back East, I remember the Pinkerton's foiling an assassination plot against President Lincoln."

"Yeah, if old honest Abe would've stuck with the company," the mustachioed man said, he probably would've lived to serve out his term. We'd a stopped that two-bit actor, Boothe, that's for damn sure."

Hicks set the plate and the spoon down on the chair next to the basket and tipped his hat to the sheriff.

"We'll be back in a spell," he said.

Thorpe acknowledged him with a quick jerk of his head and continued his conversation with the two men. When they'd gotten out on the street, Abby turned to Hicks.

"Who were those two fellows?"

"Pinkerton detectives." He continued his long strides down the boardwalk.

"Pinkertons?" Abby suddenly understood the

familiarity she'd felt about the two men. "Like that one we dealt with back in Woodman?"

A trace of a smile graced Hicks's lips. "It's called Hope Springs now. Remember?"

Abby laughed, but then turned serious.

"You think they're connected somehow with him? He hired those gunfighters to kill us."

"That Pinkerton was just a middle man. Somebody else hired him. Somebody with money. Lots of money."

"Who?" she asked. "And why?"

Hicks didn't reply, and Abby somehow got the impression that he knew the answers to her questions, but didn't want to tell her.

"Guess I shoulda killed that Pinkerton when I had the chance," Hicks said finally.

"Well, you did give him one hell of a beating."

"Girl, don't you go using curse words at your tender age."

"At *my* tender age?" Abby laughed. "Are you forgetting what I've got stuck in my boot, and that I've had occasion to use it?"

"No," Hicks said. "I ain't forgettin' that."

She looked up at him and could see he was deep in thought.

CHAPTER 7

THE DOMINION

Freddie's cries and moans had shrunken to whimpers, and Big George McManus knew that the end was near for his third born.

The inevitability of death, he thought. Nobody cheats the grim reaper.

Yet although he made no outward show of grief, which he assumed would be seen as a sign of weakness, he secretly admitted to himself that he actually felt little in the way of sorrow. Not for Freddie, nor for any of his four sons. They were his blood, that was for certain, but none was, to his satisfaction, a full measurement of the McManus manhood. Each, in a way, was lacking. Aaron was smart, but physically deformed. Burl was powerful, but essentially a big dullard. Freddie was a categorical failure devoid of any and all virtue. And Little George had his father's strong features, but was mean-spirited, bullying, and worst of all, short in stature as well as judgment. Big George had sired them all, but the weaknesses inherent in their mother had tainted his seed.

He took in a deep breath and walked to the table where the decanter of whiskey resided. As he poured himself a fresh glass, his first of the morning, he contemplated starting a new family, one with a woman of both beauty and breeding, who could give him a new heir worthy inheriting the McManus Empire.

Aaron walked into the room. His face was ashen as he approached his father with tentativeness.

"He's looking real bad, Pa. Eyes rolled up into his head, burning up with fever. The sheets are soaking wet."

Big George was rolling the fine liquor around in his mouth. He said nothing.

"We need to send somebody to fetch the doc," Aaron said.

Big George swallowed. "Wouldn't do no good."

"You don't know that. We gotta do something."

Big George took another sip of the whiskey.

His son looked up at him, eyes blazing.

"Dammit. Pa. Did you hear me?"

Big George gazed down at him. None of his boys, except for Burl, was as tall as he was. He swallowed the remainder of the liquor, feeling its burning progression down his esophagus as it settled into his gullet.

"Have Juanita change the sheets," Big George said. "Keep him dry. And give him some of that laudanum that the doc gave us."

Aaron stared at him.

"Don't you want to go in and take a look at him?" he asked.

Big George was contemplating whether he should pour himself another drink, or wait till later.

"Pa?"

"What?"

"You going to take a look?"

Big George let his irritation creep upward and curl his mouth into a sneer. Maybe this crippled pup needed another slap, not that it would do much good. He was weak to the bone. Crippled and weak.

"Now why in the hell would I want to do that?" Big George said.

Aaron's gaze critical gaze lingered until Big George felt a rising surge of anger about to over-take him.

How dare he be disrespectful? To his own father?

Containing his anger, he said, "You'd best go find Juanita. And find that laudanum."

Aaron muttered something under his breath and left the room.

Big George watched him go and shook his head. He recapped the decanter and set the glass down on the tray. It was definitely time to look into find-ing a woman of good family lines and designed for more favorable breeding. Freddie's demise would provide the perfect impetus. The comparison of the current situation to that of a chess match returned to him. The thought of the satisfaction when one of your pawns reaches the opponent's final row and get then transformed into another, more powerful piece. It was like turning Freddie, a pawn, into something more, although the image of one of his male progeny being designated as a "queen" repulsed him. That was an obvious mistake on the part of the game's inventor. The king should have been the most powerful piece on the board—A warrior king who fought his own battles, did his own killing instead of fleeing in constant avoidance to a checkmate while the more powerful queen whipped about the board slaying enemies.

That was the McManus way.

But sometimes it was better to have one's lessers doing the dirty work, setting up the inevitable triumph.

The moaning sound became audible once more from down the hall.

Where the hell was Aaron with that laudanum?

Another chess comparison flashed in his mind: the ploy of a sacrifice-piece.

His son's inevitable death would provide an edge, a shroud of sympathy that he could slip on to place him in better standing with the community, the judge, and the governor, once he got here.

It was my son Frederick's dream to see the railroad complete its loop through the land south of here, he pictured himself saying. *A railroad south of the Dominion.*

In reality, Freddie had no more regard for the railroad development than he did for a bale of hay. But the idea of promulgating this ruse would give his passing a bit of usefulness.

But first, Big George thought, I've got some more business to attend to.

It was time to realign the pieces on the board.

✳✳✳✳✳✳

OPEN RANGE JUST SOUTH OF SWEETWATER

Connor remembered the additional cartridge he'd loaded into his Colt at the barbershop as he, Hicks, and Abby rode toward Bardwell's place with his two horses in tow. He told Hicks about the sixth round.

"Better take care not to drop it then." Hicks said.

"You think I should unload it?"

Hicks shook his head. "Leave it in. You might need it if we come upon some of those Phantom Riders."

Connor checked the leather thong securing his Peacemaker and found it in place, as he knew it would be. He caught a glimpse of Hicks regarding him. Connor blushed. Rechecking his gun made him feel like a novice.

"Leastwise John Henry seemed to be a little bit more at ease after seeing that Rance fella kinda cleaned up," Connor said.

He canted his head toward his mentor for approval, but Hicks didn't reply.

Connor had brought Rance to the jail once the barbering and bathing had been completed. The lawyer's hair didn't look so much like a blown over haystack anymore. And he'd talked and listened with interest to John Henry's account of what happened.

"If he stays that way," Abby said. "But at least his hair looked better and he didn't smell quite so bad. His clothes could use a good washing, though."

"He'll look better once he gets his suit back from the undertaker," Connor said. "Don't you think so, River?"

Hicks smirked slightly. "I suppose. If he stays sober."

"I think he will," Connor said. "What do you think?'

Again, Hicks was silent.

They were traveling southeast from the town, pursuant to the directions Bardwell had given them to locate his spread. The country looked dry and hard and Connor wondered what John Henry's chances of success were in this bleak terrain even if he was able to clear himself in court. As the rounded a slightly elevated plateau the remnants of a dried up river bed wound through the yellow grass.

"That must be the river that he told us about," Connor said. "The one that McManus fella's got all damned up."

Hicks surveyed the area and motioned for them to follow the bed, as Bardwell had directed.

Much of the grass had yellowed and died, and many of the trees showed scant leaves.

"Looks like this place was real good before the water dried up," Connor said. "Still ain't too bad here and there."

"Could be an underground stream or tributaries," Hicks said. "Sometimes those can feed the surface ground."

The terrain dipped into a gradually extending declivity, and several houses and barns, set a few hundred yards apart, became visible down in the valley. Rows for cultivation had been plowed into the soil, and some sparse plants had pushed through the earth. As they drew closer Connor assessed the nearest buildings. Portions of the two closest ones appeared to be haphazardly constructed from logs and piecemeal lumber. But the frames were solidly fixed in place on both the house and the barn. A fence spanned the front portion of the property and a corral and some pens were adjacent to the barn.

As the three of them drew closer to the house an old man stepped out onto the porch holding a double-barreled shotgun. The weapon appeared old and had a patina of rust cresting one of the barrels. The man wore no hat and his curly hair formed a white, cottony nap on top of the dark skin of his face. His eyes were defiant.

"That'll be far enough," he said. "Who are ya and what y'all want?"

Connor looked to Hicks, who answered the man in a slow, assured tone, holding his hands high and not near the twin guns that were on his waist.

"We mean you no harm," he said. "We're friends of John Henry Bardwell."

The old man squinted and his grip on the shotgun tightened.

"He ain't here."

"We know that," Hicks said. "We brought his horses back."

"His horses? John Henry's horses?"

"That's right." Hicks said. "Your name Ben Green by any chance?"

The old man appeared surprised.

"How you know that?"

"John Henry said you'd probably be looking after his place. My name's River Hicks."

Ben Green's head jerked with a quick nod.

"Where's John Henry at?"

Connor could see Hicks take a deep breath before he answered.

"He's in Sweetwater. In jail."

"Jail?" Ben Green's face hardened and he rotated the shotgun toward Hicks. "What for?"

"He's accused of killing a man."

"Killin'? What's this about, mister?"

"We'll be glad to explain it to you," Hicks said. "And we've got a message for you and the other homesteaders from John Henry. But first, how about you ease that scattergun down a might?" His smile widened. "I don't like looking into them two barrels."

Ben Green hesitated for several seconds before lowering the shotgun.

"Is John Henry all right?"

"So far he is." Hicks gave him a quick rundown of what had happened. At the mention of Layton's murder and the accusation of Bardwell being part of the Phantom Riders, the old man's face twitched into a grimace.

"I met that Mister Layton." Ben Green shook his head slowly. "He come out here a few times in the past week looking around and talking to people. John Henry said he was a trying to help us. That damn McManus done got the whole valley here parched drier than a smoked beef jerky over a fire. Guess we got no hope now."

The door behind him opened and another black man stepped out holding an equally decrepit shotgun. He was much younger than Ben Green and his face was framed by an expression of simmering anger.

"What y'all want?" His question was more of a sneer.

The older man cocked his head toward the younger man.

"This is my neighbor's boy, Percy Louis," he said. "We been watchin' John Henry's place till he get back."

Hicks acknowledged the man with a nod, as did Connor. Percy Louis merely glared up at them with hatred in his eyes.

"What can you tell us about the Phantom Riders?" Hicks asked.

"They be like the Klan back in Georgia. That be where I'm from. Wearin' masks, ridin' at night, leavin' burnin' crosses on folk's property." Ben Green looked up at Hicks with an expression of sad, ironic mirth. "And McManus is a sayin' that John Henry, a black man, is the leader?"

Hicks nodded.

Ben Green laughed again, but without humor.

"All white men are no good liars," Percy Louis said. He spat off to the side, the anger still knotting the space between his eyes.

"Hush, boy," Ben Green said.

Louis spat again, this time close to Green's foot.

The old man made a tsking sound with his mouth as a solitary tear wound its way down his dark cheek. "Sooner or later you gonna have to get rid of all that hate."

Everyone was silent for a bit.

"First things first," Hicks said. "We hired a lawyer for John Henry. There's a circuit judge due in tomorrow, as well as the governor. It'd be best if some of you people could come into town, maybe try to get seated on the jury, if there is one."

"Jury?" Ben Green frowned. He'd made the word sound bitter. "Who you trying to fool, Mister Hicks? They ain't gonna be allowin' no black folks on no *jury.*" He enunciated the last word with a particular disdain. "McManus ain't *never* gonna allow that."

"I told you," Hicks said. "McManus ain't running things. There's a circuit judge—"

Ben snorted. "Mister, you got a lot to learn. He runs everything 'round these parts. The water, the election, that damn railroad ..."

"Just the same," Hicks said. "I'm sure John Henry'd appreciate seeing some friendly faces sitting in the courtroom."

Percy Louis snorted in disgust.

Ben Green's lower lip encompassed his upper in a moment of contemplation. Then he gave a curt nod.

"We'll be there, Mister Hicks," he said. "Guess we can be makin' our last stand in town just as well as being picked off out here by them Phantom Riders."

Hicks's mouth drew into a tight line. "I ain't saying that. There's no sense on rushing in there and starting trouble and getting yourselves killed."

Ben Green shot back a defiant look. "Mister, we don't got no choice. We been being promised to and lied to since the War, and now we at the end of the road. Ain't no place to go, and we ain't going down without a fight."

Percy Louis gave an emphatic nod.

Hicks and Connor exchanged uneasy glances.

✳✳✳✳✳✳

SILVER CITY, NEVADA

O'Rourke took out his watch and then peered back over his shoulder. Quint was loitering outside the telegraph office gazing at the open plain before him, the scabbard with the Sharps resting on his shoulder. This water stop was virtually in the middle of nowhere. Just the cistern, a small depot, the telegraph along with a smattering of buildings. A few tumbleweeds rotated down the space between them. O'Rourke didn't even want to dignify it by calling it a street. He popped open the faceplate of his timepiece. It was nearing half-past four and they still had hours to go before they reached San Francisco. It was already dark in Chicago, but

O'Rourke had no doubt that there would be someone manning the main office at this time because,
as the saying went, the Pinkerton's never slept.
Unfortunately, neither had he.

They'd been traveling all night and while Quint
seemed to have no problem dozing off on the uncomfortable seat of the westbound train, O'Rourke
had found it virtually impossible to get comfortable. The sharp angle of the hard, crosshatched
seat against his back, and the constant jostling of
the train car made prolonged slumber impossible.
Consequently, he felt physically exhausted as he
leaned against the counter in the telegraph office.
He almost felt like he could fall asleep standing up.

"Any word back yet?" he asked the telegraph
operator.

The man frowned and shook his head.

"Welcome to my little corner," he said. "Sitting
here all day and half the night sometimes waiting
for that key to begin its chattering."

The last thing O'Rourke wanted to do was listen
to the drudgeries of this simpleton's pathetic life. It
was better not to engage in conversation with him.

"I'm going to step outside for a bit," he said.

The telegraph operator swatted at a fly.

"All righty. I'll let you know if that reply comes
through before the train leaves."

O'Rourke put his hand in his pocket and pressed
two of his coins together. If the home office didn't
reply by then, he and Quint would simply get back
on the train and keep moving toward San Francisco. The probability that one of the operatives scat-

tered through the western states had come across any information on O'Rourke's quarry was slim indeed. But the Pinkerton's network was vast, so the chance did exist. Every operative was trained to search for information and report back to the main office. In his imagination, O'Rourke likened it to a gigantic octopus whose tentacles extended in every direction. River Hicks and the two Mack off springs, Abby and Connor, were out there somewhere, just waiting to be found.

He didn't want to refer to them as "children." Not after their conduct back in Woodman where they'd helped kill Randall Landecker and his crew. Landecker, who called himself The Regulator, had been the first man the company had hired to exterminate River Hicks. The other two, Connor and Abby Mack, were just supposed to be taken into custody. That was before O'Rourke had seen how deadly the two of them could be. Especially the girl. O'Rourke had anticipated that the boy might be formidable, having spent time under the tutelage of a gunslinger like Hicks, but the female and that handgun in her boot ... The bitch was a deadly and cold blooded little thing.

She was also rather comely.

O'Rourke allowed himself to flirt mentally with the idea of having his way with her the next time they crossed paths. He'd first disarm her and perhaps slap her around a bit before tying her wrists and legs to the frame of a solidly built bed and then—

The telegraph operator's voice intruded upon

his fancy. "I thought you said you were stepping outside." He chuckled. "Looked like you were having a real good dream there sleeping on your feet."

O'Rourke dismissed the surge of anger he felt. He swallowed, took in a deep breath. It would serve no purpose to converse further with such a shallow individual.

He turned and went through the door.

Outside the late afternoon air was dry and hot. Quint winked at him. He was sitting on a barrel next to the side of the building and had the enormous rifle out of its scabbard now and was polishing it with a rag. The brass scope along the top of the barrel shone like a polished gold piece.

O'Rourke's eyes widened.

"Is it wise to display that thing?" he asked.

Quint shrugged. "Ain't too many people about to see it, is there?"

O'Rourke realized Quint was right.

Damn, he thought. This fatigue is slowing me down so that even this once-buckskinned buffoon has a clearer grasp on things than I do.

The irritation, coupled with the lack of sleep, made O'Rourke testy.

"Perhaps you should try and find a stray prairie dog to practice on," he said. He was conscious that his tone sounded officious.

Quint squinted up at him and then slowly began to get to his feet.

"Nah," he said, holding the rifle in his left hand and stretching out his right arm. "I got something I'd much rather shoot."

With that his hand flashed upward, snatching O'Rourke's recently purchased wide-brimmed hat from his head and then flinging it away from them.

The hat sailed on the air, whirling like a dervish for about thirty feet or so before leveling out and starting a spinning descent.

Before it had landed Quint whipped the big Sharps up to his shoulder, sighted, and fired. He seemed to accomplish this in a matter of seconds. O'Rourke didn't even have the time to cover his ears.

The loud report hit him like a clap of unexpected thunder, only much louder, and much closer. His sense of hearing immediately ceased functioning replaced by a persistent and dominating humming sound circulating in each ear. His hat had ceased its smooth ride and was now tumbling end-over-end as it fell straight downward.

O'Rourke felt a burst of rage, but knew better than to confront Quint, who stood a few feet away in silent laughter. His mouth worked, forming words that O'Rourke couldn't hear or understand. Quint pointed toward the hat, which was now resting in the dirt. With an expression of utter disdain, O'Rourke stormed off in the direction of his fallen hat, his ears still buzzing.

That barbaric, odiferous idiot, he thought. Well, the bill for a new hat was going to come out of his end of the money, as he's so fond of calling it.

As O'Rourke bent down to pick up his hat he was vaguely cognizant of another burst of thunder.

The hat jumped away from him, landing about five feet away.

The bastard had shot at him.

For a moment O'Rourke thought that his bladder was going to void, and then he recovered control of himself. He thought about drawing his own gun and answering that reprobate in kind, but dropped that thought immediately.

His handgun against a Sharps' rifle would be tantamount to suicide.

Besides, the company would never approve. They'd solicited Quint's services for a specific purpose, and O'Rourke recited one of the credos: *Maintain absolute loyalty to the Company.*

He rotated his head to stare back at Quint who was now bent over and laughing very hard. He raised his right hand and waved dismissively in O'Rourke's direction.

He felt it was now safe to pick up his hat, which he did.

His hearing was gradually returning, albeit distorted, and he could almost discern the words the telegraph operator, who was now outside and standing next to Quint. The operator was yelling something inaudible as he held a sheet of yellow paper in his hand.

A telegram? It had to be the reply from the home office.

O'Rourke quickened his pace and reached the operator in about twenty more seconds.

"Here's your reply, mister," the operator said, his voice sounding like it was coming from the far end of a tunnel.

O'Rourke struggled to read the message scrawled

on the paper without his spectacles and was finally able to make out the first lines:

SUBJECTS LOCATED STOP PROCEED WITH UNDUE HASTE TO SWEETWATER CALIFOR-NIA STOP

At last, he thought. And now, the chase begins in earnest.

CHAPTER 8

SWEETWATER

On the way back to Sweetwater Hicks, Connor, and Abby rode in silence for a good portion of the way.

Finally Connor said, "Looks like there might be some trouble brewing."

"Looks like," Hicks answered. "But judging from that shotgun old Ben had, it ain't gonna be much of a fight."

Connor agreed. He hoped it wouldn't come to an all-out gun battle. He didn't want to see the old man getting hurt, and neither did he want to see Bardwell dangling from a gallows. But the thought of killing more men, even as deserving as some of the McManus crew were, sent an uncomfortable shiver down his spine.

But what in heaven's creation could he do about any of it?

It was like they were riding down the steep slope

of a mountain, always in danger of tumbling, but unable to stop.

"Well," Abby said. "The question is, what are we going to do about it?"

"That ain't the question I'm considering right now," Hicks said.

"Why not?" she asked.

Hicks let his horse advance several steps before he answered. "We kind of got dragged into this thing, and it might be a good idea if we start figuring out the best way to get out of it."

"What?" Abby said. "You mean just abandon everybody?'

Connor saw Hicks take in a deep breath. He knew River's intent was not to wind up in the middle of somebody else's land war, or water-rights conflict. But weren't they involved already?

"But what *are* we going to do?" she asked. "We can't just let them hang John Henry."

Hicks turned in saddle. "We'll cross that bridge if and when we come to it. But remember, this ain't our fight. We got way more involved than we should have."

"But—" Connor started to say.

"No buts," Hicks said, cutting him off. "We'll do what we can to see this through the best way possible. But no promises."

"I thought you said no buts?" Abby said.

Hicks turned and shot her a stern look.

"Girl, you may be blossoming into a nice young lady," he said. "But that don't mean you ain't too big for me to take over my knee and give you a paddling."

Abby pursed her lips but said nothing.

They were encroaching on the southern end of town and saw Otis Baker stumbling from his shop toward the saloon down the street.

"Ain't that the blacksmith?" Connor said.

"Sure is," Hicks said. "Looks like he's through working for the day."

"He looks drunk already," Connor said.

"Sure enough," Hicks said. He steered his horse toward the stables. "Let's put our horses away now. Abby, you stay here and get them fed and bedded down."

"What? But I don't feel like it. I got to the—oh, never mind."

"What you got to do, sis?" Connor asked.

She frowned and didn't reply.

Hicks grinned at him. "Boy, you ought to know better than to ask a female a question like that."

Connor felt his face redden.

They rode up to the doors of the stable and Hicks dismounted.

"Anybody here?" he called out.

No one answered.

Hicks pulled open the doors and walked his horse inside. Abby and Connor followed on horseback. Hicks stopped, took out a match, and lit one of the lanterns hanging on the post. Between the filtering of the fading sunlight through the open barn doors and the incandescence given off by the lantern, the interior of the stable seemed less foreboding. Hicks held the lantern in his outstretched left hand as he walked his horse toward one of the open stalls.

Abby's horse snorted and bucked slightly. She leaned forward and patted the animal's neck.

"What's the matter with your horse?" Connor asked. "Looks like she's limping a little."

"She just got spooked a little is all," Abby said.

"All the more reason for you to give her a good rubdown." Hicks hung the lantern on an angled nail that had been driven into the timber nearest his stall. After securing his mount, he slipped out and lit an additional lantern, which he hung on the timber between his and Connor's stall. The illumination was fairly substantial now.

"Make sure you put these out when you leave," Hicks said.

Abby rolled her eyes. "I know, I know."

Hicks squinted at her and then smiled. "And I know you do. Just like reminding you from time to time."

Abby smiled back at him and tied her horse to the front rail in the stall.

Hicks went back to his own horse, unfastened the cinch, and pulled off his saddle and blanket, then dropped them onto the ground.

Connor groaned. "I'm guessing that I'm gonna have to carry hers and mine back to the hotel again."

"Hers for sure." Hicks grinned. "But yours only if you trust that drunken blacksmith. And if you're gonna want a pillow tonight."

Connor grinned back and undid his saddle strap as well.

Abby was bent over inspecting the bottom of her horse's right front hoof.

"I think she picked up a stone, or something," she said. "And she wasn't limping until she was in here, either."

Hicks motioned for Connor to help his sister unsaddle her mount. Connor stepped into the second stall as Abby straightened up.

"Look at this." She held up a curved piece of iron about as big as a broken pencil. "This is what was caught in her shoe."

Connor took the metal from his sister. If you held it one way, it resembled a sharp mountain. The other way, it looked like the letter V. He shrugged and handed it back to her.

"Good thing you found it," he said. "Coulda done some harm."

"You bet your life, it could've," she said. "I'm going to keep it and show that big blowhard just how clean his stable is."

"Do it later," Hicks said. "Like tomorrow, when we'll hopefully be leaving."

Abby's head whirled to stare at him. "Tomorrow?"

"After the trial," Hicks said.

Abby and Connor exchanged looks.

Hicks stood there in front of them, then stooped to grab the horn on his saddle and then hoist it over his shoulder.

"Come on," he said. "We owe it to Bardwell to let him know his place is being taken care of."

"For the time being, anyway," Abby said. She jammed the piece of metal into her pants pocket.

Hicks stared at her for a time and then turned to

start walking out of the stable. Connor grabbed the two saddles and hoisted his own over his left shoulder before tucking his sister's under his right arm.

"Good thing I'm so strong," he said.

Abby giggled. "Or at least you will be after getting all that exercise."

He frowned and marched rapidly out of the stable to catch up to Hicks. When he was by his mentor's side he asked, "So how do you think it's gonna go tomorrow?"

Hicks shrugged. "Depends on a lot of things, one of them being our side's lawyer. How he presents himself."

Connor was hopeful that because Hicks had used the words "our side's" when referring to John Henry's position. It meant that River was becoming more invested in the overall situation. Connor secretly hoped they'd stay on to see this matter through and maybe help to resolve things. But he wasn't naïve about their chances of doing that without some blood being spilled. The thoughts of killing once again filled him with trepidation. The last thing he needed was more ghosts coming to visit him in his dreams.

THE DOMINION

Big George McManus took his customary seat at the head of the large table. He'd had the chair specifically built to be a head higher than the rest of the chairs in the room. As it was, he still sat eye-to-eye with Burl, but that was all right. His large, bulky frame was a good reminder of the McManus brand of power, and Big George always liked to be reminded of that. A white tablecloth had been spread over the rough wooden top, and several bowls and dishes had been placed in the middle along with a platter of meat. The aroma of the cooked food wafted over to him. Big George glanced around the table, seeing Aaron, Burl, and guest Matthew Tiddy, but not his youngest son. As Juanita scurried up next to him to fill his wine glass, Big George grabbed her arm.

"Wait for Little George to get here," he said.

The Mexican woman's mouth tightened as she winced.

"*Señor*, please," she said. "Your hand ... it hurts me."

Burl spoke up: "Pa, he ain't here."

McManus released the woman. "What? Where is he?"

"He rode into town," Burl said. "He's taking what was happening to Freddie kinda hard."

"What time did he leave?"

"About an hour ago," Aaron said. "He got tired of waiting."

"Waiting." McManus enunciated the word purposefully. He thought again about the similarity of the situation to a chess match and silently lamented that none of his sons had the dexterity or patience to be a master player. "For what?"

His first born didn't answer, but he didn't have

to do so. It was in his eyes, his expression: *He was waiting for you to show some remorse about Freddie.* Big George could see it on Aaron's face as clearly as if he were reading it in a book.

The ungrateful, crippled son of a bitch.

"We tried to stop him, Pa," Burl said. "Honest. But you know how he gets when he's got a mind to do something." Burl clucked his tongue and snorted. "Hell, he's almost as bad as Freddie—"

"Shut your damn mouth," Big George said. He leaned forward, pointing his index finger at his largest son. "Now you go into town and fetch him back, you hear?"

Burl's face twisted slightly, as if he'd been slapped. "Aw, Pa, can't it wait till after I eat? I done worked up a powerful hunger, and Juanita made some of that peach cobbler."

Big George slammed his palm down on the table. His empty wine glass shook.

"When I tell you to do something," he said. "You damn well better do it."

Burl's nose twitched and he wiped at it with his fingers. "Yes, sir." He began to stand up when Aaron placed a hand, his good hand, on his brother's immense forearm.

"I'll go, Burl." His eyes met Big George's. "I haven't got much of an appetite anyway."

Burl's face spread into a smile. "Thanks, Aaron. I'm as hungry as a bear."

Without another word being spoken Big George's first born stood, tossed his cloth napkin onto his plate, and walked slowly out of the room.

"You tell him to get his ass back here and not to start no trouble," Big George called after him.

Aaron made no reply, and this infuriated Big George all the more. Being disrespected by his first born in front of a servant, his second son, and this horse's ass of an attorney exacerbated the irreverence. McManus took in a deep breath as he felt his color rise. If Aaron wasn't his son, and if he wasn't needed to assume that commissioner's job …

"George," Tiddy said. "I wasn't aware until now that—"

"Shut your mouth, too," Big George said. He turned to Juanita and nodded.

She bent over slightly and poured the wine from the bottle into his glass. The smile on her face was forced, but that was good. Fear assured loyalty. Big George assessed the low cut of her white blouse over the top of her cinnamon colored breasts. She was a fine looking woman.

She'd make a good breeder, he thought. It was too bad she was a Mexican.

Tiddy cleared his throat.

Big George waited until he'd sampled the wine before telling the woman to proceed with the disbursement of the food. She busied herself going around the table, picking up the various bowls and the platter.

Big George canted his head and acknowledged Tiddy. The lawyer gave a slight nod.

"As I started to say before," he said. "Judge Robertson is due in on tomorrow's train. It's scheduled to arrive midmorning. I've already sent a telegram informing him of the situation and the trial."

"What about the governor?" Big George asked.

"He's not due in until the afternoon," Tiddy said. "We've already posted the torches so there'll be plenty of light in case the celebration extends into the dark."

"Make sure that damn photographer knows not to photograph Aaron so that his right hand shows," Big George said.

"Of course," Tiddy said.

Juanita had finished her rounds dishing out the food. Her wide eyes sought out Big George, who picked up his knife and fork and signaled the others it was all right to begin. He shoveled some of the mashed potatoes and peas into his mouth. The succulence of the gravy felt delicious on his tongue. Burl had cleaned one plate and was shoveling more of everything onto his plate again. His big jaw worked up and down, his cheeks still bulging.

"So how long do you expect this damn trial will last?" Big George asked.

Now it was Tiddy's turn to smile with the smugness of assurance.

"I don't expect it will be too lengthy," he said. "You are aware that Bardwell's engaged the services of an attorney, aren't you?"

"What?"

"That gunslinger fellow hired one," Tiddy said. "Kandy told me."

"Gunslinger? That son of a bitch that pulled them two guns on us yesterday?"

"One and the same." Tiddy had been slicing his

meat. He popped a very small piece into his mouth and chewed.

Damn, McManus thought. I'm up against Bardwell, that damn Thorpe, the tough gunslinger, and now some lawyer. "Who is this lawyer fella?"

Tiddy dabbed at his lips with a napkin and then grinned.

"James Rance."

Big George's brow furrowed and then relaxed and he let out a laugh.

"The dishwashing drunk from Demar's? The one they ran into town on a rail in his underwear?"

"Again," Tiddy said, the smugness increasing tenfold. "One and the same."

McManus leaned back and laughed long and hard. When he stopped he saw that Burl appeared to be joined with him in mirth.

"*He's* a lawyer?" Big George asked.

"Apparently, he is."

McManus scratched his ear. This was getting better and better all the time. It wasn't like a game of chess at all. It was a card game: poker.

A defendant that's blacker than the ace of spades, he thought. A gunslinger that's like a one-eyed jack, and now somebody's tossed a joker into the deck. And jokers can sometimes turn out to be wild.

He needed to stoke the home fires.

"This is turning into one of them comedies," Big George said.

"Indeed," Tiddy said. He took a deep breath. "But Rance apparently does have some legal experience. He presented me with a writ of discovery earlier today." Tiddy finished slicing a piece of meat and plucked it into his mouth. "Of course the thing was barely legible."

"Discovery?" Big George said. The space between his brows furrowed.

"It's a legal term," Tiddy said. "A delaying tactic really. It's nothing more than a bit of *habeas corpus*. A demand that opposing council, in this case the prosecutor, me, present the defense, him, with the evidence we intend to present against his client."

The explanation did little to quench Big George's confusion, or dispel his sudden anxiety.

"You saying the drunk might know what he's doing?"

Tiddy ate another slice of the meat.

"I doubt whether he's had much trial experience," Tiddy said.

"Still, it's something I wasn't counting on." McManus ran his tongue over his teeth and called for Juanita to bring him some water. When she returned he grabbed the glass and downed half of it.

"Burl, go fetch Kandy," he said.

Burl turned toward him, his mouth gaping open displaying a mishmash of half-masticated food. "Huh?"

"I said, go fetch Kandy."

"Now?"

McManus just stared at him. The answer was obvious.

"But, Pa, I ain't even got to eat none of that peach cobbler that Juanita made." He chewed some more, swallowed, then smacked his lips. "And you know how partial I am to peach cobbler."

Big George reached over and smacked Burl's huge shoulder. It was like hitting a rock pile, but it was meant more for effect than to be injurious.

"Move your big dumb ass, dammit. Be quick about it. Come back with him. And I got something for you to do as well."

"Aw, Pa." Burl's face crinkled and muttered, "Shit," under his breath. As he stood he reached over and grabbed a big handful of the peach cobbler from the pan, breaking it apart with his fingers and shoving it into his mouth as he rose. He shoved his chair back and stormed out of the room.

Tiddy used his fork to extract a piece of brown, roasted peach layered with heavy syrup from the opposite side of the container and placed it into his mouth.

"Ah, delightful," he said. "What've you got planned, Big George?"

"This damn thing has changed from a chess match to a game of five card stud," McManus said. "And it's time for us to stack the deck a little."

******

SWEETWATER

After she'd finished brushing down the three horses and making sure they had some food and water, Abby stepped out of the last one the three stalls and reached into her pocket. She removed that V-shaped piece of metal and studied it. The surface was pitted and worn. It had been put to a lot of use, yet the ends of showed the newness of some sort of fresh abrasion, like they'd recently been broken or cut. She rubbed her thumb over the edge to confirm this, and then slowly retraced her horse's path as they entered the stables. The floor was less than immaculate, with traces of scattered hay, crushed weeds, and excess dirt littering the surface. A broom was leaning against the wall and Abby grabbed it. There was no sense one of their horses picking up any more of these metal chips and maybe going lame.

No wonder that fat blacksmith Baker was stumbling around drunk already, she thought as she began sweeping. It looks to be a long time since he put in a good day's work cleaning this place up.

She felt something hard under the sole of her boot and bent down to pick it up.

It was another piece of metal. A straight piece this time, but with the same abraded cleavage on each end.

I knew it, she thought.

Frowning, she pocketed this one as well and continued sweeping, but found nothing else that could be considered inimical to the inner aspect of the horse's hooves. Abby used the broom to move the collection of detritus to the substantial pile in the blacksmith's shop area, near the anvil.

The big oaf should be paying me for the tidying up I'm doing, she thought. Or doing it himself instead of going down to the saloon and getting drunk. Or in his case, even more drunk.

Abby took both pieces of metal from her pocket and was about to drop them into the pile when something mixed in with the dirt caught her eye.

It was another, longer shard of iron, this one almost resembling the number 7, except that the top portion was at a more severe angle. She squatted down and ran the longer straight piece of metal through the heap. More fragments appeared, and each had a similar appearance as the ones she'd found. After sifting through the entire mass of rubbish, she separated two more pieces. One was another small V shaped shard, and the other a more substantial hunk that resembled a Z with an elongated top. They all appeared to have come from the same batch, and each edge appeared to have been cut.

Not sure what they were, Abby decided to keep them to show River. If nothing else, he could use them to get fat-man Baker to reduce the exorbitant prices he was charging them for use of the stable.

✳✳✳✳✳

While they were stowing their saddles in their hotel room, Connor again watched as Hicks removed the wrapped tubes from each of the two saddlebags and inspected them. After ensuring that they were intact and not leaking, Hicks rewrapped the tubes and once again carefully placed them in separate bags.

"You planning on using that to break John Henry out of jail?" Connor asked with a grin.

Hicks didn't answer.

Connor wondered if he really was considering such a move. It would get things moving in a hurry, and head off this ridiculous trial thing. But it would also most certainly end in a bloodbath, and Connor had the feeling that Hicks liked and respected Thorpe too much to allow that to happen. Connor liked the man, too. In a way, he reminded Connor a little bit of River. They were both hard, tough men and good with a gun. At least he knew River was, but had to assume that Thorpe knew how to handle himself as well.

He'd have to be able to in place like this, Connor thought.

They were almost like two sides of the same coin. Both tall, dark, strong, and tough, but whereas Thorpe wore his hair cut short, River's was long and fashioned into a pony tail. River's face had scars— all traces of past battles. Thorpe's showed some wear, but it was basically unmarked. Both men carried Colt Peacemakers, but River had two on his belt, and Thorpe only one. And both men were even-tempered and obviously wise in the ways of the world.

The town of Sweetwater could do a lot worse than Thorpe as far as having a sheriff who could keep order. If that Burl McManus took over, there'd be hell to pay for the decent folks.

After lacing the saddlebags closed, Hicks turned to Connor and said, "Let's go check on Rance."

Connor said nothing but silently hoped they wouldn't find the lawyer on the wrong end of a bottle of whiskey.

When they got to the front entrance of Demar's
Restaurant Hicks paused to look around. Connor
did the same. The street appeared relatively solitary, with only a few people milling about. On the
opposite side, the light spilled out from the open
space above the winged doors of the saloon, however, and a discordant sounding mixture of yelling,
piano music, and song emanated from there was
well. Hicks studied the sight across the street and
shook his head.

Connor continued to wonder if Rance had
managed to maintain his abstinence or if he'd suc-
cumbed to the lure of the bottle.

"Let's hope we find our lawyer boy on this side of
the street," Hicks said.

He opened the door and they stepped inside
the restaurant. The proprietor, the woman named
Rose, walked over to them. The restaurant had
about six patrons, some of whom glanced up at him
and Hicks and then turned away quickly.

The smile on Rose's face evaporated as she saw
it was them.

"You want a table?" she asked.

Hicks tipped his hat. Connor saw him do it and
did the same.

"Evenin', ma'am," Hicks said. "We're looking for
Rance."

"He ain't here," she said. Her voice was rife with
contempt.

"Know where we can find him?" Hicks asked.

She stared at him and the ends of her rather wide
mouth dipped into a frown.

"Ain't it enough that you talked him into doing something that he'll most likely fail at?" Her voice sounded brittle. "You had no business making him think that he could stand up to Big George McManus."

"He's standing up for the law," Hicks said. "And himself. Man spends his days drinking and evenings washing other people's dishes when he's got education ain't doing the best for himself."

Her frown deepened. "Whatever. Like I told you, he ain't here."

Hicks repeated his earlier question: "Know where he might be?"

"Try the damn saloon," she said, and stormed away.

As they turned and walked out of the place Hicks shot Connor a wry smile and said, "Appears she gonna be looking for a new dishwasher. Maybe you ought to think about applying for the job."

"Huh?" Connor said. "What for?"

Hicks shrugged in exaggerated fashion. "Well, the way you keep giving away our hard-earned money like you been doing, paying for Bardwell's wagon and such, I figured you'd be a good fit for some steady work."

Connor snorted a laugh. "That ain't for me."

"Didn't think so," Hicks said. "Besides, you're a lot better at making a mess than you are at cleaning one up."

Connor could tell that Hicks was joshing him, but he also knew that there was a kernel of truth in what he'd said.

They walked across the street toward the saloon and Connor was dreading what seemed most probable that they'd find in there.

As they stepped inside the noise factor increased tenfold. A scantily clad woman with large breasts stood next to a man playing a lively tune on the piano. The woman's voice was terrible and Connor was reminded of a cat in heat. The two tried to carry the melody, but for that, he reflected, they'd need a picnic basket. They were ringed by a group of other drunks, slobbering and spilling their steins of beer while waving their arms in time to the off-key tune. Connor surveyed the bar and saw it was pretty crowded. Several of the tables were filled with men playing cards, and an assortment of saloon girls weaved between the tables touching and flirting. One of them, a particularly fetching wench with long blonde hair secured in a French braid, locked her eyes on Hicks, then on Connor.

He tried to control his surprise as he saw her beauty was marred by a long scar that ran down the left side of her face from the bridge of her nose to the underside of her jaw.

Connor smiled at her.

She flicked a tentative smile in reply.

Two men appeared in animated conversation at the far end of the bar. Connor recognized one of them as the hot-headed youngest son of McManus, the one Connor had cold-cocked when he'd threatened to pull his gun and shoot it out with River yesterday. They called him Little George. The other man had been with him and the elder McManus the day before and had a size distortion of his right hand. It appeared to be much smaller than his left. They'd both departed with McManus, but Connor wasn't sure who this second man was.

Hicks was already striding toward the opposite end of the big room and then Connor saw why. James Rance, still in his ragged clothes, sat at one of the tables with a bottle of whiskey and a glass in front of him. The glass was full of an amber liquid.

Connor moved in Hicks's wake as he pushed men out of his way. He stopped in front of Rance. In addition to the bottle and glass, there were two thick books on the table top.

"I thought I told you, in no uncertain terms, to lay off the booze until after the trial," Hicks said.

It wasn't a question.

Rance looked up at him.

"So you did." His voice sounded clear, not slurred at all. "And so I have."

Hicks glared down at the man. "You want to explain what the hell you doing here then?"

Before Rance could answer the younger McManus came strutting over, his mouth stretched with a leering simper. A trace of discoloration and swelling ran at an angle along the left side of his forehead from Connor's strike the day before. McManus evidently remembered it as well, judging from the hostile glare he directed at them.

"Leave my favorite dishwasher alone, Mister Gunfighter," he said. "I was just getting ready to buy him a drink myself."

Hicks didn't look at him, but raised his left hand,

palm down, fingers extended. It was a signal for Connor to watch for the approach of a possible adversary and act if necessary. He and Hicks always talked about and worked on different signals and tactics to use in potentially dangerous situations, of which this was certainly one. Connor stepped to the side and unfastened the leather thong that secured his Colt in the holster.

"Don't be bothering me, boy," Hicks said in a low growl. "This is between me and him."

Little George McManus's face twisted with sudden rage and he lowered his hand toward his gun.

"Hey, you don't know who you're talking to," he said.

The other man, the one with the crippled hand, rushed forward and encircled Little George with both arms.

"Georgie, no," the man said. "Let it alone. He's too good with a gun for you."

"Lemme go, Aaron. Lemme go." Little George tried to shake loose, and the two of them danced over to the bar, continuing their struggle. "That other one hit me yesterday."

Keeping his hand on the butt of his gun, Connor recalled Sheriff Thorpe mentioning that McManus's oldest son was named Aaron.

That must be him, he thought.

If need be, he was prepared to draw and fire with deadly results, but considering how things had worked out the day before, the last thing he wanted to do at this juncture was kill another man, especially a McManus.

Little George had almost jerked free and Connor pulled out his Colt and held it down by his side. He could try and deliver another non-lethal blow to the younger McManus's head that would hopefully take him out of any potential gunfight. At this point, it would be better than shooting him, but they were a good twelve feet away now.

Aaron McManus still had his younger brother pinned against the bar, but appeared to be losing the battle. Just as it looked as if Little George would break free, a deep, loud voice bellowed behind them.

"Dammit, little brother. Can't you keep outta trouble?"

Connor turned and saw the huge, imposing form of Burl McManus sauntering toward them. A group of four men were with him, some of whom appeared to be the same ones who'd ridden in with the McManus contingent the day before.

A couple of patrons seated in the section near to the doors got up and hurriedly left.

"I missed out on my second helping of peach cobbler 'cause of you, Little George," Burl said.

The youngest McManus turned to look at him.

"Burl, this two-bit gunfighter's messing with me."

Burl tipped his hat back and raised his eyebrows, but before he could speak Aaron McManus broke in: "That's not exactly the case, Burl. Our little brother here has had a bit too much to drink."

Burl blew out a long breath and stepped over, putting a big arm around his much smaller sibling, forcing him up against the bar. The movement appeared effortless, but Connor saw that Little George McManus was held tight, unable to move.

"Your playtime's over," Burl said. "Pa's got something he wants us to do." He motioned for the four men who'd accompanied him to belly up the bar.

Connor replaced his Colt in its holster but left the leather thong dangling.

"I'm only gonna say this once," Burl's booming voice said over his shoulder. "I don't want nobody, ever to be speaking ill to my little brother here. If'n' anybody does, there gonna have to deal with me. Understood?"

Hicks turned toward Burl McManus.

"You talking to me, big man?"

Burl's face had an even expression on it, but his mouth twitched into a slight smile.

Connor figured he was pleased with the reference to his size. Most large men reacted thusly.

"You pretty good with them guns, are you, gunslinger?" Burl asked.

Hicks kept his eyes on the other man, his expression even. "You looking to find out?"

The smile on Burl's face dissipated.

"I'm only gonna say this once, mister." He raised his big right hand and extended his index finger toward Hicks.

"You say a lot of things just once," Hicks said.

Burl's nose twitched in perplexity for a moment, then he resumed his look of intimidation. "Come next Tuesday, I'm gonna be sheriff of this here town, and you best be gone by then."

"Or what?" Hicks asked.

"Or," Burl appeared to be searching for something felicitous to say, but was obviously having trouble thinking of a good line.

"Look," Aaron McManus said. "It'd be best if you three left. We're not here to cause any trouble."

"Looks like it follows your family like the tail on a dog." Hicks stared at all three McManus brothers for a solid eight seconds, then motioned for Rance to get up. "Grab your books and let's go."

Rance stood and uncapped the bottle. He then picked up the glass, brought it to the lip of the bottle, and then poured the amber fluid down its narrow neck, not spilling a drop. His hands were steady, his grip sure. When he'd finished, he stared at the whiskey on the table before recapping the bottle and placing the glass over the top. Picking up the two books, he stepped behind Hicks and started for the door.

Connor could see that the bottle was full now.

Hicks moved away slowly, backing up. Connor did the same.

"You *better* leave," Little George McManus yelled. "You come back and I'll *kill* ya."

"You're welcome to try, boy," Hicks said. "Anytime."

Burl McManus physically turned his younger brother back toward the bar and whispered something to him. Little George seemed to settle down slightly, but he shot a glance at Connor and Hicks that was sheer malevolence.

Connor pushed Rance through the swinging

door at the front entrance, turned, and drew his pistol. Hicks was still walking backward, his hands hanging loosely by his sides. He pushed through the doors after Connor and curled his body around the side of the door jamb.

"Looks like his big brother got him settled down some," Hicks said, peering through the opening above the swinging saloon doors.

"Would you really have killed him?" Rance asked.

Hicks slowly turned from the doors and stared at the lawyer.

"If I had to," Hicks said. "I say what I mean, and a man's only as good as his word."

"I didn't take a drink," he said. "I put the bottle and the glass in front of me, but I didn't take a drink."

Hicks stared at him for several seconds. "That's good."

Rance's eyes drifted down to the boardwalk. He shook his head.

"I wonder if I made a mistake coming out West," he said. "It seems like everything's handled at the point of a gun. The law doesn't seem to matter much here."

"Sometimes it's like that," Hicks said. "And whether you stay or go ain't the question right now. You got a man depending on you for his life, and it ain't gonna be a gun that decides his fate in that courtroom tomorrow."

Rance pursed his lips, as if deciding something. He nodded and straightened up.

Hicks watched the man, then motioned for him and Connor to follow as he began walking toward the sheriff's office.

"Let's go see your client, counselor," he said.

CHAPTER 9

SWEETWATER

As they walked into the sheriff's office Thorpe shot a glance toward the door. He was standing behind his desk checking the load of his pistol. The deputy, Lucas, was loading a shotgun. He looked startled as well. Thorpe lifted the hat off his head and hung it on the rack behind him.

"We were just fixing to head down to the saloon," he said. "Some concerned citizen just stopped in here and told us you two were about to take on just about the whole McManus family."

"Concerned citizen?" Hicks said. "I take it he was concerned for the welfare of the McManus's?"

Thorpe grinned. "Not hardly. A lot of the towns-folk, and all of the other ranchers are intimidated by McManus and his four sons. His ranch hands regularly ride into town on their payday and cause a ruckus."

"Why do folks put up with it?" Connor asked.

Thorpe blew out a slow breath. "It's the price of doing business. McManus is the merchant's primary customer. His spread is so big, he's always buying supplies. Plus, he's been controlling the water for a lot of the smaller ranchers and farmers. People are afraid of him and don't want to get on his bad side."

"That don't seem fair," Connor said.

Thorpe shrugged. "It's just the way things are."

"How's that gonna play out next Tuesday?" Hicks asked. "For the election?"

Thorpe laughed. "That circuit judge is supposed to overseeing everything to assure fairness, but I'm sure Big George will be spreading enough money around so that the ballots are all properly counted, according to his liking."

"That ain't right," Connor said.

"Lotta things ain't right," Thorpe said.

Hicks turned to Rance, who was standing there holding his two law books.

"Why don't you go confer with your client," Hicks said. "We'll join you in there shortly."

The lawyer headed for the door separating the cell block from the office.

"Lucas," Thorpe said. "You can put that shotgun away and run down to Demar's and fetch supper for you, me, and the prisoner."

The deputy broke open the shotgun, removed the two shells, and snapped it closed. He then replaced the weapon in the gun rack and walked to the door.

When he'd gone, Hicks addressed Thorpe.

"What are the chances this trial tomorrow's gonna be fair and square?"

Thorpe blew out another long breath.

"Well, it's hard to say. The judge is a good man. He won't put up with any shenanigans in the courtroom. We've had trials here before. But like I said, McManus swings a lot of weight around here and there ain't a lot of people who'll want to cross him."

"How's it crossing him?" Connor said. "It was that Layton fella who got killed, wasn't it? He wasn't any kin to McManus, was he?"

"No, he wasn't," Thorpe said. "But McManus is obviously pushing for a conviction. That's why he made that charge that John Henry's one of the Phantom Riders. That's got a lot of the townsfolk scared."

"There ain't no truth to that," Connor said.

"That's what Rance will have to bring out in court," Thorpe said. "If he can."

"What'll happen if he can't?" Connor asked.

Thorpe's face pulled tight, his reply terse: "Then John Henry'll hang."

Connor glanced at Hicks, who showed no emotion.

"Let's go talk to Bardwell," Hicks said.

Connor nodded and they walked to the door.

They stepped into the long room. There were three sets of cells, each with a cot placed against the wall. The cell block was lighted by three oil lamps set on shelves along the wall that ran opposite the cells. Connor saw Rance leaning against the cell door, a law book opened in his grasp. Bardwell stood next to him on the other side, his large hands clutching the iron bars.

Rance had his finger pressed to one of the printed pages. He stopped his conversation.

"Mister Hicks," Bardwell said. "Connor."

"We took your horses back to your place," Hicks said. "A couple men were there keeping an eye on things."

Bardwell raised an eyebrow. "One of them old Ben Green?"

"Yep."

"Who was the other one?"

"Young fella named Percy Louis."

Bardwell blew out a breath. "He can be a hot head sometimes."

"So we noticed," Hicks said.

"Figured it was them," Bardwell said. "If'n' I don't make it outta this, I'd appreciate you tellin' Old Ben to keep the horses and my belongings."

"Let's not think like that," Rance said. "We're going to fight, aren't we?"

Bardwell let out a heavy sigh. He shook his head.

"I'm not sure how much fight I got left, Mister Rance."

"We've got the truth on our side," Rance said.

"And they got the McManus brand on theirs," Bardwell said. His voice had a tone of finality to it.

He's beat before he starts, Connor thought. And that ain't good.

"The sheriff's getting you something to eat," Hicks said.

Bardwell smiled, but it was a wry smile. "Might be my last meal."

The three white men standing outside the cell exchanged glances. No one spoke.

Suddenly the crack of a shot, then another broke the silence.

That sounded close, Connor thought. Like it was just outside.

Hicks turned and grabbed the doorknob.

The staccato bursts of more shots followed sounding louder now that the door was open.

As they ran into the office area Connor saw that Thorpe was rushing out the door. A body lay half on the boardwalk and half in the street, an overturned wicker basket spilling gravy covered mashed potatoes, a hunk of meat, and sliced carrots onto the dirt.

Lucas, Connor thought. The deputy.

Another gunshot. Then another.

Thorpe grabbed at his shoulder as he slammed back against the framework of the heavy doorjamb. Blood welled through the light colored fabric.

Hicks already had his gun out and stepped to the door. He pulled Thorpe inside and shoved him to the floor. Gesturing for Connor to follow, Hicks stepped through the door in a crouch. Perhaps twenty-five feet down the street, by the saloon, a cluster of five men stood shoulder to shoulder across the street, firing handguns. Beyond them was a group of masked men on horseback. They were firing their guns as well. Hicks leveled his gun and cocked back the hammer.

"Get your damn asses out of the way, dammit," Hicks yelled.

The cluster of men in the street didn't move.

Hicks aimed but did not fire.

Connor saw why as he extended his own weapon. The gaggle of men on foot in the middle of the street was in the way. He ran down the boardwalk with Hicks walking fast on his trail.

"Slow down." Hicks called out.

Connor heard him and lessened his pace. Down the street two of the masked riders darted out from between two buildings. Another shot sounded as one fell from his horse. The other masked rider grabbed the horse's reins and began to tow the animal away.

When they got to the edge of the skirmish line, Hicks danced to the side, raised his pistol, aimed, and fired.

Connor thought he saw the masked rider towing the horse jerk, but keep on riding, galloping away through the far end of the town and then disappearing into the escalating darkness. As the cluster of men on foot ambled forward toward the body of the fallen masked rider, Connor saw that it was the two McManus brothers, Burl and Little George, and the four cowhands who'd been with them. Aaron McManus wasn't among them.

Burl got to the supine body on the street and leveled his pistol, firing one round into it. The prostrate figure didn't move.

He's already dead, Connor thought.

As if to reaffirm his unspoken words, Burl McManus bellowed a loud howl, and then yelled, "I bagged him, sure enough, dad-gummite."

He kicked the body.

People were coming out of the other buildings and the saloon now, gathering along the boardwalk, the gathering crowd buzzing with conversation. A few of them were lighting lanterns and heading for the matrix.

Burl's loud voice carried above the dissonance. "Guess we all know who's the best man for sheriff now, don't we? I got me one of the Phantom Riders."

Just as Connor neared the edge of the crowd he felt Hicks grab his shirt and pull him to a halt.

"Let's back off and see what's what," Hicks said.

Burl bent over, ripped the mask off the body on the street, and held it high over his head.

Connor struggled to see the dead man.

"See?" Little George McManus yelled. "What my father tell yas?"

His words were slurred and barely understandable.

"It's one of them damn nigger homesteaders," Little George said. "They shot Thorpe and his damn deputy, and was trying to break their leader, Bardwell, out of jail."

"The sheriff's been shot?" a voice in the crowd said.

"Somebody go get Doc Ingraham," another said.

Connor glanced back at Hicks, who shook his head slightly.

"Thorpe's wound didn't look that bad," he said in a low whisper. "Can't say the same for that deputy, though. Come on. I want to see this."

Hicks and Connor pushed through the outer

edge of the group. Several of the men stood with their lamps held high, which cast a soft, eerie illumination over the scene. The body lay about ten feet away, the face turned toward them. Lips were stretched back over white teeth covered with a crusted lamina of crimson. The glazed-over eyes were barely visible through half-open slits. Connor studied the face and a flicker of recognition struck him.

It was Percy Louis, the angry young man they'd seen out at Bardwell's farm earlier.

He turned back to Hicks who nodded fractionally and held a finger to his lips.

Burl McManus had his gun in one hand and the mask in the other. He shook the hood in Hicks's direction.

"See for yourself, Mister Gunfighter," Burl McManus said. "I always hit what I aim at."

"You sure waited till you were close enough," Hicks said. "And dead men generally don't shoot back."

Burl held up his long-barreled Colt. "Hey, I'm plenty good with this. Wanna see?"

"Well, you and your boys here fired off a lot of rounds," Hicks said. "Don't you think you better make sure you got some bullets left first?"

Burl's face fluttered with a dubious expression as he fingered at his weapon, then he frowned and slammed it into his holster.

"Next time, gunslinger," he said.

His younger brother jumped forward toward Hicks, but Aaron McManus suddenly pushed through the crowd and stopped him.

"Georgie, no," he said. "Don't."

"Lemme go." Little George McManus turned to his other brother. "You gonna let him talk to you like that?"

"Don't matter none," Burl McManus said. "Let's go back inside. I want to finish my beer."

"I'll be coming for you before long, gunfighter," Little George yelled, pointing at Hicks.

"And I'll be waiting," Hicks said.

Aaron McManus glared at them, then, with the assistance of his brother, Burl, managed to pull their younger sibling away from the scene and back toward the saloon. The four cowpokes went with them and the rest of the crowd began to scatter. Something in the street glinted in the lamplight. Connor stared at it and saw it was an elongated silver spoon, but not the kind used for eating. It was the kind attached to a fancy set of spurs. He started to go over to it but Burl McManus seemed to catch the movement out of the corner of his eye. The big man's head swiveled to the street and he stooped down, picked up the spoon, and slipped it into his pocket.

Connor turned to Hicks.

"You see that, River?"

"What of it?"

"There was a part of spur on the street. And that big McManus fella picked it up."

Hicks motioned for him to start walking back toward the sheriff's office. Three men, one of them in a nightshirt and holding a black satchel, were hurrying in that direction.

"I seen one of McManus's men wearing a set of fancy spurs when I took Rance to the barbershop," Connor said. "That one with the load of grease in his hair. Kandy. And I didn't see him with them other McManus men tonight."

Hicks continued walking.

"I imagine spurs like that are pretty hard to come by," he said.

"But don't you see?" Connor said. "If he ain't here, it's gotta mean that he was riding with the Phantom Riders, don't it?"

"Maybe," Hicks said. "Maybe not. But we'll have to see if he's wearing both of them next time we see him."

When they got to the sheriff's office they were met by Abby, who was holding her Trantor pistol in her hand. She cocked her head toward the inside of the office.

"Sheriff's been shot," she said. "Deputy's over there. Dead."

Connor saw the deputy's body lying on the office floor. His eyes showed the same vacuous display as the dead man's up the street, but without the haziness. There were two bullet holes, one in his chest and the other just under his right eye. Four men, one of whom was James Rance, stood in a semicircle next to Thorpe, who was shirtless and seated in a chair by his desk. His face was twisted with pain, but his eyes sought Hicks.

"What's going on out there?" he asked through clenched teeth as the man in the nightshirt dabbed at the wound on Thorpe's right shoulder with some bloody cotton balls. "Go easy, will you, doc."

The man in the nightshirt frowned. "Got to make sure this is sterilized." He pressed the cotton against the gash and turned to one of the others.

"Run over to the saloon and fetch me a bottle of their whiskey," he said. "I'm running low on isopropyl."

The man looked dumbfounded and the doctor said, "Dammit, move," and the fellow took off at a hurried pace.

"I asked you what's going on," Thorpe said.

"Looks like the little fracas is about over," Hicks said. "The masked riders rode out of town heading north. There's a body in the street."

"A body?"

"Fell off of a horse. Was wearing a mask. Burl McManus shot him and pulled it off of him after he was down."

"Any idea who it is?"

"It *was* a Negro homesteader," Hicks said. "We saw him earlier when we rode out to Bardwell's place. Name was Louis. Percy Louis."

Thorpe shook his head and swore.

"A homesteader?" Rance said. "Aw, hell."

Thorpe's face contorted with more pain as the doctor poured some liquid over the wound.

"Louis? He was one of the Phantom Riders?" Thorpe paused as his grimace hardened. "He was something of a hot head, but it's kinda hard to believe."

"It sure is," Hicks said. "Especially since he's been

dead for a while."

"What?" Thorpe said.

"The blood on Louis's shirt and over his teeth was all dried." Hicks pointed to the deputy's body. "Take a look at his eyes. They ain't had time to glaze over yet. Louis's were all cloudy, like the air had gotten to them for a spell."

Connor had suspected as much. "So that's why you told McManus he'd shot a dead man."

Hicks smirked. "That big, dumb ox walked up and put a bullet in him after he was laying in the dirt. You ain't gonna find no fresh blood in that wound, neither."

"Would you be willing to testify to that in court?" Rance asked.

Hicks grinned. "Sure, why not? It looks like John Henry's got himself a lawyer after all."

Rance's mouth twisted into something resembling a grin and he nodded.

Just then the door opened and the man the doctor had sent for whiskey burst through it.

"Sheriff." The man was breathless, like he'd run all the way. "There's some real ugly talk going on in the saloon."

Thorpe's brow furrowed. "What kind of talk?"

The man handed a whiskey bottle to the doctor, who set the cotton balls down and popped off the cork on the bottle. He raised it to his mouth and took a quick sip before pouring it over Thorpe's shoulder.

The sheriff grunted in pain.

"Gotta make sure this don't get infected," the

doctor said. "Now sit still."

"What kind of talk?" Thorpe repeated.

"Lynch mob talk," the other man said. "Little George McManus is getting people all stirred up, talking about how they oughta not wait for no trial."

"They can't do that," Rance said. "It's barbaric."

Thorpe groaned as the alcohol ran down his arm and formed a puddle on the rough floor boards.

"Hand me my shirt." He reached for his gun-belt, which was on the desk.

"You're in no shape to go down there, Dan," the doctor said. "I need to see how serious this is."

"See it when I get back." Thorpe started to get up but fell back against the chair and moaned in pain.

"The doc's right," Hicks said. "And Little George McManus is all fired up on booze, with his two brothers and a bunch of his cowhands with him. He's itching to shoot first and say he's sorry later."

"Help me stand up," Thorpe said. "Got to go close that damn saloon or else the whiskey's gonna whip those idiots into a lynch mob frenzy."

The doctor put a hand on Thorpe's chest and held him in the chair.

"You ain't going nowhere till I get this bleeding stopped and this wound stitched up."

Connor saw Hicks take in a deep breath, as if he was deciding something.

"Thorpe," Hicks said. "Deputize us."

"You?" The sheriff started a laugh that turned into a coughing spasm. "You're a gunman."

"You see anybody else volunteering?" Connor said.

Thorpe was breathing hard now. He stared toward the body of his deputy a few feet away. His eyes swept the floor, then settled back on Hicks and Connor. "You two know what you're getting into?"

"Don't look like we have much choice," Hicks said. "Does it?"

The sheriff's teeth clenched over his lower lip and he shook his head. He pointed to the fallen deputy, said, "Take the badge off of his chest," and then pulled open the center drawer of his desk. He reached inside and came up with another silver star, this one with *DEPUTY* stamped across the front.

Connor moved over to the body and stared down at it. Lucas hadn't been a particularly handsome individual in life, and in death his features seemed almost grotesque. A grimace was frozen on his mouth exposing a row of broken and crooked teeth. Abby came up next to Connor, knelt, and unpinned the badge. It was splattered with droplets of blood. She strode over to the desk.

"Deputize me, too," she said.

Rance, who had been standing there in silence, cleared his throat and spoke. "And me as well."

Thorpe looked at them, and then up at Hicks.

"That ain't a good idea," Hicks said.

Abby whirled to face him. "Why not? I can handle a gun. You know that."

"Yeah," Hicks said. "I do. And I'll be counting on that if Connor and me come a runnin' from the saloon. You're best needed right here. You, too, counselor." He gestured toward the gun rack. There were three rifles in it. "Load up them Winchesters and station yourselves by the window and door."

"But—" Abby started to say.

Hicks held up his open palm. "No buts. Remember?"

She compressed her lips and nodded.

Hicks turned to Connor. "Grab that scattergun and some shells. Ain't nothing better than one of those to break up a lynch mob."

Connor moved to the rack and took down the shotgun. He found six shells in the drawer on the bottom of the rack.

"This all you got?" he asked.

"Unfortunately, yes," Thorpe said. "Now both of you raise your right hands."

Connor lifted his arm and Thorpe started to recite the oath. Hicks grabbed the badge from Abby, shoved it into Connor's hand, the blood smearing his palm. Hicks then reached down and plucked the star from the desk in front of Thorpe.

"We ain't got the time," Hicks said. "Come on."

Connor broke open the shotgun, dropped the two shells into the twin holes, and snapped it closed. He then put the additional three shells in his right pants pocket. Hicks was already moving out the door, pulling a new cartridge out of the holder on his belt and opening the loading gate of his first Colt Peacemaker.

"Let's see if we can cut this mob off at the knees," he said.

CHAPTER 10

SWEETWATER

It was fully dark as they moved up the street. At least eight horses were tied to the hitching rails in front of the saloon. Noise and light spilled from the entranceway. Hicks and Connor moved up the street in silent approach with Hicks in the lead. Over the cacophony of discordance emanating from the bar, an undercurrent of a loud voice could be discerned.

Hicks slowed his pace until Connor was right beside him.

"How many rounds you got for that thing?" he asked.

"Five total," Connor said. "Got both barrels loaded and three rounds in my pocket."

"Take them out and stick them primers-up in your belt," Hicks said. "The right side of your belt so you can keep your left hand by the trigger. That way, if you fire off them two in the gun, you can just pop it open and reload a lot quicker. And don't open it unless you fired both barrels."

Connor began digging the rounds out of his pocket. "Got it," he said.

And he had gotten it, too. Hicks was continually drilling tactics into him, be it the quickest way to shoot and reload, or the best way to approach a dangerous situation.

Hicks emitted a low chuckle. "Guess I'm preaching to the choir, ain't I?"

"Preaching?" Connor said. "You?"

"Never mind. Once I get inside, I'm firing off one round to get everybody's attention right quick."

Connor finished jamming the shotgun shells into his belt. "At the ceiling, right?"

Hicks chuckled again.

"Like I said, preaching to the choir." He peered toward the saloon. "Hopefully we'll be able to close this damn place down and send them all on their way without having to fire more than the one shot. But be ready. Once we get through those doors, you move toward the wall and keep your back to it. Anybody gets in your way, either ease them away or knock 'em down."

Connor smiled. "And knock over a table for cover, once the fun starts?"

Hicks's mouth drew up at the ends into a slight smile.

"Yep," he said. "Preaching to the choir."

Connor grinned back. "Well, it ain't like we haven't done this before, a time or two."

They'd reached the front of the saloon and Hicks flattened against the wall then motioned for Connor to get behind him. Hicks then pointed to himself, and then to the other side of the door opening.

Connor nodded and Hicks swiftly moved across, stationing himself opposite Connor.

The discordant sounds of loud voices drifted through the open space above the winged doors.

"It just ain't right, I tell ya. They got the leader of the Phantom Riders in our jail, and they're putting all of us—the whole damn town, all of youse, in danger." Connor recognized the slurred voice of Little George McManus.

A chorus of supporting comments followed. He continued with his incendiary diatribe.

"We all know what we gotta do, don't we?"

Another round of inebriated agreements resounded.

"Now wait a minute, dammit," a second singular voice said. "We need to just take a step back before we do something we're all going to regret later."

Connor recognized this voice, too: Aaron McManus.

"Aw, shut up," someone yelled.

"Hey," Little George yelled. "You don't talk to my brother like that. Hear? I'll *kill* ya."

Hicks blew out a breath. "Worst comes to worse, I'm shooting that son of a bitch first."

Connor heard Little George's tone change as he said, "Comere, honeypot. I wanna take you upstairs before we go hang that nigger."

Leaning forward, Connor could see through

the slats in the swinging door closest to him. Little George had grabbed the arm of a saloon girl and was pulling her to him.

"Leave me alone," the girl cried. "I don't want to be with you right now."

"Huh? Why not?"

"You're too mean when you're drunk."

"Oh yeah? Mean like this?"

The girl screamed in pain.

Little George pressed his mouth against her neck. "You know you like it that way, honey."

"Let's get to it," Hicks said.

The girl was trying to push him away but couldn't. The others were standing around laughing.

Hicks drew his gun as he moved forward and pushed through the doors. Connor slipped in right behind him and headed for the wall. Hicks aimed his Colt upward and fired a round.

A sudden hush fell over the large room as all eyes were on Hicks. A few darted toward Connor as he brandished the shotgun.

"Whaddaya want, gunslinger?" Little George McManus said. His hands were entwined in the blonde hair of the bar girl Connor had seen earlier—the girl with the scars on her face and neck.

"We've been deputized by the sheriff," Hicks said in a commanding tone. "By his order, this place is closed. Vamoose."

"You looking for trouble, slickster?" Burl McManus said. His huge form straightened to its full erectness.

Hicks winked. "You reload your gun yet, big man?"

Burl's face twitched and his eyes darted down toward his sidearm. His tongue shot out and traced over his lips.

Connor was able to infer that Burl hadn't reloaded.

Probably got an empty or near-empty gun in his holster, Connor thought.

Burl lifted his arms and crossed them on his chest. "You're just mighty lucky I ain't had the time yet."

Hicks smirked. "Well, now that's a damn shame, seeing as how you're such a big target." His face tightened. "Now, none of the rest of you fellas get any ideas here. My partner, and fellow deputy of the law, has a scattergun and knows how to use it. Plus, we got more deputies going around the back with the sheriff."

"The sheriff was shot," Little George said. "He ain't coming here."

"That's why he's bringing up the rear, sonny," Hicks said. "Along with three more scatterguns. Now take your filthy hands outta that pretty girl's hair and let her ease away from you."

Little George tightened his grip and the girl gasped in pain again as her head was bent backward.

Hicks raised his Colt and aimed at the youngest McManus.

"It's been said I can knock the wings off a fly at ninety feet," Hicks said. "So putting one right through your pumpkin head's gonna be easy. Real easy. Now let her go."

Little George glared back at him with sheer rage.

Aaron McManus moved forward and placed his hands on his brother's shoulders. Whispering softly so no one could hear, he slowly unwound the girl's hair from between Little George's fingers.

When she was free she jumped away and ran toward the stairs.

Little George's eyes never left Hicks. Neither did the expression of anger and malice. "You shouldn't a oughta done that, gunslinger." He spoke through clenched teeth.

Hicks kept the Colt leveled at Little George's head.

"All right," Hicks said. "All of you. Skedaddle, or we're gonna start clearing you out the hard way. And I ain't usually particular, but pretty little Georgie here's gonna be the first to go down."

"And anybody makes a move or draws a gun," Connor yelled, "is gonna get introduced to some double-ought buck."

A murmur of voices circulated through the crowd.

"You heard the deputy," Aaron McManus said. "This place is closed."

The barkeep glared at Hicks, then began removing bottles, steins, and glasses from the top of the bar. Men started meandering out the door. Hicks moved to the side, but still kept his gun pointed at Little George.

"That's right," Hicks said. "Keep moving. But first I'll need a volunteer to stay and help carry that body in the street down to the undertakers."

"What?" one of the formerly unruly patrons yelled. "I ain't touching that nigg—"

Hicks pointed his Peacemaker directly at the man's face.

"I'm getting mighty tired of hearing that word," Hicks said.

The man's eyes were as huge as shot glasses. He raised his hands, palms up, and flashed a nervous smile as he shuffled quickly toward the door.

"You gonna try and shoot us all, gunslinger?" Little George McManus yelled.

"Not all of you," Hicks said as he swiveled to point the gun at Little George's face again. "But like I told you, I know who I'm going to start with."

The youngest McManus said nothing as he stared at the gun barrel.

Connor saw the man's hands were shaking. He was either going to draw or fold.

Aaron McManus stepped forward. "Mister, I'll help you move that body."

"Aaron, no," Little George said. "Don't give in to him. He ain't gonna shoot. He ain't got the guts."

Hicks pulled back the hammer of his Colt. The four distinct sounds it made as it was cocked seemed to echo in the silence that had suddenly fallen over the room.

Little George McManus blanched.

Looks like it's fold, Connor thought. He felt a small surge of relief.

"Burl," Aaron said. "Take Georgie home. I'll be along in a bit."

Burl grunted and pulled his brother toward the door. As they passed by Aaron, he grabbed Little George's sleeve and then removed his pistol from its holster.

"What you doing?" Little George said.

"Holding on to this till you sober up," Aaron said.

"You son of bitc—"

Before he could finish Burl McManus clubbed his youngest brother on the side of the head. Little George's legs went rubbery and Burl picked him up and slung him over his shoulder like a sack of potatoes. He stared at Hicks and said, "He's too drunk to fight, but when he sobers up, him and me are gonna come back."

Hicks slowly lowered the hammer of his Colt and let his arm drop to his side then winked at the big man. "Like I said before, you better be sure you've reloaded by then."

When the last of the patrons had exited, Hicks moved to the edge of the door and peered outside. Connor moved up also. From his vantage point, it appeared as though the crowd was dispersing. Men were either walking or riding away. He saw Burl McManus place his brother over the front of a horse and then mount the steed. One of the other McManus hands undid a horse Connor assumed was Little George's and towed it behind him after mounting. A retching sound began and Connor smirked as he saw a stream of vomit draining from Little George McManus. His big brother's horse jockeyed back and forth obviously uncomfortable as the puke struck his foreleg. Burl swore and rode off with Little George doing a hiccupping cough as the overburdened horse began a quick trot.

"You want some help moving that body?" Aaron McManus asked, coming up behind them. Connor saw the man was wearing a gun on his right side, but it was facing handle-out, making it accessible with a left-handed cross-draw. Then he remembered the deformed right hand and wondered about Aaron's proficiency. He had a slender build, too, which didn't exude a lot of toughness of formidability. Connor suddenly felt a pang of sorrow for him, and wondered what it was like being the oldest and least physically able in a family of bullies and braggarts. He knew from experience that type of situation wasn't pretty, but this Aaron McManus seemed to have weathered it well enough.

"Let's give the street a minute or so more to clear," Hicks said. He whistled to the bartender. "After we leave, you lock these doors and don't open them until tomorrow. Got it?"

"Hey, mister," a feminine voice called out from the staircase across the room.

Hicks glanced over at her.

Connor noticed she was the same blonde girl that Little George had been menacing.

"I think there might be one more drunk upstairs," she said, pointing to the row of room at the top of the stairs. "You wanna check?"

Hicks motioned for Connor to do so, and the girl said, "No. It's gotta be you."

Connor and Hicks exchanged looks and Connor grinned.

"Guess she's got an eye for what she likes and who she wants," he said.

Hicks glanced at Aaron McManus, appeared to size him up, then moved to the girl and went up the staircase.

Connor turned and continued to survey the street area.

Aaron McManus assumed the position Hicks had taken.

"I just want you to know that it was the liquor talking," he said. "My little brother ain't really a bad sort."

Connor was having none of it, even though he knew the man was just being defensive about his sibling. "Tell that to that girl whose hair he was pulling. Or that lynch mob he was trying to fire up."

Aaron McManus didn't reply.

After about five minutes Hicks came down the stairs alone with his gun holstered and a smile on his face.

Connor wondered what had gone on up there, but he didn't figure it had been long enough for any kind of carnal encounter. Still the expression on Hicks's face told him that it hadn't been totally devoid of significance either.

Hicks motioned to the bartender and then to the doors. "Lock 'em up."

The man grunted an agreement.

As they moved through the doors Connor raised an eyebrow.

"Find anything?"

Hicks shook his head. "Just a pillow rolled up

under a blanket. Sorta looked like it could've been somebody, but it wasn't."

It seemed to Connor that Hicks had been up there a bit longer than it would take to throw a blanket off a bed, but he sensed that Hicks didn't want to converse in front of McManus. They walked in silence to the body that still lay in the street. Connor tried to make out the state of the blood stains, but in the dim moonlight it was virtually impossible. He held the shotgun out to Hicks and then stooped to grab the body under the arms. Aaron McManus bent down and encircled the corpse's leg with his left arm. They rose in unison and began walking toward the undertaker's place. When they got there Hicks pounded on the door several times. No one responded, and he repeated the movement with harder strikes.

Finally a woman's voice called out from inside: "Who's there?"

"Open up in the name of the law," Hicks said, grinning widely. In a lower voice he added, "Never got to say that before."

Just as the dead weight of Percy Louis was beginning to take its toll on both him and Aaron McManus, Connor heard a shuffling noise inside and then the jangle of keys, followed by the scraping sound of a key being inserted into a lock. The door swung open and a man in a long nightgown stood there holding a ring of keys in one hand and a lighted lamp in the other. His head was bald on the top with whisks of white hair sticking out in all directions from the fringe on the sides. A pair of pince-nez spectacles sat on the bridge of his nose and his face lit up with a smile as he saw the body.

"Another customer, eh?" he said, holding the lamp near the corpse's face. He recoiled and took a step back. "Oh my."

"Something wrong?" Hicks asked.

"This man's a Negro," the undertaker said.

"He's also dead," Hicks said. "Step aside."

The man did so and Connor and McManus carried the body inside. The undertaker scurried along, directing them to the back of the house and cackling about who was going to pay for the services he would render.

"You're worried about getting paid?" Hicks said.

"Yes. I'm afraid I am. The Negroes haven't exactly been my most lucrative clients. And a businessman has to take such things into consideration."

"Well, we'll be bringing over another one from the sheriff's office in a bit," Hicks said.

"Another Negro?" the undertaker asked.

"No, the deputy."

"Well," the undertaker said as a smile crested the mouth on the under-slung jaw. "Am I correct in assuming that the sheriff will pay for that one?"

"Just tell us where to put this one, will you?" Connor said.

"Certainly. Place him on that table over there."

They put the body on a long wooden table. In the dim light Connor saw a set of silver tools lined up in a holder sitting off to the right. A bit farther he saw a hook extending from the wall. Even in the darkness he could tell that a set of fancy clothes hung on a hanger fastened to the hook. He looked at Hicks, who winked.

"Give me that lamp," Hicks said.

"Oh, yes," the undertaker said. "Of course."

Hicks held the lamp above the dead man's chest and pointed to the blood crusted on the front of his shirt.

"Take a look," he said to Aaron McManus.

He leaned over and perused the stained cloth.

"So?"

"Now pull open his shirt."

McManus stared at Hicks for a second, and then did as instructed. His face twitched slightly as the holes of two bullet wounds became visible.

Hicks held the lamp closer to the corpse's chest.

"There are two bullet holes," he said. "Take a look."

McManus did so.

"This man was shot in his front side," Hicks said. "At close range."

McManus was silent for a time, and then said, "So what?"

"So," Hicks continued, "you want to explain to me how a man, who's riding away from the crowd that's supposedly firing at him, gets hit twice in the front of his chest?"

McManus said nothing.

Hicks brought his free hand up and poked him in the chest twice.

"And," Hicks said, "while you're at it, explain to me why your two brothers, along with those other ranch hands from the Dominion, were spread out across the street shooting at those Phantom Riders and blocking me from getting a good shot at them."

"What are you insinuating?" McManus asked. "That my brothers intentionally wanted those ne'er-do-wells to get away?"

"I'm saying they were blocking my aim. And they were firing way too high to hit anything."

"And they sure couldn't shoot a man in his front from behind," Connor added.

Aaron McManus stood in silence for close to half a minute.

Hicks turned to the undertaker and held the lamp close to his own chest.

"You see this badge?"

The undertaker's head bobbled up and down, like a ball being bounced by a child.

"I'm giving you a lawful order not to move the body of this man from this room," Hicks said. "There's going to be a trial tomorrow and I may want to show this to the judge."

"Well," the undertaker said. "There is a bit of a time factor to be considered. It is late autumn, and the days still tend to get a bit warm. And we all know what happens to the dearly departed in the heat, don't we?" He flashed a weak smile and when Hicks didn't reply or agree he went on. "It unfortunately becomes a matter of … Well, odor. It tends to worsen as the heat of the day commences. So I'd rather, if we have to, place the unfortunate individual out back by my outhouse until such time as—"

"You're worried about the smell?" Hicks said.

The undertaker shrugged and nodded.

"Well, I am too," Hicks said. "I'm also worried about horseflies eating away at the wounds and destroying evidence. You keep him in here, and you keep him covered up. Got it?"

"Well, yes," the undertaker said. "But the odor—"

"If I find out you didn't do what I told you," Hicks said. "You'll have more than a bad smell to worry about." He glanced over at the hanging suit. "But I'll tell you what I will do. I'll take that fancy-go-to-meeting suit with me and hang it in the sheriff's office for you. That way the odor won't settle too deep into the clothes."

The undertaker rubbed his hands together in what appeared to be frustration.

"But—"

"No buts," Hicks said, and gestured for Connor to get the clothes on the hanger.

Looks like Rance's got his court duds back, Connor thought.

✳✳✳✳✳✳

THE DOMINION

Big George McManus heard the approach of the horse and peered out the window. Kandy rode up on his big, golden stallion and reined the animal to a stop by the front hitching post. He had a frown on his face as he swung down from the saddle. McManus moved to the door and had it open before Kandy could knock.

"About damn time you got here," McManus said.

Kandy grinned. "Had to change horses, boss."

"Where are the rest of them?" Big George stepped back to allow him entrance.

"Tidying things up," Kandy said, removing his hat. "Jasper got shot."

"What?" The gesture of respect did little to assuage the anger McManus was feeling. It meant that someone didn't follow his instructions. "Dammit. He stay on his horse at least?"

"He did. Till we made it outta town, anyway. He was hit pretty bad so I slung him over my saddle till we got to the canyon."

"And you left behind what you were supposed to?"

"One dead nigger homesteader." He grinned. "That part went just like you wanted. Even had him sitting on one of Bardwell's horses beforehand."

"How bad's Jasper?"

Kandy's eyebrows rose and fell. "I don't expect he'll make it through the night. The rest of the boys are feeding him booze to keep him numb right now. Ah, I don't suppose you want me to go fetch Doc Ingraham, do you?"

McManus answered the question with a telling frown.

"How'd it happen to Jasper? I told Burl to have all of the men make sure they kept their aim way high."

"It was that gunslinger fella," Kandy said. "Came outta nowhere."

The gunslinger, McManus thought. It was getting pretty clear that something had to be done about him.

"You think you could take him in a fair fight?" Big George asked.

Kandy shrugged. "I reckon. But from what I seen, he's pretty damn good. But I mean, I probably can."

There was a trace of doubt in his voice. Big George considered this and placed a hand on the other man's shoulder. Kandy was his most capable man, but that gunslinger was like greased lightning in a bottle.

"We'll deal with him when the time comes," McManus said. "When things are in our favor."

Kandy flashed a smile.

Big George could sense the other man's relief.

"There's something else," Kandy said.

"Now what?"

Holding his hand up and pointing downward at his boots, Kandy said, "I lost one of my spurs."

McManus snorted and smiled, then, as the realization of what this possibly could mean, let the smile dissipate.

"Where?" he asked.

"I ain't exactly sure," Kandy said. "I'm thinking it was after we rode out, but it coulda been while we all was still in town."

McManus swore. "That ain't telling me a lot. Them damn things are so noticeable …" He blew out an exasperated breath. "Why in the hell were you wearing them in the first place?"

Kandy's gaze moved to the floor.

"Sorry, boss," he muttered. "I was gonna take 'em

off, honest. But it took us longer than we thought to bag that nigger and then get him set onto that horse once we got to town. I plum forgot."

Big George stared at him balefully, saying nothing.

After a few seconds Kandy flashed a half-grin. "You shoulda seen how we done it. I had Jasper down the street between two buildings holding the dead nigger on the horse, just waiting. Then we come riding by from the other end a shooting. Couldn't a worked out any better. That stupid deputy was walking along with a food basket and couldn't even get his gun out. I bagged him good. Twice." He paused to lick his lips, like he was relishing the residual taste of a cinnamon stuffed muffin. "Then Thorpe come stepping on out and I shot him too, but I think I only winged him. We passed by the saloon and Burl and Little George was there waiting and formed a line right across the street, just like we planned."

"You mean like I planned," Big George said.

"Ah, yeah, like you said boss."

"What about Aaron? Was he there, too?"

"He was, but I didn't see him do no shooting."

Big George grunted in approval. He knew Aaron couldn't shoot worth a tinker's damn, and that's why he'd explicitly told Burl not to include him in the ruse.

Overall, McManus was pleased. Except for a few minor snags, like the spur and Jasper getting shot, things had gone well. The Phantom Riders had made their attempt to break their leader out of jail, and in the process shot the sheriff and his deputy.

And all this occurring on the eve of the trial. The deck had been stacked. It would give Tiddy more than enough nails to pound into Bardwell's coffin. Regardless, the two-bit shyster had said a guilty verdict was all but a foregone conclusion. But still, even with a stacked deck, there was always a chance of an unlucky deal.

"You say you winged Thorpe?" McManus asked. "How about that deputy?"

"Head shot. He looked to be a goner."

The sound of distant hoof-beats became audible.

Must be Burl, Little George, and the boys, McManus thought. He hoped that Burl had done as instructed with the rest of the plan.

Juanita came running into the room crying. McManus whirled.

"*Señor, Señor,*" she cried "Freddie. *Es muerto.* He is dead."

Kandy's mouth pulled into a taut line as he looked up at McManus.

"I'm right sorry to hear that, boss," Kandy said.

McManus shook his head fractionally.

He hadn't been shocked by the words. He'd been prepared for them. It was almost a relief to hear them finally spoken, and they didn't even sting that much. He'd come to terms with his third-born's death, and, all things considered, it wasn't such a bad feeling. One less complication for him to worry about down the road, and it also presented an opportunity. With the governor arriving, the somewhat untoward nature of Freddie's last confrontation in town, as well as his unseemly reputation, would be put to rest under the cloak of a sudden demise. The focus would be on Big George McManus courageously bearing up under the strain of having to bury his son.

The thought of playing the martyr had never appealed to him, but this was one time where it could work for him.

Milk the situation for all its worth, he thought. Lord knows that boy cost me in time and money and status with all of his damn tomfoolery. Especially with them damn saloon girls he was always messing with.

The approaching horses had stopped in the front courtyard. Big George went to the window and saw Burl dismount and pull someone from the front of his horse. It appeared to be Little George. Burl cradled him in his arms and barked some instructions to the men with him. Suddenly Big George was worried that his youngest son had been shot. He strode to the door and pulled it open.

Outside the night air was cool.

"What happened to him?" Big George asked.

"He's drunker than a skunk," Burl said, carrying the still limp form through the doorway. "Me and Aaron had to disarm him and knock him out to keep him from getting himself killed."

"What? You laid hands on your brother?"

"Had to, Pa. Like I told you, he was outta his head. Gonna try to draw against that damn gunslinger."

Dammit, thought Big George. That gunslinger again.

"Put him over on that chair," he said.

Burl walked across the room and laid his brother down as easily as if he were setting down a cup and saucer. He stood up and turned back to the other two men with a broad grin.

"Hey, Kandy," he said, reaching into his pants pocket. "I got something for you." He pulled out the long spoon of the silver spur. "Seems one them Phantom Riders left it in the street after they finished shooting up the town. I picked it up so's nobody'd see."

Kandy nodded a "thanks" and accepted the item.

"You're lucky," Big George said. "Now get rid of those damn things and don't let me see you wearing them until after all this is over."

Kandy nodded again and headed for the door.

"That all the thanks I get?" Burl said.

Kandy left without any comment.

"What the hell's the matter with him?" Burl's head flicked as the sound of a keening wail drifted out from back in the house. "What's that?"

"Juanita," Big George said. He tried to muster up an affectation of the grief he actually did not feel. "It's Freddie."

"Freddie?" Burl's jaw dropped open.

Big George thought his second born resembled a bewildered horse.

"He's gone," Big George said.

Tears welled up in Burl's eyes. "Aw, damn. And I wasn't even here."

Big George placed a hand on his son's shoulder.

"He went quietly in his sleep," he said. "He wouldn't even have known you were there."

Burl wiped at his eyes, and then his nose as he straightened up.

"Guess you're right. But I'm still mad as hell." Burl punched his big fist into the palm of his left hand with a resounding smack. "I want to *o* something."

The last thing Big George needed at the moment was another of his sons making a rash move when they were so close to tying this all up with a nice, pretty bow.

"You just keep your head," he said. "There's a reckoning coming, but we got to do things smart."

Burl looked at him and his huge head rocked up and down in silent agreement.

"So what we gonna do with Freddie?"

"Bury him," Big George said. "And then figure out our next move."

✳✳✳✳✳✳

THE B & D RAILROAD, CALIFORNIA

O'Rourke poked his finger through the one of the twin holes in his wide brimmed hat as the train continued its rocking journey through the darkness. At least the lamps in the car provided enough light for him to assess the damage. The holes were clearly visible and made the hat as conspicuous as a mouse on a wedding cake.

So much for the tenant of maintaining anonymity, he thought.

He heard a snort.

"You still got your britches in a bunch over me shooting that damn hat?" Quint asked.

The bounty hunter was sitting across from him with his own hat titled over his face. The man's long legs intruded under the seat on O'Rourke's side.

"I was *not* amused," O'Rourke said.

"Hell, if'n' I'd a knowed how prissy you was gonna be about it, I'd a put a couple more through it."

O'Rourke frowned and Quint laughed. He reached into his pocket and removed his pipe and tobacco pouch. After packing the bowl, he padded his pockets until he came up with a match. The train began slowing amid the accompanying squeal of brakes and metal wheels skidding on iron rails.

"Looks like we're due for another water stop," Quint said. He flicked the primer of the match with his heavy thumbnail and held the flame over the open portion of the pipe bowl. "I ever tell you about riding these rails with rich folks so they could stop and shoot the buffalos?"

"Several times," O'Rourke said. He saw by Quint's reaction that he had not reacted favorably to the retort.

Well, that's too damn bad, O'Rourke thought. He doesn't have to like it. And he's got too much time invested in this venture to up and quit.

O'Rourke watched as Quint puffed on the pipe, getting it going. He blew twin plumes of smoke out of his nostrils.

"Well, rather than me telling you what you already heard," Quint said. "Maybe it's time you gave me the lowdown on just who I'm supposed to shoot for you when we get to this damn town. What's the name of it again?"

O'Rourke winced at Quint's loud tone and careless verbiage. There was one passenger in particular O'Rourke was concerned about: a middle-aged man in a blue suit wearing spectacles, seated only three seats away. The man appeared to be well educated and was reading a thick book by the lamplight. Additionally, he had the aura of importance and authority about him, and he was not slumbering.

Definitely not the kind of person O'Rourke wanted to be within earshot of slipshod conversation.

"Sweetwater." O'Rourke paused and pretended to stretch while his eyes danced around the interior of the train car. The official looking passenger had seemed to take no notice. Neither had any of the other passengers seated around them, most of whom looked to be sleeping or at least trying very hard to slumber. O'Rourke knew it was not good form to discuss company business in the presence of possible prying ears. He gestured for Quint to stand and then headed to the end of the car where there were no people. Quint followed, leaving a trail of foul smelling tobacco fumes.

O'Rourke's eyes shot in both directions and, when he was satisfied that there was no one around, reached into his jacket pocket and removed a folded piece of paper. To his dismay, it felt damp to the point where it was almost sodden. He realized that he'd been sweating profusely, and blamed the buffoon next to him for causing him so much consternation.

Shooting holes in my new hat, he thought.

His chagrin increased as he unfolded the paper and found that the printed letters on the WANTED poster had bled onto the drawing of the pictured face making it virtually undistinguishable.

"What the hell's that?" Quint asked.

Not wishing to display his faux pas, O'Rourke quickly refolded the paper and said, "It's a picture of the man we want. Evidently, it got a bit damaged."

"From you sweatin' like a hog, no doubt." Quint blew a cloud of smoke into O'Rourke's face, causing him to cough.

The bounty hunter snickered.

"Whatever," O'Rourke said, finally managing to regain a clean breath. "And I'll thank you not to do that again. I'm very sensitive to tobacco smoke."

"You can thank me when you pay me. Now who the hell is it we're gunnin' for?"

This buffoon speaks in such a loud tone, O'Rourke thought. Damn him.

He surreptitiously glanced around again, looking for anyone who might have overheard. They were far enough away from the other passengers that he felt reasonably sure that no one had been eavesdropping. Leaning closer, despite the obnoxious pipe odor, he said in a hushed undertone, "There's a man, a gunslinger. His name is River Hicks."

CHAPTER 11

SWEETWATER

Abby heard the scratching of a key in the lock of the hotel door and immediately sat up in the bed and gripped the Winchester. Outside it was still dark. She worked the lever as the door slowly opened and then she heard River's low whisper.

"I don't particularly want to get shot this early in the morning, so I'd appreciate it if you'd aim that someplace else."

Abby lowered the gun. "And just how was I supposed to know it was you?"

She was still miffed that last night Hicks had told her to go back to the hotel room while he and Connor stood guard at the jail all night in case the Phantom Riders returned.

"Why can't I stay there too?" she'd asked. "I can shoot as good as him."

While she actually didn't totally believe she was

a superior marksman and gun-hand to her brother, she'd said the words out of anger and spite. And she'd looked directly at Connor when she'd uttered them.

Hicks had walked her back across the street as he explained to her that he needed her up in the room to provide much needed support. He called it "taking the high ground," and reminded her that he'd explained the concept to both her and her brother numerous times.

She remembered that he had, but that didn't make the bitterness any easier to swallow.

Realizing she couldn't win, she'd acquiesced, but only reluctantly. She'd stayed awake most of the night, but eventually got bored just staring at the empty street. Eventually she'd sneaked downstairs and removed a pen, inkwell, and paper from the front desk and gone quietly back upstairs. Then, after lighting the lamp, she'd taken to doing some drawing. The five pieces of metal that she'd found in the stable had been bothering her. She'd saved them all and took them out, arranging them on the top of the dresser in different designs. Something was there. She was certain of it. They fitted together in some way. It was like working one of those picture puzzles she'd seen once.

So she'd taken to arranging them and then sketching the patterns. After about an hour she'd come up with what she thought was the answer, and she couldn't wait to tell River.

Outside, somewhere in the town, a rooster crowed.

"What time is it, anyway?" she asked.

"A little before dawn," Hicks said. "I just came up to tell you that me and Connor gotta ride out for a bit."

"Ride out? Where?"

"We gotta check on something." He struck a match and lit the wick of the lamp for her. Then he took notice of a wrapped handkerchief sitting on the dresser. "What's this?"

Abby sprang off the bed. "Some pieces of metal I found in the stable. That big dumb blacksmith ain't too good at cleaning up. And, I think I figured something out."

Hicks held the lamp next to the stack of papers.

"These look kinda interesting," he said. "What're they supposed to be?"

"That's what I've been trying to tell you," Abby said. "Remember that piece of metal that my horse stepped on yesterday? In the stables?"

Hicks nodded.

"Well," she pointed to the handkerchief. "I found four more pieces in there yesterday when I was cleaning up." She pulled open the handkerchief and picked up one of the metal pieces. "Look at the edges."

Hicks ran his finger over the end of one long piece.

"It's kinda rough," she said. "You can tell it's been cut from something it was part of, can't you?"

"Looks like it."

"Well," Abby continued. "It got so boring in here last night, I tried to figure out how they fit together. Like the pieces of a puzzle." She pointed again to the paper, which had a pair of jagged lines that were the mirror images of each other. "I was drawing different patterns."

"You're a pretty good artist." He set the lamp down and headed for the door. "I'm running behind. I need you to go down to the sheriff's office and help him and Rance get ready for the court trial."

"But, why can't I go with you and Connor?"

Hicks shook his head. "It's more important that you stay here till we get back. With Thorpe shot and his deputy dead, Rance and Bardwell need somebody who knows one end of gun from the other." He grinned and gestured toward the Winchester on the bed. "And I know you do."

"But—"

He held up his hand. "Remember what I said before? No buts."

Glumly, Abby folded her handkerchief with the metal pieces and jammed it into her pocket before picking up the Winchester.

I didn't even get a chance to tell him anything, she thought. It's always like that. Connor and him get to do all the fun things. Her lips puckered into a pout.

"Well, are you at least gonna tell me where you're going and what you'll be doing?" she asked.

Hicks smiled. "We're going looking for a lost canyon."

✳✳✳✳✳

"A lost canyon?" Connor said as he and Hicks rode out of Sweetwater at a fast trot toward a slice of pinkish orange encroaching against a slate gray sky.

Hicks didn't answer. He was periodically studying the ground as they went.

"That's what that little gal wanted to tell you last night?" Connor asked.

"Her name's Columbine. And she was grateful for us saving her from Little George McManus. I guess him and his brothers can be kind of mean to a girl, especially when they're drunk."

"Yeah? And that's all she wanted?"

"Well, she wanted a whole lot more from me." Hicks winked at him. "But I told her I was regrettably tied up, upholding the law for the night."

"I'll bet she was disappointed." Connor grinned. "So what else did she say?"

"She told me about the lost canyon. And—" Hicks reined his horse and pointed toward the ground and said, "Look there."

Connor saw several half-moon impressions in a barren section of soft earth. He marveled at Hicks's ability to track and studied his moves every chance he got.

"Looks like they go up that way," Connor said.

As they rode northeast, Hicks continued with his story: "Columbine said that one of the McManus boys, Freddie, the one that got stabbed, took her and another girl to the canyon a while back and kept them there for a night or so." He paused to frown. "Had their way with them. Cut her up real bad."

"That Freddie's a dirty son of a bitch, ain't he?"

"He is. And the devil's most likely waiting right now with a special place in hell for him."

"Let's hope so."

"What else she say?"

"That the reason he cut her up was she seen some of his boys cutting up flour sacks."

"Flour sacks?" Connor thought for a moment, then he understood. "For making masks. So McManus is behind the Phantom Riders?"

"Makes sense, don't it? Especially with would-be sheriff Burl stretching that line of his buddies across the street to keep us from shooting at them last night."

"And him picking up that fancy spur that belonged to that Kandy fella." Connor snorted. "That big, lazy ox wouldn't pick up anything otherwise."

"Tracks veer off that way." Hicks pointed to the left. They followed.

"So this lost canyon … It's on that Dominion spread?"

"I expect. From the way she described the place, it sounds like a small box canyon. Has a couple of wooden shacks, a spring, and enough grass for a bunch of horses to graze there."

Connor had seen those gorges and ravines before, but never one like Hicks described.

"If it's that big, how come Sheriff Thorpe and his posse didn't find it?"

"It's hard to see, unless you know it's there," Hicks said "It's in what they call a declivity."

Connor's brow furrowed. "What's that?"

"A low point in the ground." Hicks gestured toward the horizon. "See there? Looks flat, don't it?"

"Sure does."

"Well, it ain't really. It's curved. And the surface is uneven in places. You seen canyons before when we were in Arizona, remember?"

"Yeah, but not like what you're describing."

"It's the same thing. Water and weather run through the ground wearing away the soil and rocks. Some places wear away, and others are stronger and they form an escarpment."

"A what?"

Hicks smirked. "A cliff. From what Columbine said, this one was probably caused by an underground river. Wore away the ground, formed the canyon."

"How'd you learn so much stuff, River?"

"The result of a misspent youth," Hicks shot him a wry smile. "I had me a lot of schooling once."

Connor always felt amazement at the depth of his mentor's knowledge.

"Appears old man McManus has a particular inhospitable dislike for folks coming onto his land."

Hicks pointed to a large, flat sign with black letters spelling out its message:

THE DOMINION
ABSOLUTELY NO TRESPASSING
YOU WILL BE SHOT ON SIGHT
BY ORDER OF BIG GEORGE McMANUS

The *McM* brand was burned into the wood below the warning.

Hicks stared at the sign for a long half minute, then he grinned.

"The man values his privacy, all right." He gestured toward the trail of the horseshoes. "But it don't look like that sign stopped the Phantom Riders, does it?"

As they went past the sign Connor surveyed the area before them.

"Looks kind dense," he said. "Lots of trees and high grass. How we gonna find it?"

"Columbine said to look for a couple different things. One was that sign back there. She also said there's a tree shaped sorta like a wishbone. Then the entrance to the place. It's supposed to look like an upside-down V. And it's surrounded by flowers."

"Flowers? What kind?"

Hicks winked. "Columbines."

Despite his fatigue of having stayed up most of the night, Connor suddenly felt invigorated. The chase always did that to him. As they rode perhaps 500 yards more Connor noticed the ground became dry and hardened, making the tracks harder to discern. Hicks slapped him on the shoulder and said, "Over there."

He glanced up and saw the tree with the twin trunks branching upward from a solid base forming a Y shape—like a wishbone. The ground sloped downward at the base of a hill. Then he caught a glimpse of it: a profusion of colors— reds, whites, yellows, purples, mixed into a nape of green, scaled the upward slant of an upside-down V. Flowers ... Columbines ... A whole passel of them.

"Is that it?" Connor asked.

"I expect." Hicks pointed the left. "Head up that way."

"But the entrance is over there."

"We're not riding into some narrow space where we got no room to turn around if we have to in a hurry." He pointed to the ground. "No tracks coming out."

"You think them Phantom Riders are still hiding out in there?"

"It's a good bet. Despite Burl McManus and his boys blocking the street, I got off a shot and think I winged one of them."

"So how we gonna handle this?" Connor asked.

"We're going to scout the rim above it so we can look down and see what we can see."

They rode up the sloping incline adjacent to the upside down V. After they'd gone about a hundred yards, Hicks gestured toward a cluster of shrubbery surrounding a scrawny tree. He rode over and dismounted, then tied the reins of his bridle to a jutting branch. Connor did the same and they crept to the edge of the escarpment. Hicks crouched down and flattened out onto his belly as he got a few feet from the edge. Connor crawled up next to him and peered over the side and down into the widening crevice in the earth.

Approximately forty feet below them lay a small box canyon. To their left was what appeared to be a long, narrow passage way that wound between overhanging outcroppings of rock. It extended back toward the entrance, but was hardly visible due to the overlapping of the bulging sides. The area to their right expanded outward into a circular enclosure about a hundred yards long and maybe sixty yards wide. A pool of standing water lay off to one side and a group of ten horses were tethered together to a rope strung between two posts near the pond. Five saddles had been slung onto a fence line next to the tethering point. There was grass on the ground as well. Two wooden shacks, the smaller one hardly much more than an enclosed lean-to, sat opposite the horses; a chimney was on the roof of the larger structure. A privy was behind it. A broken whiskey bottle lay on the ground in between.

Below all was quiet although the ears on a couple of the horses pricked upward.

"Looks like they picked up on our scent," Connor said.

Hicks continued to study the scene then turned his head toward him.

"It also looks like their riders are still down there, most likely sleeping off a drunk."

"How we gonna handle this?"

Hicks was silent for the better part of thirty seconds or so, during which he kept glancing back and forth.

"I got me an idea," he said finally. "But it ain't gonna be easy."

✶✶✶✶✶✶

SWEETWATER

Abby finished wiping the ink off each of the five metal pieces and replacing them in her handkerchief. James Rance stood next to her holding his fancy, Sunday-go-to-meetin' clothes with an expansive grin on his face. Although she didn't want to say anything to him, she felt the suit had retained the scent of the dead. She kind of liked him, though, now that he was cleaned up. And he'd been very complimentary to her after she'd shown him her drawings and explained their significance. In fact, he'd gone so far as to say she'd helped immensely.

"This is really significant," he said. "Make sure you bring the ink well and a cloth as well as all of those pieces."

"I can do that," she said. "But I don't really want to talk in front of all those people."

His brow furrowed. "Unfortunately, you'll have to. I can't introduce the evidence myself without calling you to testify."

Abby felt the dread encroaching upon her, as sure as if someone were spreading a shawl over her face.

Rance raised his hand and patted her shoulder. It was gentle contact, but it sent a strange shiver through her.

"It'll be all right," he said. "I promise."

She nodded and marveled at the change that had come over him. He hadn't had a drink since River had spoken harshly to him the day before, and with the haircut and bath he'd taken, he didn't smell so bad anymore, despite the aromatic suit. His face was long and kind of handsome in a tenderfoot sort of way, but his jaw was covered with a modicum of burgeoning stubble.

Sheriff Thorpe shifted off the bunk on the other side of the office and blinked. He held his arm stiffly and grunted in pain as he pulled on his boots and then tried to get up. Rance immediately set his suit down on the desk and went to help the sheriff. Abby fingered the dark cotton fabric as it lay there and wondered how the clothes would look on Rance. It was too bad he didn't have some charcoal and wax to shine up his boots a bit, but she didn't suppose anybody in this town would notice. It was going to be enough of a shock seeing Rance sober and all dressed up. She hoped it would make the difference and get John Henry acquitted. In her heart she knew he couldn't have killed that man.

"Thanks, Rance," Thorpe said, hobbling along. "Still feeling a little woozy. If you could help me out back to the outhouse, I'd appreciate it."

"Sure thing," Rance said.

"And, Abby," the sheriff said. "If you could run out to the pump and get us some water so we can shave?"

Abby straightened up and grabbed the bucket in one hand and the Winchester in the other and went to the door. Outside the main street was deserted, but the sun was now hanging over the eastern horizon like an orange ball that hurt her eyes to look at.

Sighing, she wondered what Connor and River were doing.

******

THE LOST CANYON

Connor tightened River's leather gloves over his own hands and gripped the rope. He and Hicks had tied their two lariats together to form a length long enough to allow him passage down the side of the cliff to the floor of the lost canyon. The hardest part, he knew, was going to be getting over the prominent outcropping at the top of the escarpment.

"You ready?" Hicks asked. His face appeared taunt and almost grim looking. Connor figured that Hicks would have much rather made the decent himself, but common sense dictated that Connor was the better choice. He was younger and more agile, not to mention a few pounds lighter, although not by much, the way he was growing. Still, if the outcropping gave way causing the climber to fall, Connor felt he could survive the jump more so than Hicks. Plus, River was the better shot, and having him on the high ground with the Winchester was a safety factor against any of the Phantom Riders waking up and starting trouble.

Connor nodded, flipped the coil of rope behind him, and started his backward walk over the crest of the cliff. He'd gone but a few steps when he began to feel an immense pressure drawing him downward. The rope crackled over the bulging rock as Connor's boots struggled for purchase. Slipping and sliding with each downward step, he suddenly felt himself suspended in the air as the side of the cliff jutted inward. Connor dropped several feet, the leather gloves heating up as he gripped the rope in a near-free fall, resisting the urge to cry out. He swung his legs, trying to catch the rope and curl it around his boot to slow the descent, but it proved as elusive as a sidewinder slicing through the high weeds. For what seemed like an eternity he spun around and around in dizzying fashion as he slid, his palms feeling the burn now even through the gloves. Finally one of his feet snared the swirling rope and Connor closed his legs together, clamping his boots hard against each other, the rope in between.

His descent slowed considerably and he saw that he was nearly at the bottom. After clenching the rope so hard as to come to a complete stop, Connor hung suspended about fifteen feet above the ground, his body slowly rotating, giving him a three hundred-sixty degree view of the canyon. He felt his senses return to normal and then lowered himself down the rest of the way.

It was good to be on solid ground once more, even though the sandy surface felt somehow moist and soft under his boots. He gave the rope two sharp jerks, signaling Hicks that he had reached the bottom successfully. After feeling the acknowledging pull from Hicks, Connor pulled the end of the rope upward forming a large loop, and secured it with a bowline knot. It was part of their plan that if he needed immediate extrication, he was to place the loop under his arms and yell, "Wishbone," at which time Hicks would slap the flank of the horse, to which he'd tied the other end of the rope. Connor would be pulled up the side of the cliff at a rapid pace while Hicks provided cover fire with the rifle from up top.

It wasn't a perfect plan, and Connor had his doubts that it would work. For one thing, he was worried that he'd never be able to keep from smashing into the overhang of rock above him, and even if he could, the abrasiveness of the surface would no doubt be excruciatingly painful.

Best not to let it get to that point, he thought as he undid the leather thong securing his gun and removed the Colt from its holster. He crept along in a crouch, looking and listening.

Nothing moved ... The only sound an occasional snort from one of the horses.

Easy, boy, he thought. I'll be getting to you in a bit.

The soil under his boots squeaked with a rasping sound as he ran. He made it to the larger of the two structures and peered in one of the windows, which was just a squared out open frame cut into the wall. It was dark inside, but he could hear the sound of several men snoring.

Sleeping off a drunk, he thought. Just like River figured.

Connor moved toward the second building, pausing to pull open the door of the outhouse slightly. It was empty.

Moving the smaller shack, he stopped beside the door and readied himself. After a quick intake of breath, he pushed open the door and moved immediately inside, hooking to the right. Hicks had taught him never to stand in an open doorway.

"You'll silhouette yourself," his mentor had told him. "Giving anybody inside a real nice target to shoot at."

Light poured inside sweeping over a pair of extended legs. Connor leveled his pistol at the figure and cocked back the hammer, but as the door swung back slightly, his eyes adjusted to the dim lighting and Connor saw that the man wasn't moving at all ... Not even with breathing. A large stain spread out on both sides of the supine figure and Connor heard the buzzing of flies. As he moved closer the man's face became perceivable: lips curled back over gnarled teeth in a rigor grin with flies crawling over the slack cheeks and onto the half-open, hazy eyes.

Looks like River did more than just wing one, Connor thought.

Glancing back over his shoulder, he checked for any sign or sounds of movement behind him.

So far all was still.

His eyes shot around the room and saw a six-gun next to a pile of tangled cloth on a nearby table. After sticking the gun into his belt, he examined the pile of cloth. Upon closer inspection, he saw that it was actually eight of the Phantom Riders masks. Leaning against the edge of the table was something else: a long, round bar. It was a branding iron with the letter P inside a circle ... The Phantom Riders' brand. As he picked it up he caught a whiff of stench and scrutinized the end of the iron.

It stank and, holding in the sliver of light provided by the open door, he could see what appeared to be dried blood and something else on the end.

A dead man's skin, maybe?

Connor saw a crumpled four sack on the floor and grabbed it. He stuffed the masks and the branding iron inside the sack and went to the door. This time he heard something: footsteps in the moist clay … a hacking cough … a loud fart, then a grunt of displeasure.

Someone was heading for the outhouse.

It wouldn't do if he caught a glimpse of the dangling rope.

Connor waited until he heard the door to the privy slam shut, and then he moved quickly to the side of the outhouse and set the sack down.

Inside he could hear the sounds of the occupant reliving himself. After hearing more grunts, the occupant became silent, and then Connor heard what sounded like vomiting.

No time like the present, he thought, figuring it would give him the advantage if the vomiting man had his back to the door.

Jumping around to the front side Connor pulled open the door and saw the man inside crouched over one of the two holes puking.

He stepped closer and grabbed the long mane of hair with his right hand, pulled back, then slammed the man's forehead down onto the wood as hard as he could.

The man howled in pain.

Connor repeated the slamming move.

Another grunt emanated from the man.

Connor then brought the barrel of his Colt down onto the man's head three times. The first two sounding like sharp knocks, the last more sodden. The man groaned once and heaved a sigh.

Connor kicked him in the side and when he heard no response, assumed the man was out, at least for the moment.

But how to secure him?

Then it came to him. He stepped out of the outhouse and closed the door. Moving next to it, he put his back against the side wall and shoved. It wobbled once and then the bottom lifted upward. Connor twisted his body and, careful not to fall into the pit, continued to push the wooden structure onto its side. It flopped down and he rolled it so that the door was on the bottom. When the occupant regained consciousness he'd have to wait for someone to roll the privy over, or else try to wiggle through one of the holes. Chances were also good that he might be able to kick his way out, but Connor wasn't planning on waiting around to see which option the man would choose. Instead, he stepped around to grab the burlap sack. The pungent odor rose upward from the hole next to him and it was so strong that Connor was momentarily worried it might rouse the others in the larger shack. He wasted no time worrying about it as he ran toward the group of horses. When he got to them a couple of the horses snorted and brayed in alarm.

They're smelling my fear, he thought, and paused

to stroke the neck of the closest animal. The move quieted the beast and the anxiety in the others seemed to lessen appreciably.

Connor turned and looked to the top of the escarpment.

Hicks rose from his crouch and waved.

Connor waved back and pointed to the horses, then to the passageway out of the canyon.

Hicks nodded and disappeared. The dangling rope began to creep up the side of the cliff, snapping and whipping to and fro like an ascending snake.

Connor holstered his gun and studied the hobbling line. It was strung between two posts and had each of the ten horses secured to it by roped nooses. Moving to the far end, he took out his knife and cut the end of the rope securing the line to the post. The horse closest to him stepped back and forth, obviously feeling the freedom of the restraining line. Connor reached up to stroke the animal's snout, but the beast pulled away. He walked slowly but steadily up to the front of the tether line and stroked the nose of the first horse. This one seemed more amenable to the touch.

"Okay, boy," Connor said in a gentle whisper. "I'm gonna take you and your friends outta here."

He slit the end of the rope securing the tether line to the front post then moved alongside the first horse, still holding the rope in his hand. After petting the animal a few more times, he slid the burlap sack over the beast's back and onto its opposite side. The horse snorted once, but stayed in place.

So far, so good, Connor thought as he grabbed

a hank of the horse's thick mane and jumped upward and onto the animal's back. The horse bucked
slightly, but was apparently used to a rider. Riding
bareback was something Connor had grown up
doing, so he was used to managing an animal without a saddle or bridle. He looped the rope around
the horse's long nose and doubled it back, giving
himself a bit more control. Then he brought the
heels of his boots into the beast's flanks, urging it
forward. The others behind began to follow their
leader and Connor encouraged a brisker pace as
they approached the narrowing passageway. He
had to duck his head as they entered it and the
clopping of the hooves made an echoing sound that
he was certain would wake the dead.

Or at the very least, the group of slumbering
drunks, he thought.

The horse was obviously familiar with the trek
and trotted with alacrity through the winding crevice, the others following. The lighted, upside-down
V at the entranceway grew closer and closer, and finally, after what seemed like an eternity to Connor,
the semi-darkness evaporated and they burst into
the sunlight. The air felt clean and fresh on his face.

He saw Hicks with their horses about fifty feet
away.

River was astride his mount holding his Winchester to his shoulder. Connor continued to ride
past him, towing the ungainly team. As he passed
he heard the report of the rifle. A couple of seconds
later a horrendous roar sounded behind him that
almost knocked him to the ground. Turning, Con-

nor saw a thick black and brown cloud of rising smoke where the upside-down V had been.

He pulled back on the horse's mane, slowing the animal, which had begun to bolt away from the explosion. As the pace slowed to a trot, Hicks came riding up next to him, slipping his Winchester into his scabbard and grinning widely.

"I knew damn well that nitro would come in handy one of these days," he said.

"What about them back in there?" Connor asked.

Hicks smiled as they looked back at the cloud of dust that was still settling around the now crushed opening.

"Damn shame to destroy all them pretty flowers," Hick said. "But I doubt any of them Phantom Riders will be climbing out anytime soon."

CHAPTER 12

SWEETWATER

Inside the sheriff's office Abby watched as Thorpe struggled to get into his tan, chambray shirt. She stepped forward and gently lifted the material over his shoulders.

"Let me help you," she said.

Thorpe seemed to stiffen slightly, but nodded as she adjusted the shirt and buttoned it up.

"I'll take it from there," he said. "Thanks."

She backed away and watched as he labored to stuff the shirttails into his pants.

I could have done that, she thought, and almost said so, feeling a bit mischievous.

After all, Thorpe was a rugged, handsome man. It was obvious that the wound on his shoulder was bothering him, but he nonetheless buckled the gun-belt around his waist and secured the holster to his leg with the dangling twin leather strands. As he straightened up, his mouth worked its way into a smile. She was standing by the side of his desk with a frown on her face.

"Something wrong?" he asked.

"I'm just wondering how you're going to manage to draw that gun if you need to."

Thorpe's smile tightened and it was obvious that he was in significant pain.

"Well, hopefully, I won't have to," he said. "If my two deputies get back. Where did you say they were going?"

"To look for a lost canyon." Abby shrugged. "I wanted to go with them, but River said for me to stay here and help you."

"I can sure use it," he said. "But I'm afraid I could use the two of them being here more."

Abby felt a bit miffed at the comment. She bent over, pulled up the leg of her pants, and withdrew the Trantor pistol from her boot. Holding up the gun, she said, "Listen, I can shoot if I have to."

Thorpe's eyebrows rose in unison. "I don't doubt that, but please, keep it under wraps. We'll not be allowing any guns in the courtroom."

"No guns?"

"Except for me and my deputies. Especially with emotions running so high after that Phantom Riders raid last night."

"You don't believe that John Henry's involved with them, do you?" She replaced the Trantor in her boot, thinking it would be better if no one knew she was wearing it anyway. It wasn't as if she could execute a quick draw, so the veil of concealment was her ally.

Thorpe shrugged, then immediately winced.

"Ah, it don't matter none what I believe. At this point it's gonna be up to the jury."

As he spoke Rance and John Henry pushed open the door and entered the office area. Abby could tell that both of them were nervous, although John Henry's face had an almost serene expression.

"And how many Negroes you think'll be on that jury, Mister Thorpe," Bardwell said.

Thorpe didn't reply.

Rance patted Bardwell's shoulder. "I'll do my best for you."

Bardwell's eyes moved to the lawyer. "I ain't doubting that you will, Mister Rance. And I appreciate you taking up for me." He looked back to the sheriff. "You'd be doing me a might big favor if'n' you was to turn your back and let me slip out the door 'fore this thing gets started."

Thorpe shook his head. "You know I can't do that, John Henry. Besides, how far you think you'd get? Even if you managed to get a horse and gun, it would give McManus and his bunch the excuse to hunt you down. And as a wanted man, charged with murder, there wouldn't be nothing I could do about it."

"And running would make you look guilty," Rance said.

Bardwell transferred his stare to the floor, and Abby wondered if he was contemplating making a break for it. He wore no restraints and could no doubt easily overpower both Rance and Thorpe, especially in his weakened condition.

And I'm certainly not going to shoot him, she thought.

"Our best chance is to face this in the court-room," Rance said. "The law's on our side."

That brought the trace of a smile to the black man's lips. "Sure don't seem like it at the moment."

"Trust in Lady Justice," Rance said. "She wears a blindfold and holds a scale. The truth will come out. It has to."

"I been told that before," Bardwell said. He in-haled deeply. "But you're right. This is the only chance I got."

Thorpe stood there watching him for a bit and then the sharp sound of a distant train whistle reverberated in the distance. The sheriff moved to the window and pulled back the heavy wooden shutter, peering out through the crack.

"That'll be the morning train coming in," he said. "Judge Robertson will be on it." He closed the window, came back to the desk, opened the top drawer, and removed a pair of iron shackles.

Bardwell's head jerked back, as if he'd been stuck.

"I ain't got a choice about these," Thorpe said. "We're going to have to move down to the Grain Exchange. It's the only building big enough to hold a trail and accommodate all the spectators."

"Everybody's gonna want to see the show, huh?" Bardwell extended his arms and held them out in front of his body.

Thorpe slowly slipped the iron bracelets over

the black man's wrists.

"My daddy wore these back before the War." Bardwell shook his head. "The overseer never did put none on me. Said I was too young and they'd just shoot me if'n' I ran off. Guess things ain't too much different now."

"It's just regulations, John Henry," Thorpe said.

Bardwell nodded fractionally. "I'm just glad he ain't here to see this." His head shook and his lips twisted back into a wry smile. "He sure was proud when I joined the army, became a buffalo soldier. He sure was proud."

Abby felt like pulling out her Trantor pistol and forcing the sheriff to let John Henry go.

Thorpe locked the bracelets in place and told Abby to check the street.

Abby went to the door and as she opened it saw a cloud of dust rising from the eastern edge of the town. Seconds later she heard the thundering echo of approaching horses. She strained her eyes to try and discern exactly who was approaching, and then she spotted the two riders in the lead and motioned for Thorpe to join her.

He strode to the door and asked, "Who are they? Can you tell?"

"I can tell all right," she said, opening the door a bit wider as her brother and Hicks rode by with ten riderless horses all tied to a tethering line.

"Looks like your deputies made it back in time for court after all," Abby said.

******

As the train rolled to a stop entering Sweetwater junction, O'Rourke watched the distinguished looking passenger in the blue suit remove his spectacles and place them in a black case. O'Rourke pretended not to be too obvious as the train ground to a halt and the other man stood and set a black valise on the seat next to him. There were gold-embossed letters along the side of the valise: *JUDGE HORATIO ROBERTSON.*

A judge?

This complicates matters, O'Rourke thought.

With the specially prepared wanted poster of River Hicks now illegible, and no mention of either of the Mack twins on it, carrying out the executions might be brought under more scrutiny, especially where the girl was involved.

Maintain anonymity.

The Company tenet suddenly held more significance than ever for him now.

Quint's long, lanky form was stretched out on his seat, with his boots on the seat next to O'Rourke's pant leg. He couldn't care less about the seat, but hoped none of the boot-black had rubbed off on his suit. The snoring ruffian stirred awake as people started getting up and stretching. The long scabbard containing his rifle was tucked against Quint's side and O'Rourke stood up quickly to obscure it as the judge strode past them. O'Rourke didn't think the man had noticed the rifle.

The quickness of the move was not lost on Quint. He stood and scrutinized the back of the passing man.

"He somebody we should be concerned with?"

O'Rourke shook his head and shot his eyes from side to side.

No one seemed to be paying much attention to them.

"Get your stuff and let's get off this damn train," O'Rourke said.

Quint grabbed his rifle and the carpet bag that contained his buckskin clothes and moccasins. O'Rourke stood blocking the way from the seats to the aisle while several other passengers shuffled by. When he felt there was sufficient space between the judge and themselves, he pushed his way into the aisle, cutting in front of a woman with three small children. The woman uttered a gasp, and Quint paused, doffed his hat, and gestured for her to pass in front of him.

As they descended the steps from the train and onto the platform, O'Rourke checked the judge's progress. Suddenly, he saw a man leading a group of horses into a corral across the way. The man turned and O'Rourke recognized him.

Connor Mack.

That meant two things: they were indeed in the right place. The report by the preliminary team scouting the location for the governor's arrival had been right. The quarry was indeed in Sweetwater.

And secondly, River Hicks was, in all probability, close by as well.

O'Rourke recalled the ease and aplomb with which Hicks had slain Randall Landecker, the professional gunman with the extraordinary reputation, when O'Rourke had last located the elusive trio. Hicks was a terror with a gun.

And he'll most likely recognize me if he sees me, O'Rourke thought.

He'd changed his hat, which now had two holes in it, making it more distinctive, thanks to the uncouth barbarian. That was different from the customary derby that he'd worn the last time Hicks had seen him. But O'Rourke still wore the same navy blue suit which was practically the company uniform.

Maintain anonymity.

He was going to have to suggest a variance in the dress code to the higher-ups in Chicago.

"Well," Quint said in a loud tone. "What we waitin' for? The cows to come home?"

O'Rourke whirled and spoke in a low voice.

"Keep your voice down. That cowboy across the street. The young one with those horses. He's one of the ones we want."

"Well, hell," Quint said, gripping the handle of his Sharps. "Why don't I see if'n' I can take him right now, then?"

"No," O'Rourke said quickly. "Put that away. The main one we're after, that Hicks fellow, he's got to be around here, too."

Quint's face crinkled with a squint. "Shootin' this one'll flush him out."

"That's exactly what we *don't* want. We'll wait until the two men are together, where you can get off two quick shots in rapid succession. We can't afford to have either one of them, especially Hicks, escape to confront us."

"Why not?"

O'Rourke continued to glance around. He didn't see Hicks, thank God. Turning back to Quint, he said, "Because I told you. He's good with a gun. Very good."

Quint winked as he made a clucking sound with his tongue. "I guess then I'll just have to be smarter."

"Precisely," O'Rourke whispered. "We'll take out the two of them, and then take our time with the girl."

Quint grinned, showing his tobacco-stained teeth. "Sounds good. Been a while since I had me taste of a woman."

Connor Mack had his back to them now, lacing up the gate of the big corral. It would be propitious for them to move along with the dwindling crowd rather than be the last ones left standing on the platform.

O'Rourke muttered for Quint to follow him and to "Keep your head down."

That seemed to embolden the ruffian seemed to stand straighter. O'Rourke could hardly wait for this unseemly partnership to be concluded. They mingled with the departing passengers from the train. The judge paused and was staring at a building across the way. It was a sturdy looking structure with a sign reading *Sweetwater Junction Grain Exchange* above a set of double doors on the front. After checking to assure the street was free of traffic, the judge started across. A young woman in shirt and pants stood by the door and spoke to him as he stepped onto the boardwalk. O'Rourke noticed the winding braid of auburn hair hanging down her back as she turned to speak to the judge.

It was Abby Mack.

Luckily, she gave no apparent hint that she'd seen O'Rourke, but with her and her brother in such close proximity, could River Hicks not be far behind?

Luckily, a group of five riders were galloping up the main thoroughfare providing a spectacle of obfuscation.

O'Rourke quickened his pace, not wanting to alert Quint to the girl's location. It would no doubt give the rash buffoon another excuse to call attention to them. They had to keep moving, not be noticed, get to a place of concealment, and then figure out their next move.

The main street curved slightly, bearing to the left up ahead and O'Rourke saw the high, peaked tower of a church with a large bell inside.

The high ground, he thought, and smiled. The perfect place for Quint to make his long distance shots.

✻✻✻✻✻✻

Abby watched as Big George McManus and four others rode down the main street toward her. Three of the other men were McManus's sons, and the fourth one was the handsome cowboy they called Kandy. She also saw a group of maybe half a dozen blacks walking down the boardwalk toward them. After opening the door for the judge and pointing inside, Abby called to Sheriff Thorpe. He came to the door just as McManus and the others had finished tying off their horses to the hitching rails. The group of blacks was almost upon them as well, and Abby recognized old Ben Green in the lead, carrying his ancient, rusty shotgun. Abby glanced to her left and saw Connor heading toward the front of the Grain Exchange in a quick trot. Big George McManus stepped onto the boardwalk and tipped his hat to Abby, but his face reflected anything but cordiality.

She kept her expression neutral, but she wanted to spit upon him. He represented everything she'd come to hate: power, dominance, cruelty …

McManus turned and regarded the approaching blacks and frowned, but before he could say anything, Sheriff Thorpe stepped through the door.

"You and your boys are welcome inside, McManus," Thorpe said. "This is a public trial. But you'll have to check your guns first."

"Check our guns?" Little George McManus said. "We ain't gonna do that."

"Then you ain't coming inside," Thorpe said. His face was firm.

"Says who?" Big Burl McManus asked, stepping forward.

The third McManus son, the one with the dark hair named Aaron, stood at the rear of the group saying nothing.

"Now what we got here?" The handsome cowboy, Kandy chuckled as Ben Green and his entourage got to the door.

"Sheriff," Old Ben said. "We come here to serve on the jury, if'n' you'll have us."

"Jury?" Little George McManus said. He slapped Kandy's shoulder. "You hear that?"

"Button your lip," Thorpe said. He extended his arm in front of Big George McManus and ushered the group of blacks in, saying, "You're welcome to come in, Ben, but you'll have to leave your guns on that table just inside the doors."

Ben Green nodded in agreement and held his shotgun at arm's length as he went through the doors, followed by the other blacks.

"You're letting them in before us?" Little George said.

"They're in compliance," Thorpe said.

"You can't make us give up our guns," Burl said. "You got no authority."

"I've got all the authority I need, as long as I'm still wearing this star," Thorpe said. "And it's by order of the judge. You're lucky we didn't run Little Georgie in last night for damn near instigating a lynching."

Big George McManus smirked and clapped Thorpe on the shoulder. The blow was engineered to look like a friendly gesture, but obviously carried more force than was appropriate.

Thorpe grunted in pain.

"Oh my," Big George said in an overly exaggerated tone. "My apologies, sheriff. I heard you got shot last night. Clumsy me." His teeth flashed under the bushy mustache.

Abby saw a stain of red beginning to work its way through the fabric of Thorpe's shirt. She was anticipating how quickly she could bend down to retrieve the Trantor pistol from her boot when Connor arrived, a bit out of breath, and asked, "Everything all right, sheriff?"

"Everything's real fine," River Hicks said, stepping out from the doorway. "As soon as Mr. McManus and his boys here unbuckle their gun-belts." He drew his Colt from its holster and opened the loading gate, conspicuously sliding a cartridge into the last open space on the cylinder. "Ain't that so, Big George?"

McManus glared at Hicks and for a moment Abby thought there was going to be trouble, but then McManus emitted a laugh and began unbuckling his gun-belt.

"We got no problem complying with the law," he said. "No problem at all. As long as justice is done."

The other McManus's and Kandy followed suit.

Hicks and Thorpe exchanged glances as the four men moved between them, each dropping his gun-belt with weapon onto the table.

CHAPTER 13

SWEETWATER

Connor and Hicks stood on opposite sides of the big room as it filled up with people. It had been a laborious process to make sure that no one brought a gun into the courtroom, except for the two deputies and the sheriff, who sat in a chair by the back. Thorpe's face was ashen, and despite him placing a handkerchief over the wound on his shoulder, the crimson spots continued to work their way through the woven material of his shirt sleeve.

"This court of the state of California is hereby in session," the judge said, pounding his little wooden hammer, called a gavel, on the table. He was a heavyset man in a dark blue suit and wore some gold-rimmed spectacles on his broad face. "How does the defendant plead?"

Rance stood and said, "Not guilty, your honor."

He actually looked kind of good in that undertaker's suit.

Connor had watched with fascination as the courtroom procedures got underway. He'd never been in a courtroom before, much less seen a trial. The room was big and expansive, with the judge sitting at a table up by the front of the room, the light from a big window pouring in from behind him making him look almost like a statue that moved. He was facing two other tables. Rance and Bardwell sat at the one on the judge's left, and McManus's lawyer, Maxwell Tiddy, sat on the right. An empty chair was up by the left side of the judge's table, and two rows of six chairs for the jury were lined up about ten feet away from that.

McManus and his three sons were seated in the first row of the spectator seats, but Connor saw that Aaron McManus had separated himself from the others. Several more cowhands had come in and sat next to Kandy, who was directly behind McManus. Connor had been glad to see that a handful of black homesteaders, led by old Ben Green, had shown up and hoped some of them would be picked to sit on the jury, but that was not to be. After the judge asked for volunteers to serve as jurors, at least twenty people stood up, some of whom were the blacks. Each person was questioned by the judge as to his ability to render a fair and honest verdict, and then questioned by the two attorneys. Using language that Connor didn't quite understand, Tiddy was able to disqualify all of the blacks. Rance, on the other hand, used a similar tactic to eliminate some of the cowhands that were obviously in league with McManus.

"Mr. Tiddy," the judge said. "Do you wish to make an opening statement?"

Tiddy rose from his seat at the table and smiled broadly. "I do, your honor."

He strode over the open area in front of the judge's table and then turned so he was facing both the jury and the spectators.

"Gentlemen of the jury, we are gathered here today to see that justice is served," he said. "The prosecution will prove, beyond the shadow of a doubt, that two days ago, one John Henry Bardwell, the defendant, and a Negro, one who was dishonorably discharged from the army for cowardliness, and striking his commanding officer ..."

Connor shot a glance at Bardwell, who stiffened, but remained silent.

"Did commit the heinous crime of murder of one Howard Layton," Tiddy continued. "And did so in a grotesque and vengeful manner. The prosecution will also prove that this crime was brought about by the defendant's greed and anger at the decedent due to an ongoing property dispute upon which the *late* Mr. *Layton* ..." Tiddy paused and smiled again, as if pleased by the rhyme of his words. "Was to have ruled against him in a court of law."

Tiddy continued talking for several minutes more claiming that Bardwell was the leader of a band of killers known as the Phantom Riders, "who have been carrying out a wave of terror over the community of Sweetwater and the surrounding ranches." Connor thought the words began to sound abstract and repetitious. He began to scan the courtroom, looking at the faces of the people in the audience. Most of them seemed bored, a few were actually dozing. Connor caught the eye of his sister and saw her fierce expression. She was taking this whole thing very hard, and he wished that she would have stayed at the hotel in case trouble arose. But he knew better than to ask her. Not only would she have refused such a request, but he also knew that Rance intended to call her as a witness. Connor knew that he and Hicks were also on the list to testify.

A sudden burst of applause filled the room as Tiddy took a bow.

"Order in the court," the judge said, banging the little mallet again. When the applause ceased, he said, "Mr. Rance, does the defense wish to make a statement?"

"We do, your honor." Rance stood and walked to where Tiddy had been standing. When he started speaking he looked nervous and there was a quaver in his voice.

"My client had been accused of a crime he did not commit. We will show that he did not commit these crimes and ..." He paused, as if searching for something more to add.

A burst of laughter emitted from the audience and the judge banged the gavel on the table.

The room became deathly quiet and Rance seemed frozen, unable to speak.

"They'll be none of that," the judge said in a sharp tone. "Mr. Rance, do you wish to continue?"

"Yes, your honor. The defense will show that

John Henry Bardwell is innocent of all charges. Thank you."

He wasn't too fast outta the gate, Connor thought, trying to buoy his spirits by remembering that the race was far from over. But he couldn't help wondering how John Henry was feeling.

Tiddy started out by calling the first of three McManus ranch hands to the stand.

After having the man place his hand on the Bible and swear to tell the truth, the judge told him to sit in the empty chair by the judge's table.

Tiddy moved up close to him and nodded. After stating his full name as Pete Koors and admitting that he worked for Big George McManus, Tiddy asked him what had happened on the day in question.

"We was out riding the range," the man said. "Looking for strays from Big George's herd, when we come up on that there Nigra, Bardwell, stringing up that fella Layton. We seen what he'd done, and started chasing him."

"Now when you say, you'd seen what he'd done," Tiddy said, "what exactly did you see?"

"Well." Koors shifted in his seat. "We seen Layton was strung up, you know, hung from a tree, and he had a brand on his face."

"A brand?"

"Yes, sir. It was the Phantom Riders' brand."

Rance jumped up and objected. "How does this individual know that this particular brand belongs to anyone?"

"Everybody knows that brand," Koors yelled

back. "We seen it often enough. It's the one from the Phantom Riders."

A flurry of objections and accusations flew back and forth before the judge got things settled down again.

He told Rance to sit down and for Tiddy to continue.

"And then what happened, Mr. Koors?"

"The Nigra, he took to running once he seen us a coming. Then his wagon flipped over, and I thought we had him, when these other fellas, them two in here wearing them deputy badges, come ridin' up and started shooting at us."

"And isn't it true that one of your party was in fact shot by the defendant during this altercation?" Tiddy asked.

"Sure is. Lloyd Miller. He's dead, too."

"Objection, your honor," Rance said, getting to his feet. "It has not been established exactly who shot Lloyd Miller."

"Sustained," the judge said. "The jury will disregard the witness's last statement regarding who did the shooting."

Tiddy paused and raised an eyebrow. He reminded Connor of an actor in a play, prancing about and using exaggerated gestures. Connor was disgusted by the entire affair, and felt like crying out, but both Thorpe and Hicks had cautioned him against any such outbursts. He swallowed his emotion, but knew that Tiddy was obviously twisting the fact to suit his own purposes.

The testimony went on for a few minutes more

and Tiddy said he had no more questions.

Pete Koors started to get up, but the judge told him to "Sit back down."

The ranch hand's face twitched and he slid back into the chair.

"Mr. Rance?" the judge said. "You have any questions of this witness?"

Rance got to his feet. "I do, your honor." He walked over to the chair where Koors was sitting. "Mr. Koors, how long have you worked for Mr. McManus?"

The witness shrugged. "I don't know. About six months or so."

"And he's treated you pretty well, hasn't he?"

Koors seemed to relax a little. "Sure has."

"Have you been a good, obedient employee of Mr. McManus?"

"Emplo-what?" Koors said, his brow furrowing.

Tiddy jumped to his feet. "Objection, your honor. This line of questioning goes beyond the scope of my examination."

A murmur of assents sprang from the spectators.

The judge tapped his gavel once again and sustained the objection, adding, "Get on with it, Mr. Rance."

Rance's lips drew together into a tight line, then he said, "You pretty much do or say anything that Big George McManus tells you to do or say, don't you, Mr. Koors?"

Tiddy jumped up again and yelled another objection. Rance turned and the two began to argue. The courtroom erupted in a cacophony of muttering. The judge slammed the gavel down once more and called for order.

It went on in a similar fashion as Tiddy called the other two ranch hands. Each gave an almost identical accounting, and both lawyers repeated their performances. Connor thought the entire thing was an absurd exercise in futility. Hicks walked over to him and winked.

"Don't let this circus get to you," he said in a low whisper.

Connor puckered his mouth. "I thought this was supposed to get at the truth," he whispered back.

"Usually it's a case of the first liar never having a chance," Hicks said, tapping him on the shoulder. "Just keep your head when it's your turn."

Tiddy said that he had one more witness to call, and asked for Otis Baker to take the stand.

The blacksmith rose from the rear of the spectator section and strode to the front. He was still clad in the same clothes that he'd been wearing two days ago when Connor had first seem him, except that his distinct body odor was now more prevalent. He raised his right hand and was sworn in.

"State your name and occupation," Tiddy said.

"I'm Otis Baker, blacksmith and stable owner."

Tiddy asked a few other questions leading up to Bardwell's appeal for Baker to fix the broken wagon tongue.

"I told him I'd do it," Baker said. "But had another job, so he'd have to leave his wagon at the shop for a spell."

"And did he do so?"

"Yep."

Tiddy paused and gestured to the twelve members of the jury. He then walked over to his table and picked up a sack. He withdrew a long iron bar with a circular brand on the end and walked back to the witness.

"Have you ever seen this branding iron before, Mr. Baker?"

The blacksmith nodded. "Sure have. I found it in his wagon." He raised his big hand and pointed toward Bardwell. "It was stuck under the seat, and I seen it when I went to fixing his wagon."

Tiddy stood still, holding the branding iron in his hands and turning it slightly. "And would you describe the emblem on this iron?"

"It's like the letter P," Baker said. "The one the Phantom Riders use."

More murmuring emanated from the spectator section, and the judge pounded his gavel once again. When it stopped, Tiddy walked over to the judge's table and asked that the branding iron be admitted as evidence.

The judge looked to Rance, who offered no objection.

Bardwell grabbed Rance's arm and whispered something, but the lawyer only patted the black man's hand and spoke to him in an undertone. Bardwell sat back hard in his chair.

"Do you wish to cross-examine the witness?" the judge asked.

Rance stood. "Not at this time, your honor, but I reserve the right to recall Mr. Baker."

The blacksmith's eyes shot over to the judge. "What's that mean?"

"It means take a seat in the courtroom," the judge said. "And don't leave."

The blacksmith got up and walked back to his chair in the spectator's section.

"Before the prosecution rests, your honor," Tiddy said as he moved toward the judges table and placed his hand on the Bible. "I have one statement to make, which I am doing under oath. We all know that there's a pending dispute here in the area regarding water rights. The principals in this dispute are George McManus and the defendant, John Henry Bardwell."

He turned slightly and gestured toward the defendant. "To save the court's time, I would offer that I was present two days ago, the same day Howard Layton was murdered, at the Dominion, the ranch of Big George McManus. Mr. Layton came there that morning and informed me personally that he had made a decision in this case, and, that he had decided in favor of Mr. McManus." He paused and curled his head toward the table of the defense. "Mr. Layton also stated to me that he felt it incumbent upon him to advise Mr. Bardwell of this decision." He paused again and lifted an eyebrow. "This was apparently the last time he was seen alive."

"Objection," Rance said. "The prosecution is testifying in his own case."

"Regrettable, but necessary, your honor," Tiddy said. "How else am I to import was a witness to what was an obvious motive in this heinous crime?"

The two attorneys argued back and forth, with the judge eventually allowing Tiddy's testimony to stand.

Rance shook his head vehemently and asked for a dismissal of the charges.

The judge refused.

"Do you wish to offer a defense at this time?" he asked.

"We do, your honor," Rance said. The flush was evident in both of his cheeks.

He first called Connor to the stand and went through the account of what had happened when they had come upon Layton's body and then assisted Bardwell. At the conclusion, the judge asked Tiddy if he had any questions.

"Just one, your honor." The short, bowl-shaped lawyer stood and flashed a smile. "Mr. Mack, or should I say *Deputy* Mack, you did not witness the actual murder of Howard Layton, did you?"

Connor felt a burn of anger flush his cheeks. "No, sir."

"And, my apologies to the court, I do have a few more questions after all." Tiddy paused and licked his lips. "You came upon the scene *after* the defendant was engaged in a gun battle with the aforementioned McManus ranch hands, did you not?"

"Yes, sir."

"And you and Mr. Hicks," Tiddy paused to glance over at him. "Took it upon yourselves to intervene, not knowing what had previously transpired to cause the gunfight, correct?"

"That's right, sir."

"And, just for clarification, neither of you were duly authorized deputies at this time, were you?"

"No, sir, but—"

"No further questions," Tiddy said.

The judge ordered Connor to leave the chair and asked Rance if he had any other witnesses.

"Yes," he said. "I call Miss Abigail Mack to the stand."

Connor watched as his sister stood and walked proudly down the spectator's aisle, her head held high, carrying her bundled handkerchief in her hand.

After leading Abby through the same line of questioning that he'd done with Connor regarding the events of the last few days, Rance then said, "I'd like to turn your attention to yesterday afternoon. You said that after you returned from the Bardwell farm, you had occasion to care for your horses at the stable owned by Otis Baker?"

Before Abby could answer, Tiddy hurled and objection: "Relevance, your honor?"

The judge turned to Rance, who said, "If your honor will grant me a little leeway here, this is integral to our defense."

The judge's brow furrowed, but he said, "Very well. Proceed."

"And did you find anything out of the ordinary during this time?" Rance asked.

Abby held up the handkerchief. "These pieces of iron."

Tiddy again objected and the two lawyers danced around in verbal confrontation. Finally, the judge ruled that Rance could continue.

Rance unwrapped the handkerchief and held the individual pieces up one at a time in front of the judge. "You'll note, your honor, that the edges of these pieces appear to have been cleaved off of some other surface."

The judge adjusted his spectacles and then said, "So noted."

"I ask that these iron pieces be admitted as defense exhibit A," Rance said.

"And I again object," Tiddy said. "Citing relevance, your honor."

The judge regarded Rance, who said, "My next witness will clarify this entire matter, sir."

Judge Robertson sighed and tapped the table once more with the gavel.

"I'll allow it on the provision that you do just that, Mr. Rance."

Rance smiled and said, "I call Deputy River Hicks to the stand."

Hicks walked from the far end of the room carrying a burlap sack. After being sworn, he set the sack between his boots and leaned what was obviously the end of a branding iron against his leg. Connor searched the spectator section for Big George McManus. The rancher's face suddenly looked drawn and tight as he leaned back and motioned for Kandy to come closer. The two of them whispered, and then Kandy got up and left the court room.

This is going to be good, Connor thought.

He watched and listened as Rance led Hicks through the events of that morning: the tracking of the Phantom Riders' tracks, the discovery of the lost canyon, Connor's descent into the box canyon, and the retrieval of the branding iron and masks.

Rance picked up a mask in one hand and the branding iron in the other and held them up for the jury, and then the judge to see.

"You'll note that this iron has the same design as the one previously entered into evidence by the prosecution," he said.

"So noted," the judge said.

"You will also note that there appears to be some residual material on the end of this brand." Rance brought the emblem to his nose, sniffed, and shook his head. "Smells like burnt flesh to me."

Tiddy rose and said, "Objection."

"So noted," the judge said.

Connor noticed that the judge was hunching forward in his chair now.

"I would now like to call your attention back to the prosecution's exhibit A, the branding iron purportedly recovered by Otis Baker." Rance walked over to the judge's table and picked up the branding iron. "You'll notice that the emblem here has some distinct markings on several areas of its surface." He showed the iron to the judge, and then walked over to the jury and did the same. "It appears, does it not, that these markings indicate a severance of some sort."

One of the jurors, a store owner, pursed his lips and nodded.

Rance walked back to the center of the floor and motioned to Abby.

"For the next portion of the defense, I will need the assistance of Miss Abigail Mack."

Abby stood and Tiddy jumped to his feet.

"Your honor," he said. "This is nothing more than some second rate theatrics."

"Objection noted," the judge said, "And over-ruled."

Abby walked to the defense table and picked up a box that was on the floor next to Rance's chair. She took a square board with two holes through it from the box and then moved the chair next to the table, laying the board flat between them.

Rance asked the judge for use of his inkwell.

The judge raised an eyebrow as he handed it across the table.

Rance then took the branding iron that Baker had recovered and slipped it through one of the holes in board. The emblem fit snugly against the flat surface.

Turning back to the judge's table, Rance requested two sheet of paper.

The judge reached into his valise, removed the two sheets, and gave them to the lawyer.

Walking back, Rance took a handkerchief from the pocket of his suit jacket and shook it.

"Your honor," Tiddy said. "How much longer are you going to allow this charlatan to make a mockery of this trial?"

"Sit down, Mr. Tiddy," the judge said in a stern voice.

Heaving a theatrical sigh, Tiddy crumpled into his chair.

Rance walked over to Hicks, who handed him the branding iron recovered from the lost canyon. After slipping it into the second hole in the board, Rance dabbed some ink onto his handkerchief and wiped it over the two emblems. He then quickly pressed one of the sheets of paper to each of them. When he withdrew the paper two distinct impressions were visible. Rance turned and held the paper toward the judge, the jury, and then to Tiddy and the spectators.

"As you all can see," he said in a loud voice. "The two brands are virtually identical. Are we all in agreement that this is the sign of the Phantom Riders?"

A murmur of agreement emanated from the spectators.

Rance walked back and retrieved the wrapped handkerchief containing the iron pieces and held it up in conspicuous fashion.

"I'd now I'd like Miss Abby to place these pieces that she found into the emblem of the branding iron allegedly recovered from the defendant's wagon while in the blacksmith's shop."

Tiddy jumped up but the judge slammed the gavel down hard on the table and ordered him to resume his seat.

The lawyer sat down and Connor noticed a brocade of sweat was forming on the man's brow.

Abby set each of the five metal pieces into the circular emblem.

Rance gave her the ink well, the stained handkerchief, and a fresh sheet of paper.

After dousing the handkerchief with more ink, she wiped it carefully over the assembled pieces and the emblem, and then pressed the blank sheet to the metallic surface. Bringing it away, she turned and held the paper above her head.

A gasp emanated from the spectators, and Abby turned slowly, rotating toward the judge and then the jury. Connor began moving toward the rear door as Hicks had earlier instructed him.

As she turned Connor could still see the clear inked impression of *McM*—the McManus brand on the paper.

Big George McManus leapt to his feet.

"This don't prove nothing," he yelled. "For all we know, the Phantom Riders could've stole one of my irons."

"Did I mention before that the lost canyon is on the Dominion?" Hicks called out from the witness chair. "Maybe you just left one laying around there."

"The witness is out of order," Tiddy yelled, as a commotion suddenly began.

Otis Baker knocked over several chairs as he hastily stood and began running toward the rear doors.

"Stop that man," the judge yelled.

Connor shoved one of the McManus ranch hands off his seat. Whirling, Connor grabbed the chair's back and slammed the legs into the big blacksmith as he ran past. Baker went down like a roped steer.

CHAPTER 14

SWEETWATER

After Connor and Hicks had dragged the black-smith back to the front of the room the big man began to sing like a bird in a cage, at first professing ignorance, then innocence, then finally complicity in the planting of the Phantom Riders branding iron in Bardwell's wagon. The judge gave Baker a stern look that made Connor glad it wasn't directed at him. Despite his size Baker began to blubber like a schoolgirl.

"Listen," Judge Robertson said, raising the gavel and pointing it like gun. "I want to know who gave you that branding iron and what they told you to do with it, and it better be the truth, or there'll be hell to pay."

Baker's mouth twitched and he looked first at Big George McManus and then to Tiddy, who jumped to his feet.

"I object," he said.

The judge swiveled the aim of the gavel toward Tiddy. "Overruled, counselor. Now sit down."

The lawyer's mouth worked and he peeked over his shoulder at McManus.

"It was him," Baker said, pointing at Tiddy. "Him and Big George's man, Kandy. They brung one of their irons down to me and told me to cut off the extra pieces. Make it like I done before."

"Before?" The judge's brow furrowed. "Are you saying you're responsible for making that other iron as well?"

Baker's eyes darted around the courtroom again. Connor could see Big George McManus's face was vivid with rage.

"Yes, sir," Baker said. "I made a bunch of them irons for Big George, putting his M C M brands on 'em. Then a couple a months ago, Kandy come to me and told me that Big George wanted one of 'em changed. I asked what for, and he said for me to make it a P markin' on one of them branding irons. Told me to just cut off some of the letter parts on the first one I made."

"You're a damn liar!" Big George McManus yelled. He got to his feet. "I ain't gonna sit here and listen to this."

"Sit down, Mr. McManus," the judge said, striking his gavel several times. "Or get out."

McManus replied with a guttural snarl and a dismissive wave of his hand.

"I guess I'll do that, judge. This is mockery of justice."

He turned and stomped out of the courtroom, his sons and entourage following.

Connor glanced at Hicks who gestured toward the back door where Thorpe was standing. The table with the guns was just on the other side. Connor started toward the center aisle at a brisk walk, and Hicks was moving that way as well.

"Mr. Bardwell," the judge said. "Please stand."

Both Rance and Bardwell stood and the judge addressed them: "The case against you is dismissed. You're free to go."

Rance put his hand out and Bardwell shook it.

Tiddy rose from his chair, head down, and began to stride toward the aisle when the judge called out, "Just a moment, Mr. Tiddy. You have to answer to the accusation that you suborned perjury."

Tiddy made no indication of slowing or stopping.

"Deputies," the judge called out. "Place Mr. Tiddy into custody."

Hicks drew his gun and cracked the lawyer over the head. The plump little man crumpled like a marionette whose strings had been severed. Connor and Rance picked Tiddy up and dragged him back to his chair.

Several other people jumped to their feet and the center aisle was suddenly jammed. Big George McManus was already through the door, and Burl McManus bumped into Thorpe, knocking him to the floor. The group of black homesteaders were now milling around Bardwell, clapping him on the back. Ben Green was in tears.

"You're a free man, John Henry," he said. "You hear? A free man."

Bardwell embraced the old man.

Near the rear door Abby was already helping Thorpe to his feet.

"You want me to go after them, sheriff?" Connor asked when he and Hicks had pushed through the crowd and made their way to the door.

Thorpe's face was a twisted grimace. He shook his head.

"Let's see what the judge wants," he managed to say. "We've got Tiddy for now."

"I guess you'll be using those iron bracelets on him this time," Abby said.

"That'll be a pleasure." Thorpe's grimace turned into a rather tight smile. "But we'd better check outside first."

Connor was cognizant of the people behind them starting to gravitate toward the exit as well.

"We'd better make sure McManus and his boys aren't waiting out there with their guns drawn," Hicks said.

Thorpe nodded and they stepped through the foyer. Connor saw a scattering of guns, mostly the antiquated shotguns of the homesteaders, still on the table. He peered through the front window and saw McManus and his sons lined up across the street, but their guns were all holstered.

Thorpe walked onto the boardwalk and then went down the steps. Connor and Hicks trailed behind him.

"McManus," Thorpe said. "The trial's over.

Bardwell's been acquitted. Now I'm giving you fair warning not to try and start any trouble."

Big George McManus raised one eyebrow and chuckled.

"I ain't in the business of starting trouble, Thorpe. Nor am I running away from it, either."

"Then it'd be best for you and your boys to get outta Sweetwater," Thorpe said.

"We will. But first we got something to attend to." Big George's lips drew into a frown. "You know I had to bury my son this morning?"

"I'm sorry to hear that," Thorpe said. "But he brought that on himself."

Connor could hear a commotion behind him and turned his head slightly. John Henry and Old Ben Green were coming out of the front doors of the Grain Exchange, followed by several of the other homesteaders.

"You," Big George McManus yelled, lifting his arm and pointing his finger. "You killed my son."

Bardwell stopped and the group of homesteaders halted behind him.

"I'm right sorry that it had to come to that, Mister McManus," Bardwell said. "But he didn't give me no choice, and it was a fair fight."

Burl McManus stepped forward. "A fair fight? You stabbed him with a knife."

"His own knife," Bardwell said. "He pulled it on me. Everybody in town here seen it."

"That's right," Thorpe said. "Your brother pulled a weapon."

Burl McManus grinned and he unbuckled his

gun-belt and handed it to his younger brother. "Well, I ain't got no weapon. And I'm fixing to get me some satisfaction, *an* some justice." He glared at Bardwell then spat.

Hicks pulled out his Colt and Big George Mc-Manus swiveled toward him.

"No guns this time, gunslinger. Let the nigger fight his own battles."

Before the sheriff could say anything Bardwell stepped forward, stripping off his shirt.

"Let him come. I'm tired of him calling me names, and I ain't running no more."

He handed his shirt to Ben Green and stepped to the center of the street. Burl McManus removed his hat and handed it to his father. A few of the home-steaders issued cries of, "Go get him, John Henry," and, "Whup him good."

Aaron McManus stepped forward and tried to put a hand on his brother's shoulder.

"Burl, no. This isn't the way."

Big George shoved Aaron away.

"Don't you touch him, you pathetic, weak-mind-ed cripple," Big George said. "Watch how a real McManus man handles things."

Aaron stared at his father, then stepped back, his face a mixture of hurt and anger.

Burl McManus and Bardwell were circling each other now in the center of the street, their fists clenched.

"I'm gonna break your neck, black boy," Burl McManus said.

Bardwell said nothing.

Connor leaned closer to Hicks. "We gonna let this go on?"

"Don't seem like we have much of a choice," Hicks said. "And John Henry deserves a chance to fight back a little after all he's been through. Now spread out a little in case it turns into a shootin' match."

Connor edged to the side opposite Hicks and stepped up onto the boardwalk next to Abby. Her face was taut with concern. Connor had his concerns, as well. Burl McManus was the size of a bear, his upper body as big as a barrel. On the other hand, Connor had also seen the power Bardwell had exhibited when he'd lifted the wagon. McManus was substantially bigger and heavier, but Connor wasn't sure who held the advantage as far as sheer strength.

Burl McManus suddenly jumped forward, his arms outstretched, and tried to grab his opponent. Bardwell darted to the side, using his open palms to push the bigger man's arms away, but McManus was quick for a man his size. He swung a backhanded blow that collided with Bardwell's shoulder, knocking him slightly off kilter. As he stumbled, McManus whirled and lashed out with a kick, catching the other man on the thigh. Bardwell twisted and fell to the ground. McManus rushed him, both arms extended, but Bardwell managed to scramble away and regained his footing.

"He's already running from you, Burl," Little George McManus yelled out.

Burl McManus didn't slow his pursuit and pivoted, still going after his foe. This time Bardwell proved more elusive, nimbly sidestepping and delivering a solid punch to McManus's exposed side.

The big man grunted and swung his huge body around. If he'd felt the punch he didn't show it. He reached out and managed to seize Bardwell's left arm then squeezed.

Connor saw a flash of white teeth appear in a grimace on the black man's face.

Instead of trying to pull his arm out of McManus's grasp, Bardwell stepped forward as he smashed his right fist into the other man's nose.

A spout of blood flew from McManus's nostrils and seemed to hang suspended in space for a few seconds.

The bigger man grunted and his lips peeled back in a feral roar.

"I'm gonna kill you for that, nigger."

Bardwell managed to pull his left arm free and sent two more punches into McManus's substantial girth. These blows, like those before, seemed to have no effect. Instead, McManus lumbered forward, his thick arms encircling Bardwell's body. The black man managed to get his own arms free, but McManus tightened his grip around Bardwell's torso, pulling him close against him in a bear-hug.

Connor could only imagine the pain such a grip would cause. He thought about pulling his gun out and putting a stop to it, but remembered what Hicks had told him before: *Never get involved in another man's fight … Unless you have to.*

Did he have to now?

He wasn't sure.

After a deep breath he decided all he could do was wait.

Got to follow River's lead, he thought.

The crowd gathering around the combat had grown and Connor caught a glimpse of a man in a navy blue suit—the kind that dudes wore, but this guy had on a wide-brimmed western style hat, and it was pulled low, partially obscuring his face. But there was something almost familiar about the fellow.

Bardwell emitted a groan and both Big and Little George McManus yelled encouragement, urging Burl to "Break his back."

Connor returned to scrutinizing the fight.

Bardwell had placed both of his hands against McManus's face. The muscles of his ebony arms stood out like a bronze statue that Connor had seen in a book once. Both combatants seemed frozen in time, and the crowd had hushed. The only sound audible was the ragged breathing of the two of them.

Abby seemed transfixed, too, her eyes wide open and staring.

Finally a snorting burst of air broke the silence, and McManus suddenly released Bardwell and took two halting steps backward, shaking his head. The blood was still flowing from his nose and was now dappling his white shirt like a collage of red pansies scattered over a white tablecloth. Bardwell was leaning over from the waist, obvious traces of fatigue and strain showing in his face. His breathing was very labored. McManus lurched forward, his fists looking like two massive sledgehammers. He was panting as well.

Bardwell's left hand shot out slamming into his opponent's already bloodied nose. McManus's head jerked back and Bardwell followed up with a smashing right hand to the other man's temple. For the first time McManus seemed to wobble, but he recovered almost immediately and grabbed Bardwell again, this time pushing his upper body down and encircling his neck.

"That's it, Burl," Little George McManus yelled. "Break his damn neck, just like you done before."

Burl McManus shot his brother a grin and a nod, his mouth framed with crimson.

"We can't let him do this," Abby said, bending to reach for her pistol.

Connor grabbed her and pulled her erect.

"Don't do nothing yet," he said.

Both Bardwell and McManus had ceased all movement. Only the grating sound of two men's ragged breathing and periodic grunts could be heard.

Little George McManus emitted a gleeful squeal: "He's gonna break the nigger's neck."

Connor wanted more than ever to put a bullet into that son of a bitch.

Slowly Burl McManus's lips began to peel back from bloodied teeth and his right arm, the arm encircling Bardwell's neck, slowly started to edge downward.

Both of Bardwell's hands were encircling Mc-

Manus's right wrist. The black man jerked free and spun to the side, ducking to McManus's right and then bringing his arm straight upward in a lightning-fast motion.

McManus howled in pain. Bardwell continued to twist the other man's arm and a gut-wrenching snap, as intrusive as a gunshot, punctuated the wail. The arm fell limply to McManus's side. Bardwell sent a two punch combination to his opponent's face and temple. McManus's head snapped back and his knees buckled, the rest of him folding down on top of his legs like a house coming down. He lay in the dirt for several seconds, then managed to brace himself with his left arm and struggle to his knees, clutching his right arm. He looked toward his father.

"Pa," he muttered. "He done broke my arm."

"Hit him again, John Henry," one of the homesteaders yelled. "Beat him good."

"He got it coming," another homesteader cried. "All them McManus's do."

Bardwell stood over his sunken foe and stared down at him, then slowly shook his head.

"Ain't no more need to hit him again," he said, and turned to start walking away.

"No!" Little George McManus said, pushing his way through the throng of spectators, his hand already raising his gun.

Hicks's draw was quick, cocking his Peacemaker as he brought it up, then firing.

The youngest McManus twisted and fell as his father stared on in horror, then turned to run at Hicks.

Connor drew his Colt and was about to fire when he suddenly caught a glimpse of the face of the man in the navy blue suit. Recognition came like the crack of a whip.

It was the same Pinkerton man they'd confronted back in Woodman.

And he was standing behind Hicks waving his hat.

"Behind you," Connor yelled.

At the same time Big George McManus jumped forward, Hicks ducked. Suddenly McManus's head exploded like a pumpkin struck by an axe, a scarlet mist blossoming in the air. A second later the sound of a heavy, distant report rolled over them like distant thunder.

Hicks whirled, his gun still drawn, and obviously caught sight of the Pinkerton man. Hicks lashed out with his fist.

The Pinkerton man's mouth popped open, his jaw seemingly jutting to the side of his face, and he stumbled backward, slamming against a hitching rail, and then tumbling down into a pile of fresh horse manure on the street.

The rumbling sound of stampeding horses shook the ground. From between two buildings four men on horseback, one of them Kandy, came galloping toward them, their guns drawn.

"Get Abby inside," Hicks yelled to Connor.

Connor grabbed his sister by the arm and dragged her up the steps and through the front door of the grain exchange.

"Let me go," she demanded, trying to reach her

Trantor pistol.

"There's somebody out there with a rifle shoot-ing at us," Connor said. "Now stay inside here."

Her eyes flashed anger, but she nodded.

He stepped to the door and saw that Kandy and the three other McManus men on horseback were in front now.

One of the black homesteaders fell, clutching his chest.

Hicks came bursting through the door.

"Did you see him?" Connor asked. "It's that same Pinkerton man we seen at Woodman."

"I seen him, all right," Hicks said. "Shoulda killed him the last time we met up with him."

"You think he's got somebody with him?" Connor asked. "Sure looked like he was signaling somebody."

"I expect he was," Hicks said. "Saw a glint of something down the street. In that church tower."

"Think it's the shooter?"

"Well, I doubt whoever it is up there is reciting the gospels."

Before Hicks could say anything else the sound of several more shots came from the street area. Connor saw the McManus crew firing their guns at the scattering homesteaders. Thorpe had his gun out and was firing at them.

"River," Connor said, but Hicks was already pushing back through the doors. Connor followed, his gun ready. He cocked back the hammer.

Hicks shot one of the riders. Connor saw Kandy turn and aim his gun at Hicks.

Connor brought his Peacemaker up and fired.

Kandy's handsome face registered surprise as a neat, round hole suddenly appeared between his eyes and he slumped forward and then rolled off his saddle and down onto the street. Bardwell grabbed one of the remaining riders off his horse and as the final one jerked his mount around and aimed his gun at John Henry, the loud roar of a shotgun echoed.

Old Ben Green stood off to the side, a trail of smoke winding up from one of the twin barrels.

"Guess that thing works after all," Connor said with a grin.

His voice sounded distorted ... far away, and he knew it was from being in the close proximity of so many gunshots. He felt Hicks tugging his arm, pulling him back through the doors of the building.

"Come on," Hicks said. "We got to work our way down to that church."

Connor knew he had five rounds left in his gun, having earlier placed a cartridge in the chamber he normally left empty for safety reasons. Now he was glad that he'd followed Hicks's example and done so. He trailed Hicks through the expansive room. It was empty save for Rance, Judge Robertson, and Tiddy, who was hunched over in his chair, his face in his hands.

"What the hell's going on out there?" the judge demanded.

"They're settling things out of court," Hicks said as he kept moving.

"Stay inside here, judge," Connor said. "There's a

man with a rifle shooting at people."

The judge recoiled visibly, but his head bobbled up and down in agreement.

"I'll keep watch on Tiddy," Rance called after them. "Good luck."

Hicks came to the rear door and shoved it open. Connor followed and saw there was a clear path, more or less, down behind the row of buildings that lined the main street. Each structure was punctuated by one or two privies. Connor hoped there wouldn't be any loose stools or open pits, but then realized they had more serious things to be worried about. The report from that rifle had sounded real loud, even at a distance. It had to be a heavy caliber with a lot of range.

Hicks was ahead of him by about thirty feet. Connor quickened his pace, remaining careful to keep his Colt un-cocked and his finger away from the trigger. He didn't figure that the gun would go off without being cocked, but the thought of the hammer being over a live round was troubling if it got dropped. Still, he knew he might very well need an extra shot in this situation.

They'd run perhaps a hundred yards behind the buildings when Hicks slowed and stopped at the corner of one. He was breathing hard from the run, as was Connor, but he thought he had a bit more wind left than Hicks. He was still taking in a plethora of deep breaths, however.

"I think we're ... beyond that church ... now," Hicks said, gasping a bit as he spoke. He moved through the three foot space between the buildings toward the street, flattening out against the wall as he went, then stopped to do a quick peek.

"We got to be real careful," he said. "And be fast as we cross that street. If he's up there in that tower, and I suspect he is, then he's got a full range of seeing, as well as firing."

Connor came up beside him and gazed across the street at the church. The sun shone brightly on the front of the building. It was a huge, two-story, wooden framed structure with a tall bell tower at the peak of the roof. A huge bell hung in the center of the tower, which was open on all four sides under a small, gabled roof. At the base of the bell tower a circular window containing a patchwork of differently colored glass sections had been set into the wood.

"Damn," Hicks said. "If he's up there, it'll be like shooting fish in a barrel once we go out there."

"What we gonna do?" Connor asked

"Easy," Hicks said with a wry grin. "All we got to do is figure out a way to get across there without getting shot."

"Maybe he ain't up there no more," Connor said. But he was feeling the doubt even as he said the words. "Could be he's on the run now. If he's working with the Pinkerton man, he musta been aiming at you and knows he missed his shot."

"Maybe. But he also might be waiting up there to finish the job." Hicks took a deep breath. "And don't know if he has anybody with him in there. For all we know there might be more than just him and the Pinkerton."

Connor recalled their encounter with the Pinkerton man and his hired gunman, Landecker back in Woodman. There'd been two assistants with him, in addition to the Pinkerton. Connor and Abby had killed two of them because it had been unavoidable. He almost regretted now that they hadn't done the same to the Pinkerton man as well. But cold-blooded killing wasn't their style.

"So you're thinking there are more there than just the rifle shooter?" he asked.

"Don't know for sure," Hicks said. "But right now we have to operate under that assumption."

A shiver of fear ran up and down Connor's spine and he momentarily studied his mentor. Was it all right to feel scared? Was it unmanly? He shook off the anxiety.

River's never scared, he thought. So I shouldn't be neither.

Taking in a deep breath, Hicks said, "Get ready. I'll go first."

"Wait," Connor said, gripping Hicks's arm. "We don't know what they look like, do we?"

Hicks flashed a quick grin. "Just look for somebody with a big, old rifle."

Connor heard the sound of running footsteps behind them and whirled, raising his gun.

John Henry Bardwell appeared in the space between the buildings holding a Winchester rifle at port-arms. He was still shirtless and as he crept closer Connor could see the hairs on the man's chest standing out in small, black coils. His face and body were bruised and bloody.

Connor lowered his Colt and grinned.

"Saw you two go running back here," Bardwell said. "Thought you could use some help."

"We sure can," Connor said, pointing to the weapon. "Where'd you get that."

Bardwell's mouth showed the trace of a smirk. "From that man Kandy's horse. Didn't figure he'd be having no more use for it."

"I think the shooter's up in that church tower," Hicks said.

Bardwell nodded. "Makes sense, if'n' he's got a good rifle. Most likely a Sharps, from the sound and the distance of that shot before. You think there's more than one?"

"Don't know," Hicks said. "But either way, we got to figure how to get across that street."

"How about I go back a ways?" Bardwell said, jerking his thumb over his shoulder in the direction from which they'd come. "Go up through some of these other buildings. Draw his attention by giving you some cover fire."

"You'll be putting yourself at a lot of risk," Connor said. "If he's got a Sharps."

Bardwell flashed a quick smile. "After all you done for me, I figure I owe it to you."

"It's as good a plan as we're gonna get," Hicks said. "Go on back. We'll give you about thirty-five, forty seconds, then we'll make our move when we hear your first shots."

Bardwell turned to go, then stopped.

"I just thought of something," he said. "If'n' he's still up in that tower, ringing that bell might throw him off a bit."

"It might," Hicks said.

"Maybe I can ring it a few times with this." Bardwell held up the rifle.

"Good idea," Hicks said. "Watch yourself, John Henry."

Bardwell waved with his left hand, turned, and ran toward the rear.

"Start counting to forty," Hicks said. "Then listen for that bell ringing and be ready to move."

Connor began mentally ticking off the numbers, one, two, three, each one more or less representing a second. After he reached twenty-five he stopped.

"He's a good man, ain't he?" he said.

"One of the best," Hicks replied. "Them buffalo soldiers usually are."

Connor was about to ask Hicks if he'd known any other buffalo soldiers when the crack of a rifle, a Winchester, not a Sharps, sounded.

The bell reverberated.

Hicks waited until the second shot, which was followed by a roaring sound of the heavier caliber report mixed with the ringing, and then pushed through a cluster of tumbleweeds and high grass and onto the street. Connor was right behind him, looking up the entire time, but only seeing the bouncing view of the church and its tall tower. The twin doors on the building's entrance were elevated from the board walk by three steps. Two thin, metal crosses had been nailed to each of the two doors.

Another shot from the Winchester cracked, and the bell echoed again.

Good job, John Henry Connor thought. That means he's still alive.

But neither did it mean that he hadn't been hit. Connor hoped that wasn't so, but tossed all those concerns out of his mind and ran faster, almost passing Hicks by the time they'd traversed the wide street and ascended the three wooden stairs. Both of them bumped into the front doors of the building. They paused for a few seconds. More shots came from the Winchester at ground level, more reverberations from the church bell, and then superior to them all, another roar from the Sharps.

They both stood by the doors, trying to catch their breath. Both guns were silent now. Only the fading repercussions of the ringing sound lingered in the air.

"Let's go get him outta that damn tower," Hicks said.

He grabbed the front handle on the door closest to him and pulled back.

The door didn't budge.

Hicks tried again, harder this time, but to no avail.

"Aw, hell. He must've anticipated somebody fig-uring out his position and barred the door," Hicks said. "We got to find another way in."

"Where?"

Hicks grinned. "Be a damn shame to bust out one of them pretty, stained glass windows, wouldn't it?"

Connor studied the door and then said, "Got me another idea."

He holstered his gun and pulled out his knife

as he straightened up. He dug at the blade into the slight gap at the bottom of the hinge. After a few seconds the retaining cap popped off and Connor went to work in the second hinge. There were three hinges in all, and once the bottom portions had been removed, it then became a simple matter of sliding the pins up and out of the holding brackets.

Hicks gave him a wink. "Good way to ruin the cutting edge of your knife, boy. But if this works, I'll buy you a new one."

Connor pressed the tip of the blade between the outer edge of the door and the jamb and tried to work the door loose. It still wouldn't budge.

"Dammit," he said in a whisper. "Must be a latch on the door holding the bar across on the inside."

Hicks squinted and gestured toward the corner.

"See if you can pry up that window."

Connor moved to it and jammed the blade between the window frame and the thick sill. He pushed upward but the window refused to budge.

Another shot rang out from street level and the bell clanged once more.

The Winchester.

No return fire came from up above.

Connor knew that could mean a number of things.

The shooter could be waiting, or he could have moved, or he could be dead ...

A huge hole tore through the center of the door closest to Connor accompanied by a flurry of spiraling wood chips and the unforgettable sound of the Sharps rifle.

So the shooter wasn't dead. Apparently he'd moved to ground level. And he knew where they were.

The rip in the door was large and Connor estimated that the bullet was a big one.

Got to be a fifty caliber, he thought.

Hicks swore, pushed Connor off of the steps, then dove to the other side. He used his gun to break out a portion of the stained glass window on the right side of the door and fired a round through the opening.

"Guess he's down from the tower," Connor said.

"Come on," Hicks yelled and shoved Connor to his left. They ran to the corner of the building and stopped. They froze there, glancing up at the door. It seemed unlikely that their adversary would take the time to undo the door barricade and come out that way, but the windows remained a persistent threat.

Hicks clapped Connor on the shoulder and pointed.

There was a dark, shadowy space, perhaps only a few feet wide, between the wall of the church and the adjacent building.

Connor did a quick peek and said, "Looks clear."

He started to go down it but felt Hicks grabbing his shoulder. As he glanced back he saw Hicks shake his head.

"It's a killin' tunnel. If he's gone outside, chances are he'll be waiting for us to get into the middle of it. He could probably get us both with one shot, as big as that damn rifle of his is."

"But what we gonna do? If he's on the move?"

"We do what he least expects," Hicks said. He ran back and ascended the three steps to the front door. Reaching up, he ripped one of the thin metal crosses from its placement and shook out the nails that had secured it. Hicks then jammed the longer, bottom section of the cross into the space between the twin front doors and lifted it up. It passed upward smoothly at first, and then stopped after meeting some resistance.

The bar, Connor thought. It's hit the bar.

He saw Hicks grimace and push up harder. He seemed frozen in place for several seconds and Connor prayed that the shooter inside wouldn't send another fifty caliber greeting through the door again. He ran up the steps, thrust the barrel of his gun through the hole in the bottom of the brightly colored glass, and fired off two rounds.

Hicks's hand holding the cross lurched upward and Connor knew that the bar had been dislodged. He fired a third round as Hicks grabbed the door knob and pulled. The right side section of the double doors fell backward. Connor flattened against the outside wall and surveyed the inside of the church. There were rows of heavy benches on both sides of the room, with a center aisle leading up to a raised platform and a wooden pulpit. Hicks pointed to himself, and then to the right.

Understanding the message, Connor nodded and prepared to go left.

Hicks thrust himself forward, firing his gun as he ran. Connor did the same, but didn't fire. He had only two rounds left and didn't have time to reload. He wished he'd gotten into the practice of wearing two guns, like Hicks always did. But that was a consideration for another time, if he survived this one.

He dropped to the floor and crawled several feet before ripping off his hat and daring a glimpse over the thick wooden frame of the last pew.

The pulpit was bathed in an array of bright colors, and Connor realized that the high, afternoon sun must be shining through one of the stained glass windows up above them. Suddenly a figure rose up inside the prismatic cone of light beside the lectern.

The next few moments unfolded in slower than normal motion, each second seeming as if it were the tick of ten:

The figure in the light raised a long barreled rifle.

The hole in the end of the bore seemed to stare directly into Connor's face, like the malevolent eye of some feral beast.

A burst of fire and smoke rippled from the end of the barrel.

The top edge of the heavy wooden pew next to Connor's head erupted in a vortex of crushed wood and he jerked his head to the side.

For a few seconds he could hear nothing, like someone had clapped him on the ears, and a wave of silence overtook him as a flurry of slivers stitched their way over the right side of his face.

He recoiled, swallowed hard, and heard twin

gunshots, one lesser than the other, resonating.

Down at the pulpit, the man in the light twisted spasmodically as the big gun slipped away from him. The glint of a smile, or was it a grimace, showing crooked, stained teeth, twisted upon his face.

Still bathed in the light, he stumbled backward, the colors disappearing from his body as he fell to the side.

Hicks, holding a smoking pistol, rose and began running down the center aisle. A split second later Connor was running after him, his ears still ringing, the right side of his face burning, his gun pointing at the supine man on the raised platform. He scanned the rest of the church and followed the long ladder attached to the wall that led up to the tower. A rope hung down from the bell. Connor reached out and grabbed it to steady himself and he felt the vibration of the bell coming to life once more. Or so he thought. His hearing still hadn't totally returned. It became evident that there were no more assailants up there.

Two rounds left, he kept telling himself. Two rounds left.

The sound of the bell ringing, somewhat distorted, suddenly intruded.

Hicks fired again and the figure lying on the platform twitched. A red pool was spreading on the planks beneath him. He tried weakly to lift the immense rifle, but Hicks moved too quickly and stepped on the end of the barrel. The grimace twitched into a smile on the dying man's face.

"Been waitin' on ya," he said. "The dude told me

you were good." Then slowly, his features mollified into an almost beatific serenity as all alertness faded from him.

Hicks reached down and pulled the Sharps away from the body, then jammed his finger in the still open eye of the downed shooter. Seeing no reaction, he straightened up and said, "He's dead."

"I wonder who he is?" Connor said. "Or was."

His own voice sounded like he was talking through the open end of a tin can attached to a string.

Hicks shook his head. "Let's go ask that damn Pinkerton man."

Connor heard the sounds clearer now. Someone running up the steps by the front door. He turned to see John Henry Bardwell burst through the doors. He regarded them, took in a deep breath, and asked, "You got him?"

Hicks nodded.

"Good," Bardwell said with a laugh. "I was getting tired of ringing that bell and I'm plumb out of ammunition."

They all laughed.

In the distance a train whistle blared.

CHAPTER 15

SWEETWATER

As the three of them walked down the main street toward the other end of the town they saw the train pulling into the depot, the black cloud surging upward from the engine's smokestack into the bright blue sky. The teeming crowd of people was still gathered in front of the Grain Exchange, busy moving horses and corpses off the main street area. A man with a black valise knelt over one of the bodies in the dirt. Several more littered the street where they had fallen. The smell of gunpowder hung in the air, mixed with the coppery scent of blood and the stench of death. Abby was standing in front of the building holding her Trantor pistol on the Pinkerton man who was seated on the ground next to an empty hitching rail. His fancy white shirt and navy blue suit were stained with the brownish smears of manure. Some errant spots decorated the side of his face as well.

Her eyes widened when she saw Connor's bloody cheek and jaw.

"Are you all right?" she asked.

"Never better," Connor said. "Except for these here splinters."

The judge stood on the top step of the Grain Exchange, his arms akimbo. Next to him Maxwell Tiddy sat all hunched over, his hands in the iron shackles that had once secured Bardwell. Rance smiled and waved, a Winchester rifle resting on his shoulder. Sheriff Thorpe gestured to them as they approached.

"I take it you got him?" he asked.

"We did," Hicks said. "How many people you got hurt here?"

Thorpe heaved a sigh. The dark red stain on his right sleeve was starting to show signs of drying.

"We're still making a count. Big George McManus is dead. So is his son, Little George."

"And his cowhand, Kandy," Connor said, pointing to a body that had been dragged off to the side. The eyes in the handsome face stared up vacuously.

"How about Burl McManus?" Bardwell asked.

"His brother, Aaron, took him over to Doc Ingraham's," Thorpe said. He pointed to the kneeling man with the valise who was stuffing some bandages into the shoulder of one of the wounded homesteaders. "Doc left him up there and came to tend to some of these folks. Said he doubts Burl will regain much use of his arm."

Bardwell clucked in disgust. "That shouldn't

happen to no man, even the likes of him. I'm right sorry about that."

"Hey, don't feel bad," Connor said. "That big son of a bitch had it coming."

"Maybe so," Bardwell said. "But that still don't make it right, what I did."

"It wasn't like he gave you much choice." Hicks looked at Thorpe. "Guess this means he's not gonna take your job next Tuesday."

Thorpe chuckled. "I guess not."

Across the street at the railroad depot Connor noticed three men standing on the platform. Two of them wore navy blue suits and had derby hats. The third man was older and a bit plumper, with muttonchops sideburns and a tall top hat. They seemed to be conferring in conversation, occasionally glancing at the remnants of the disturbance in the street. One of the men in a navy suit stepped down from the train platform and began walking toward them.

"What was that fella's involvement?" Thorpe asked, gesturing toward the subdued Pinkerton man and held up a short-barreled Colt Frontier Revolver. "He had this in a shoulder rig."

"He's the one that hired that shooter back in the church to kill us," Connor said.

Thorpe's brow furrowed. "You got any proof of that?"

"That's a totally ridiculous and fabricated charge, sheriff," the Pinkerton man said. "In fact, if you'll check, that man there is wanted for murder. The younger one is as well." He glared at Abby. "As is this little witch."

"Shut your mouth," Abby said, pointing the pistol at him.

Thorpe's eyes darted toward Hicks. "Murder?"

"Sounds like a bunch of horse shit to me." Hicks sniffed the air. "Smells like it, too."

"It's true, sheriff," the Pinkerton man said. "I swear it."

"Yeah?" Thorpe frowned. "All I know is, these two men are both my deputies, and they're some damn fine ones, too. You must be mistaking them for someone else."

The man in the navy blue suit from the train platform had finished making his way through the scattering of people and stopped, his head jerking slightly in apparent surprise as he caught sight of the seated Pinkerton man.

"O'Rourke?" he said. "Is that you?"

The seated Pinkerton man frowned and said nothing.

"You know this man?" Thorpe asked.

"Yes, he's William Francis O'Rourke. One of our operatives." The man paused and pulled back the lapel of his navy blue jacket to display a large silver badge affixed to his belt inscribed with the block lettering: *PINKERTON NATIONAL DETEC-TIVE AGENCY.*

"We're here as escorts to Governor Perkins." He pointed upward to the once-proud banner strung across the street. It was now sagging lugubriously.

"I talked to a couple of your associates the other day," Thorpe said. "Now, what exactly is this fella supposed to be doing here?"

"Don't answer that," O'Rourke said. "This is company business. We don't have to talk to any two-bit sheriff."

"Yeah, I think you best keep your mouth shut, mister," Thorpe said. "Consider yourself under arrest until I get this thing sorted out."

The other two men from the train depot had managed to wind their way through the crowd. The one in the navy suit leaned forward and whispered to his associate, but the man with the top hat smiled brightly and said, "Good afternoon. I'm Governor George Perkins, and I'm delighted to be here in Sweetwater."

His politician's smile remained in place despite the disorganization of the surroundings.

When no one spoke, he continued. "And I'm certainly looking forward to meeting Big George McManus. He's been a great contributor to my campaign. Is he around here?"

"Sure is, governor," Hicks said. "I think you'll find him laying over there. He's the one with the big hole in his head."

EPILOGUE

SWEETWATER
TWO DAYS LATER

Connor finished draping the twin bags of supplies over the saddlebags on the pack horse they'd acquired and gently patted the animal's flank. The right side of his face ached, but it was a good ache. He knew it was healing after Abby and the doc had finished plucking all the wood splinters out of it. She was already on her horse and silently shooting him daggers for taking so long. Hicks was mounted as well. Connor went to his own horse, checked the cinch, tightening it slightly to compensate for the customary inflation his horse usually had whenever he was saddled, then took a long look around the main street of Sweetwater. This was one place he was glad they'd be leaving.

But the departure was also bittersweet. He thought as he looked at Thorpe, Bardwell, and

Rance moving toward them. Bardwell carried a leather scabbard with the Sharps rifle in it.

"Just thought you'd like to know," Thorpe said. "I won reelection by a landslide."

"Burl McManus didn't get one vote," Rance said with a grin that seemed to split his face. His eyes were clear and his gait was crisp and sharp. Perhaps that meant that he'd still refrained from imbibing. He was wearing the same fancy suit they'd taken from the undertaker's place, and Connor silently wondered if the clothes still smelled like the dead.

"Sounds like the people around here know when they've got a good man," Hicks said. He reached into his shirt pocket and pulled out his deputy badge and flipped it to the sheriff. "Been meaning to give that back to you."

Thorpe caught it with his left hand.

Connor reached into his pocket and pulled out the badge he'd worn. In truth, he'd intended on keeping it as a reminder of all they'd been through, but he realized now that it wouldn't be right. In any case, he'd cleaned all the blood from it, and polished it to a sparkling sheen. It shone the sunlight with a reflective brilliance.

"Here's mine back as well, sheriff," he said.

Thorpe reached out and took the star.

"I wish you'd consider staying on for a spell," he said, shrugging slightly. "You both did a real fine job, and it's gonna be a bit before my good arm's back to normal."

"I felt like the fox guarding the hen house," Hicks said. "It ain't like that Pinkerton man was telling the truth, mind you, but I'm hardly a choir boy."

"What's gonna happen to him?" Abby asked. "He deserves to be in jail."

"Well," Thorpe said. "I do intend on holding him until I can complete an investigation. But with that rifle shooter dead, and him not being forthcoming, it's gonna be hard to make a good case against him."

"Don't seem right," Bardwell said.

"A lot of things ain't right," Hicks said. "But hopefully things will be turning around for you all here."

"I think they already are," Thorpe said. "And it doesn't mean that I can't hold Mr. O'Rourke for a week or two or three while I finish my investigation."

"I'd appreciate that," Hicks said with a chuckle.

Thorpe chuckled too. "Of course, it'll probably take twice that long to get that stink out of my cell block."

They all laughed.

"Yeah," Bardwell said. "It think a new day's dawning around here."

"With Big George McManus dead," Rance said. "It appears that his oldest son, Aaron's going to be taking over the Dominion, and he's already sent word that he's tearing down the dam so the homesteaders and other ranchers can have access to the water."

"He was always the best of the lot," Thorpe said.

"Maybe you should deputize John Henry, sheriff," Abby said.

"Appears he armed for it," Hicks said, gesturing

toward the Sharps.

"We'd never have made it without him," Connor said. "Back at the church."

Bardwell shrugged. "Hey now, I didn't do all that much. I'll be glad to help out a bit, if'n' you need me, sheriff. But I got my hands full just trying to make do with my farming."

"And I'll help out as well," Rance said. "At least until I can get my law practice going."

Thorpe raised his eyebrows.

"I want you all to know I took the oath," Rance said. "The temperance oath. I'm through with the bottle. Forever."

"Well, good for you," Abby said with a smile. She looked to Hicks, who tapped his finger to the brim of his hat in a mock salute.

"Working as a deputy will give me a real feel for the law outside of a book," Rance said.

"And it also beats the hell out of washing dishes," Connor said, grinning.

✳✳✳✳✳✳

After shaking hands with each of the three men, Connor swung up onto the saddle and the riders headed out of town at a slow trot. They road past the last of the town's buildings, and then began to go parallel to the railroad tracks which stretched northward toward the infinite horizon.

"Where we heading, River?" Connor asked.

"North," Hicks said. "The same direction we were headed before we stopped off here."

"Oregon?"

Hicks didn't reply.

Connor and Abby exchanged wary glances.

"Toward that reckoning you were talking about?" Connor asked.

Hicks was still silent and Connor wondered if he was ever going to answer.

"Yep," Hicks said finally. "Toward the reckoning."

Connor had known what the response would be even before the words had been spoken, but the curiosity burned within him. He wondered just when Hicks was going to give them a full explanation of what they were riding toward.

Maybe it was time to speak out.

"When are you going to tell us about it? About why we're riding north? And about the reckoning?"

He glanced toward Abby.

She nodded.

Hicks seemed to be considering his response for the better part of a minute, and then said, "When it's time."

Sensing that this conversation was at an end, Connor didn't try to push things any further. He looked to Abby once again, and saw her face had a look of resignation, but also one of satisfaction. After all, the three of them were a family.

They rode on in silence for a long while before Connor spoke again.

"Well, whatever it is we're riding toward, River," he said. "We're with you."

The horses trotted a few more steps.

"I know that," Hicks said.

Family, thought Connor. Bonded together by choice, more so than blood.

And by the blood they'd shed together.

Watch for Gunslinger: Killer's Ghost, the next installment in the Gunslinger series by A.W. Hart.

ABOUT THE AUTHOR

Michael A. Black is the author of 19 books and over 100 short stories and articles. He has a BA in English from Northern Illinois University and a MFA in Fiction Writing from Columbia College Chicago. He was a police officer in the south suburbs of Chicago for over thirty years and worked in various capacities in police work including patrol supervisor, SWAT team leader, investigations, and tactical operations.

His Ron Shade series, featuring the Chicago-based kickboxing private eye, has won several awards, as has his police procedural series featuring Frank Leal and Olivia Hart. He has also written two novels with television star Richard Belzer of Law & Order SUV. His hobbies include the martial arts, running, and weight lifting.

In addition to his own novels, Black is currently writing novels in a highly popular adventure series under another name.

Made in the USA
Monee, IL
03 November 2020